Praise for *Devils of Fear*

'An action packed, intricately plotted, deeply thoughtful story.'

'A complex, fast moving, and yet poetic novel.'

'A journey through both inner and outer landscapes.'

Authors note

Hi there.

If you're reading this, thank you. As you may or may not know, this is my first real book. Of course, I've put as much effort into it as I could, but some things may have slipped between the cracks.

So let's ignore those, alright?

Thanks.

This book has been my passion project for almost two years, and the fact that you can hold it in your hands and read it makes me so, so thankful. So again, thank you.

And you may notice some inspiration from other media, most of which is from the world of animation, particularly Japanese.

Most noticeable, the strong influence of Tatsuki Fujimoto's '*Chainsaw man*'. Brilliant series by the way.

But I digress.

I may know you, or I may not. Either way, I hope that my words can bring you excitement, joy, interest, or really

Disclaimer.

This is a work of fiction. All acts depicted are completely fictional in nature and do not hold any concrete resemblance to the real world. All names, incidents and scenarios are a product of the author's imagination. All statements, stunts and dialogue are completely fictional. All locations are either fictional or real and used in a fictionalised way.

Any information or material contained herein is included for entertainment purposes only and should not be relied upon in any accuracy.

Trigger warning.

This novel contains implied and outright gore, along with content and ideals that may not be suitable for all audiences. Furthermore, reasonably graphic violence of both hand to hand and weaponised combat is depicted herein.

This edition published 2025.

The right of Elias Virkar-Yates to be identified as author of this work has been asserted to him in accordance with the Copyright, Designs and Patents Act 1988.

This book has been typeset in Times New Roman and Courier New.

anything at all. As a student working up to exams, I feel so lucky to have so many brilliant people supporting me as I work my way into the world of writing.

So, here's my list.

Firstly, thank you to my mother, for always backing me every step of the way and giving me the best guidance I could have asked for, and also for generally being incredible.

Thank you to my grandmother, for being the source of my feedback at each and every moment, and for being as supportive as can be.

Thank you to my father, for everything he's done for me and for my life, and for being my pillar to lean on no matter what's happening, and to whom I promise will all the truth I have that the father depicted in this book has no relation to him *at all*.

Thank you to all my friends, for all the fun we've had and will continue to have.

And thank you to my sister, for that brilliant cover photography, and for always keeping my ego in check.

And thank *you*, dear reader.

Hopefully it'll be worth your time.

P.S, Ikari is pronounced ee-kah-ree.

'I say that I am stronger than fear'

- Malala Yousafzai

An all original
story, an exploration of
emotions

Elias Virkar-Yates

DEVILS

OF

FEAR

PROLOGUE

Fear.

To be scared of something.

In this world, fear hides in every corner. Every nook and cranny, every crevice hidden in the shadows. In fact, fear often basks in the open, clear for everyone to see.

Screaming.

Shouting.

Crying.

Fear manifests in many ways, it always has done. From the moment a human, an animal, a living being is born, it unconsciously or consciously understands the idea of fear. Humans who have dedicated their life to studying ideas and concepts may believe they understand it fully, but the only way to truly understand fear is to feel it. To stand before something, trembling, every fibre of your being begging you to escape. In that moment, one can then truly understand what it means to *fear*.

Fear takes on many forms, some verbal, some philosophical.

But never before has it taken *physical* form.

Or so the world thought.

Hidden in those same shadows, those same nooks and crannies, things were being born. Darkness pooling together, feeding off the emotions of the humans and creatures around it. The more fear felt toward something, the greater and greater it grew.

Unbeknownst to the world, their fears were gradually becoming creatures. And for the longest time, these creatures existed as if they were invisible. They were no more than animals, creatures who rely on instinct and nothing more. And as animals do, they fought amongst each other. After what may have been centuries, or what may have been minutes, a singular being rose to the top. And as the fear felt toward it grew and grew as the human population grew, its power surged.

Until, it reached a tipping point.

A point of no return.

The being became self-conscious.

It could think, it could plan, it could theorise. It developed a personality, shaped by the twisted thoughts people had about it all the time. Through their fear, the people had unknowingly created a terrible monster.

And the monster waited, as more and more fears became like it. They formed a hierarchy and created an organisation.

Once, a husband and wife dared to challenge them after discovering their existence. They poured over every tiny detail, every speck of dust. And they discovered something.

These creatures could be reasoned with. They could be… useful.

And, as a pair, they signed the first contract.

A contract, a way to turn fear into raw, tangible power, with these creatures as the catalyst.

With that power, the duo faced the creatures head on. And they got so, so close. But, at the last hurdle, they fell.

In the time that followed, others tried. But none got anywhere near as close as they did.

Many centuries passed, and religion began to grow. As it did, and the influence of faith spread across the globe, these creatures were given a new name.

Devils.

And now, millennia later, in an island nation off the coast of east Asia, in a world in which the existence of devils is known to only a few, a world-shaking incident will take place.

The incident in which the existence of devils is thrust into the limelight, and the whole world will know of them.

The incident in which the mission of that couple all those years ago will once again be attempted.

And it all begins with the moment that two children - isolated, wild, plagued by their own minds, and shunned from society, take their first steps into the world of devil hunting.

PART ONE;
TO SCORCH THE
EARTH

I: CHILDREN AND DEVILS

30th August 2018

–NAMELESS–

The night sky stretches out above me, an endless inky sea of black sporadically pin pricked by dull stars. Like some ancient tapestry, woven to remind us all that there is always something bigger, something more important than even the greatest of things.
Staring at the sky I wonder what I could've been.
What if dad had given me a chance?

What if my power had awoken?

What if I had lived up to what he wanted me to be, what he *needed* me to be?

What if… what if…

My moment of speculation is snatched away in an instant as a sharp thorn pierces my heel and I get flung back to reality. Right now, I need somewhere to sleep. With a sigh, I watch my breath billow out in white clouds before me. Just keep moving, there will be something eventually. A clearing, or a soft patch of grass. The trees loom out of the shadows as I walk, the dark forest closing me in on all sides, the deafening silence battering my ears down. A shiver trickles through my body. Glancing at the battered, dirty blanket on my shoulder reminds me of how desperate life has become. I really do have nothing, nothing at all. Except of course, my contract. That contract that never worked. And because of that, I failed him. I failed my father, leaving him with no choice.

Was that my fault though?

If my contact had worked, if…

Maybe things would have been different, maybe we could have been a happy family.

But then his deeds caught up to him, and his debt.

He was taught a lesson, one about how the Yakuza are ruthless.

Then again, they haven't come after me, and it's not like he had another son to pay for it. And when he died... I was only 13 when it happened. That is burned into my mind, the sight of my feet surrounded by those splashes of red.

The memory comes rushing back to me, from four years ago. I feel a sort of disconnect, the sharp sadness dulled by time. But still, one emotion remains with me every time I recall that day.
Frustration.
If only my *damn* contract had worked, if only my powers had awoken, he would still be here today. If I had the strength I should have had, I could have stopped them. But instead, when dad realised they were going to come for him, and that I wouldn't be able to protect him, he left me here.
And not long after, he was dead.
Involuntarily, I scream.
I scream, every drop of that built up anger pouring out and echoing through the darkness.
And something begins to build up within me, this frustration morphing into a feeling I don't recognise, a feeling that isn't quite an emotion.
Like an anticipation, bubbling just beneath my skin.
And it rises up and up, almost threatening to break through.
Wait.

Is this… is it finally happening?

Well, it's about time.

This happened once before, once before on that fateful night.

If only it wasn't too late to save dad. If only this had happened a bit earlier that night in those woods.

But, that time is long gone now. So I let it bubble up, I let it boil over.

Run wild, my contract.

Run wild, damn devil that waited too long.

***

17th January 2014 – Four years prior

The man stands in the kitchen, pouring himself a glass of wine. He watches the blood red liquid slowly climb the wall of the glass. He thinks of nothing but this, his escape from everything that seems to be catching up to him. The rim of the glass gently brushes his lips, the viscous liquid sliding toward them.

A sound interrupts his almost ritualistic drinking. Someone knocking on the door. It sounds as if they're punching it. He pads over to the door, his crimson slippers shuffling along the varnished floor. The door swings open.

"Can I help you?"

The stark moonlight gives form to two figures, standing there.

Two men, an older figure with a beard, dressed in a suit, and a large, mountain of a man in a sports tracksuit.

That's all he sees before a fist smashes into him. His jaw breaks with a sickening crack. His eyes roll back in his head. A lightswitch flicked to dark. A sound akin to dropping a sack of vegetables rings out into the night as he slumps to the floor in the doorframe.

"Get him inside. The bastard is gonna get what's coming to him."

The old suited man steps over his body before having a brief look around the house. The heartfelt lighting shows nothing he cares for. He disregards this place, that in his eyes, is nothing. Just a pile of rock. Here, in this useless place, or there?

He makes his choice.

"That old house in the woods. We can do it there."

The man's voice is smooth as molasses. He rubs his wiry beard. "Justice at last"

"What abou 'is kids?"

The man in the sports tracksuit's voice is like a hammer against iron, the voice of a brawler.

"The matter of Ikari will be addressed later."

A smile flourishes on his wrinkled face.

"You know what, I'm in a playful mood. Drop him in the old barn. And please, show some decency."

"I'll try ma est"

"Good, very good."

That quiet smile returns, the curling corners of his mouth reaching for the dark sky.

"Everything is going to plan."

***

"Awake at last, are we?"

Panic builds within the man. He knows that voice. That smooth, poisonous voice. His eyes snap open.

"You've caused us a lot of trouble, you know, Uzumaki."

Uzumaki's heart is trying to beat out of his chest. His eyelids are heavy, and his muscles burn to move his arms, but to no avail. He finds himself bound to a rough wooden chair. He strains his eyes and mind, but try as he might, doesn't recognise where he is. The building is decrepit; moss on the floor, vines on the wall.

"H-how did you find me?"

"A master never tells his methods. You should know that, devil speaker. You know, sometimes I wonder if you are a devil yourself. After all, you show no remorse for your actions. Ruining your son's future. The way you treated that boy, and look what happened to him."

He speaks through a rich man's laugh as Uzumaki spits his response.

"It wasn't my fault!"

"Wasn't it now? The brats completely messed up in the head, thanks to your failures as a parent. And even disregarding Ikari, what about your other son?"

"I don't know what you're talking about, old man."

"Oh really? Is that how you try to live? Just trying to forget. Forget the amount of times you lied and lied to *us*. Forget the boy you abandoned without–"

Uzumaki practically roars–

"SHUT UP!"

"The boy you tried to contract one of the twelve fears to? The boy you cast aside simply because he didn't fit your image of a living *weapon*? The boy the flame devil seemingly rejected? The boy you never even bothered to *name* before you left him?

"*Please.*"

Uzumaki whispers, his words heavy with fear.

"The boy had a purpose, and he didn't live up to it… it was my only choice…"

The old man laughs cruelly.

"Your only choice? That's bull, and we both know it. The boy failed to be your tool, to be your sword. So you left him to die."

With a sneer, he grasps for something at his belt, speaking in a tone of hatred.

"You disgust me."

A slow, deliberate movement. Cold, hard steel against his forehead. He sees the Yakuza man's finger tense.

"Looks like time is finally up, *devil speaker.*"

He presses the end of the gun harder, digging into his skin.

"May you rest in hell with all *our* friends."

Click.

***

–NAMELESS–

My heart pounds in my chest, my feet barely feeling the thorns I trample, my breath like a steam train off the rails. The gunshot rings in my ears. I have to know what happened. Who, or what was just killed? I run faster and faster, desperate to reach the source of that terrible sound. The rumbling of a car driving away is faint but certain. I see a clearing up ahead. An unfamiliar sense, a sense I haven't felt before is flaring up. A desire that isn't my own, some strange instinct wrestling for control of me. My own blood seems to burn.

What is happening?

Is it possible that it's finally happening?

No, that's impossible–

Before I can finish the thought I reach the clearing. The trees box me in, and it seems less of a clearing and more of a prison.

The lone structure waits. Something within me feels out of control, like a wild dog rearing to escape its cage.

Approaching the door, I see it's bolted and shut fast. I think about trying to kick it down before suddenly I snap out of my strange trance as I look down and see what I'm standing in.

My dirt-smeared feet are surrounded by a pool of thick, crimson, *human* blood. Without warning, I open my mouth and let out a guttural shriek. My eyes widen and I run.

Run.

Run.

And don't stop. I run because for some reason I can't understand, I feel responsible.

I feel responsible for that, there's something deep within my mind that seems to blame itself–

And so my feet pound the ground, kicking up dust behind me as I run and run away from that place, deeper and deeper into the woods. I trample brambles and trip over roots as I head further and further from that clearing, wishing I could erase that sight from my mind.

***

31st August 2018 - Present day

–IKARI–

I watch the car drive until it turns down a side road, the sound of the engine slowly fading into distant yelling. Having just handed over everything I earned recently, the hatred for them is stronger than usual today. I turn and start to walk. Hands in pockets, head down. Empty can, dead mouse, cigarette butt, blood stain. Nothings changed in forever, the streets are still a mess around here. Like sewer rats came above ground and founded a neighbourhood. Trudging through the slums I near the edge of the woods, patches of greenery breaking through the wall of beige shapes.

Involuntarily, my mind wanders back to the past.

It feels like that sight is etched into the back of my eyes, the stark white walls of the hospital. A singular distant family member crying, my father acting as if he cares as he speaks to the doctor in hushed tones.

But, when they finally came over to me, it was far worse.

A diagnosis.

Dissociative identity disorder.

Two people, one head.

Me and... somebody else.

Another me.

But not me.

I remember it all too well, the first time he arrived. He barged through the door soon after my mother was declared terminally ill, with possibly a few years to live. That was when he came. He took my eyes, my body, my thoughts. He made them all his own. And when he finally went away, it was the strangest feeling. Like waking up from a coma, only to find that you had been awake and active this whole time.

Except it wasn't you.

Like, it was your body. But not *you*.

And after that, it was a trip to the hospital. A strange questionnaire, then a conversation with a faux nice man in a padded beige office. Then, I was told to lie down, and wait.

Cut to the aforementioned scenario, then the doctor handed me something.

Medication. 8 years worth. 1 tablet a month.

That was 6 years, 8 months ago now.

14 tablets left.

14 months.

And after that, things may get interesting.

But I will never forget the doctor's final words.

Never, and I repeat never, taste your own blood.

Apparently, that is my 'trigger'. As for why, that tidbit of information was mysteriously withheld. It still keeps me up at night, that does. But I can do nothing except speculate–

I trip over my feet, and stumble for a moment. Regaining my balance, I smile drearily.

I should get back to reality, huh.

Almost home now, let's see what's for dinner.

***

The door to my sad excuse for a house swings open and I step in. The barn is small and full of junk; a crate, broken furniture, smashed beer bottles. I step past that and come to my living space. Well, I suppose that's a bit of an exaggeration. My bed is two old crates with some torn sofa cushions on them, my desk and table a cardboard box. I step to the money jar and shake out some coins.

Clink. Clink. Clink.

Almost enough for a used fag. Brilliant. Looks like it's another slice of bread for dinner.
Oh well. Life comes at you fast.
Thanks to my sad excuse of a father, I owe the Yakuza so much I'll live in debt for the rest of my life. Like I said. Life comes at you fast.
I sit back, grab my sole piece of bread, and fall into a daydream.
Lying on a large sofa in the living room of a modern appartement in downtown Tokyo, my girlfriend is making a delicious dinner. Life is good. A fixed mind. No devils to fight. No street gangs, no smears of red on every wall. Just the good life. The happy life. I slip into a slumber, smiling to myself.
Lying to myself.

***

The gnarled hands of a dream clutches me, pulling me in. *I'm back at the old Dojo, staring down the half rotted punching bag. The thought of strength is like a lure, pulling me toward this place. It seems so strange, being back here. Before this, it had been my father taking me to my biggest fight ever, the national championships in the U13 bracket. I've almost forgotten those days, when people used to call me a prodigy. Destined for the world's best, they said. How long ago that seemed, even though it has barely brushed 4 years. But as for the fate of that fight, it had been doomed since the first day of that month. Just by chance, I had forgotten my medication. And it was only as I was taking blows in the ring that I remembered. But by then, it was too late.*
And as I spotted a kick, reacted slowly, and took it straight to the face, a sickening crack had rang out through the ring. As that referee was screaming in my face, as the crowd jeered, as my opponent was roaring insults, I noticed. A single drop of blood crawling down my face. Perching on my top lip. I raised my hand to brush it away, but it felt a thousand miles away. I opened my mouth to warn people, but the drop simply rolled that extra millimetre, onto my tongue.
And after that, I remember nothing.

28

Until opening my eyes some time later to the sight of chaos. The wails of sirens accompanied by ambulances and police, all here, at the Dojo.

Why?

I see a body wheeled away on a stretcher, a white sheet laid on top. It fails to cover a red boxing glove hanging out the side, and the limp bicep of a shoulder adorned with crimson.

What happened here?

With no warning, I feel my shoulders seized from behind me. A gruff policeman marches me outside and slams me against a car. The shock plugs my ears, but I think I'm hearing my rights? Something about silence, lawyers and embassies?

The door to the car opens, and I find myself bundled into a time worn seat.

But why? What did I do?

I look at my hands, looking for reassurance in my shiny blue gloves.

Only to find them stained completely red.

The door of the car slams, we pull away and—

Urghh.

I slowly open my eyes, looking up at the mouldy ceiling. That dream, it just won't leave me alone. And every time, it feels just as real as the last. And each time I wake up from it, I can never remember what happened while I blacked out. I only remember that drop of blood. I really should just forget it. It was so long ago, after all.

Another day, another devil. What is today?

Oh, yeah. The first of the month.

Pulling on the same shirt I've worn for the past week, I head to the other side. My own scent is starting to make me nauseous. I need to steal some more clothes… shuffling through the maze of junk by the back of my barn I find my battered old converse. Heading back inside, stepping over my broken glass defence to enter the 'safe' area. There are still only two things here, one of which is a battered old katana my parents gave me for Christmas. I doubt they ever thought my livelihood would depend on it though.

The once bright red tsuka is so faded it can barely be called coloured. The blade, however, is my ultimate possession. I keep it spotless, so clean I can see myself in the layered steel. The other thing here, a small white bottle. It once had lettering on it that is lost to time and wear, but I know what it is. The lid opens with a soft popping sound, and I fish out a small white pill.

No need for water at this point.

Down the hatch, and keep him sealed for another month.

Sometimes I wonder, what kind of person is he?

But then, I remember that night in the ring, and I cast that question away.

Ah well.

13 tablets left.

Not long now. Life has become a ticking time bomb, slowly counting down the days until it all blows up in my face.

Alas, it's time for work.

Still somewhat groggy, I make my way to the river. The one moment I feel clean is almost here and I need it more than ever today. Plunging my head in the water almost puts me into shock, but it sure as ever wakes me up fast. I feel the fast-rushing water dredge all the slit and sweat out my hair and eyes, tense my muscles, and get me ready for my god awful job.

**

"Really? You want me to get the spider devil?"

"That's it son. Or you could use your old method… I mean ya cant sell another kidney or ball but maybe some skin?"

His voice is somehow gruff and yet almost teasing. I hate that voice. And the spider devil? Seems slightly above my pay grade, but…

Above the pay grade means more pay if I do it.

"Fine. Spider devil it is."

"Good lad"

The masked black market representative. My theoretical employer. I hate him, whoever he is, but the sad truth is that I need him. One day, I swear I'll bring the Yakuza to their knees. One day. But for now…

"So where is it then?"

The fabric of the mask pulls tight as he bears a grin.

"Warehouse on Supuritto Av. The 3rd one along."

"I'll see you here with its head."

Not letting him say goodbye, I turn away. Gonna be a decently long walk. Spider devil huh? This feels like it'll be a tough one… after all a *lot* of people fear spiders. But I can pull through. Like I always do.

After all, I don't have much of a choice.

Pull through, or die.

***

This neighbourhood is even rougher than mine, if that's possible. Drug needles litter the floor, tags of violent gangs are graffitied on almost every wall. I need to be in and out as fast as I can, no doubt about that. Now, where is it…

Supuritto, Supuritto, Supuritto!

3rd warehouse along… found it.

The door to the barn creaks open, flakes of rust falling off mid turn. The darkness inside seems absolute, yearning to swallow a new victim. I take a tentative step inside, alert as ever. Light. I need light. Spotting a grimy window far above me, I have an idea. Picking up a rock, I take a deep breath and level my arm. Draw back… Throw!
CRASH!
I wince with the loud noise, but I got what I wanted. A single shaft of moonlight piercing the darkness.
And the moment my gaze falls on that thing, a gasp escapes my lips.

***

"Really? You sent the sucker after the spider devil?" All the men around the table burst out laughing.
"A 12 Fears? He's screwed!" The words are slurred, the breath stinks of booze.
"Yeah he's got no chance! What devil does he even use?"
"Nothing but a knackered old sword. 'Parrently he's 'self taught' with it as well!"
The low lying laughter roars up again.
"A self taught swordsman huh? Well that's one little boy the world won't miss…"

Seated at the head of the table, one man remains distant from the conversation, and sits quietly.

The Yakuza man isn't listening. He looks out the window, staring at the warm black sky.

Because he knows.

He knows who else will hunt that devil. He knows who Ikari will meet there. And he knows that they will do exactly what he wants. Perhaps, sometime in the future, they might even come after him. How amusing that would be…

Oh yes. Tonight is a good night.

He smiles, admiring the patch of the yakuza on his suit cuff. It really is one of his favourite sights, the emblem of a butterfly resting on a simple katana.

***

A single man kneels in the centre of the room, a strange weapon at his side. Mysterious silvery strands lead from his joints into the echoing darkness above, a small pool of vermillion shining in the light.

"Hello?"

Hello, hello, hello…

My own voice spirals around me, ringing in my ears.

"Are you ok?"

Ok, ok, ok...

"What happened here?"

Here, here, here...

Out of options, I guess.

Approaching slowly, I enter the circle of light surrounding him. Out of the corner of my eye, I see one of those unsettling threads jerk backwards. In a flash, the man's arm lashes toward me, the glint of some weapon in his hand. Leaping back on pure instinct, I barely avoid the slash. Bringing my hand to my face, it comes away sticky with vermillion liquid. A hairline cut across my cheek. He's fast. But still–

What is that weapon?

More threads twist and pull, raising the man to his feet. Like a puppet.

His right hand grasps that odd blade, his movement granting me a better look. A semicircular edge, mandible-like spikes at each end. As he raises his head, one of the threads attached to the top goes limp, letting his head drop to one side. It rests on his shoulder, as his empty eye socket meets my full ones.

A fight against a dead man?

A first for me, I suppose.

Oh well.

Can't be picky now.

He's right handed, so standard form.

Left foot forward, knees slightly bent, facing the opponent from an angle.

Wrapping my right thumb under the tsuka just below the tsuba, I let my fingers curl around the remaining portion of the grip.

Left hand on the top of the saya, using the left thumb to slightly push the blade out.

My stance is ready. So I lock eyes with my opponent's shoulders, just like my martial arts days.

And I wait for him to make the first move.

***

—NAMELESS—

I run from the burning forest towards the city. Charred ground crunches underfoot, the silver moonlight showing me my path like some estranged guide. The cold night air clashes with the burning heat inside me as drops of sweat form on my skin, like condensation on a mirror.
Something is nearby, and my instincts are driving right toward it. My senses are still searing, the flames I just released flowing over my feet. Something, some sense or

emotion I've never felt before is bubbling up, threatening to take control. This sense, it feels almost sentient. It knows where I'm going. Towards a fight. And it's itching to boil over, to flood my mind. Just wait, wait a little longer. My face twists into a smile against my will, and that strange feeling of being used begins to overwhelm my thoughts.

***

–IKARI–

Muscles burning with tension, I wait for his move.
Wait.
Wait.
My right eye twitches with the need to blink, and my momentary squint triggers his move. Like a flash of lightning, the strings pull tight and fling him toward me as if his puppet master was in a rush of rage. As he flies, moonlight glints off that strange blade arcing toward me.
Wait.
Wait.
6 feet, 5 feet, 4 feet…
Wait…
2 feet, 1 foot…
Deep breath in.
Now.

He flies into range, swinging for a killing blow on my head. He lashes with such speed I hear his bones crack, a toy being handled with anger. Pure instinct takes over, and my feet seem to move on their own. My left foot snapping away leaving a trail in the dust, bending my body parallel to his. His blade comes down, finishing the arc, and I see an opening. My left thumb flicks out, pushing the tsuba[1], left hand pulling my saya back.

My right hand clasping the grip, right foot sliding slightly forward, right arm pushing away and bringing my blade with it.

The blade is almost fully out as my right elbow bends inward.

And finally, my arm snaps outward, my foot slamming the floor.

Flick his blood from my blade, the motion of the chiburi almost robotic.

Exhale.

Cut complete.

A thin line of red appears across his torso.

And, all too slowly, his body divides.

One side from the other, right hip to left shoulder.

From one man, to two halves.

---

[1] Tsuba - The ornate guard of a katana
Saya - The traditional katana sheath, often made of lacquered wood
Chiburi - A move that gets blood off the blade

With that, I win.

But, something's off. He was too weak to be a devil of something as feared as spiders. And as if it was reading my mind, the air thickens with anticipation.

For a moment, nothing.

Silence, not a sound–

"Most impressive"

A voice booms from above, and almost jumping out of my skin, I look to the source of the sound. It speaks?

Never had one that speaks before. Does that mean it's stronger, or weaker than usual? Something tells me I could take a good guess at which one it is.

'Suppose it's time for conversation.

Might be nice, I guess. But probably not.

And so I call out to the shadow above, my voice filling the barn.

"Finally revealing, huh?"

The echo has lessened slightly, but that eerie effect remains all the same.

"Well considering what you did to my puppet, I think it's necessary."

"Fair enough. So, are you planning on showing yourself–"

The air pressure surges, imploding all the remaining windows–

Moonlight floods in as the darkness clears away, revealing rafters completely covered in webbing. Thick, impenetrable webbing. Something falls from them, a flit of brown rushing toward the floor. With a soft, and clearly practiced landing, they hit the ground.

My gaze settles on the figure who just dropped in front of me.

The devil takes on human form, I guess. Again, that's new. Dressed in a brown hooded cloak, it speaks.

"Your strength surprises me, lone swordsman."

My strength surprises it? Was that some kind of evaluation, some kind of test? But then again... I smile, and respond.

"Considering it only took one cut, it seems you're easily impressed.."

The devil laughs, a jarring sound like a knife grating on jagged stone. The air seems to thicken with tension as it raises its oddly delicate hand to its face.

And with an elegant motion, drops the hood.

***

–NAMELESS–

I'm getting closer, I can feel it as if I was a homing pigeon finally returning. And yet, this is a direction I've never been in. And strangely, feet licked with flame, stark moonlight leading me through the night to some unknown thing, I find myself lost in thought.

I wonder what the terms of my contract are, or what a 'contract' really is at all? After all, I never got to ask my father.

All I know is that the devil I'm bound to is strong, strong enough to need secrecy. According to that old hag who called herself a seer stumbling on the edge of my woods, the devil was one of the 12 Fears. 12 Fears? I mean, I think there's a few more than twelve...

And, is this all not so strange? I'm like some weird edgy kid, talking about his 'inner beast'. But... this is real. And to tell the truth, it's terrifying–

Snapping out of my own thoughts I realise this anticipation and adrenaline is surging more and more. Whatever lies in wait at the end of this is not far now. A fight? A person? A task?

Well, I can guess which one out of those three it might be–

***

–IKARI–

"You seem surprised, Ikari."

The voice is soft, warm. Like a mother, picking her child up after a tumble.

"My n-my name? How do you know my name?"

Stuttering badly, my nerves are clear to see–
"I know lots of things, Ikari."
There's a strange emphasis when she says my name, enunciating the syllables all bouncy like. And like a hammer blow to my forehead, the weight of her words hit me after a moment.
"Oh y-yeah? If you k-know so much, why aren't you ugly l-like the rest of your k-kind?"
As I stagger over each word, I can't help but notice a simple crest that adorns her chest. A little patch of fabric, a simple embroidered logo. A butterfly on a katana? Before I can ask her about it, she responds.
"How amusing… you're a funny one. However…" She walks closer, just a few inches from me, cupping my face with her hand, "I have a slightly different agenda"
Her touch is warm, and she seems too sincere–
Too late, I see the flash of a blade. I have time to make a noise of confusion–
"Huh?"
But time seems to slow to a crawl. I can't move in time–
And then–
Crimson spurts from my chest. I fall to my knees, hacking blood as some retched cough shakes my lungs. Vision fading, blackness reaches into my mind. And I remember.

With no warning whatsoever, it all comes back to me.

I remember my fathers face, the sound of his shouting, and the sound of his laughter. The way my mothers fingers had suddenly lost strength, her hand slipping from mine. The few friends I had, the small bits of fun we got up to before it all came crashing down. All I wanted was to live a normal life. To walk around with a singular, unsplit mind. Even to work a boring office job and live in one of those weird american housing areas with the same lawns and stupid flags and expensive eggs. All I wanted was to be free of it all.

No such luck I guess.

Thanks a bunch, all you imbeciles. Dad. The gangs. The hospital workers. Even mum, cause even when she could walk she wasn't exactly exemplary.

But most of all - thanks for nothing, fate.

My grip on my sword fails as it slips from my hand, clattering to the floor. Consciousness slipping away, all I can think is how I really hope the blade didn't chip...

And then, as if I'm hallucinating, a wall of flame rushes past my face, searing the hairs on my nose. I find the strength to focus my eyes and see the lethal woman flung against the wall by the fire. It's like a strange dream. Do people dream after death? Maybe people like me do?

Someone is shaking my shoulder. Why? I'm trying to sleep…

2: HUNTERS

–NAMELESS–

In the rush of adrenaline, I can barely take it all in. The flames that spewed from my palm, the boy kneeling in a pool of red. By the looks of it, his own blood. Help him, or follow up my attack?
I should attack again now, but–
The boy slumps to the floor, hitting the ground with a low thump.
Ah, damn it.
Rushing over to him, I drop to one knee. Momentarily registering the katana resting on the floor, I realise the

mirror-like shine of the blade lets me see myself for the first time in... how long has it been now?

Well, let's leave it at what feels like forever.

Wide, bloodshot eyes. Matted hair. Burns and blemishes on every inch of visible skin.

The shock of my own face takes me away from reality for a moment, flinging me back to the last night I ever spent in the only house I've ever lived in.

I remember that house, the way I was never allowed to leave my room. Never allowed to make my presence known to the other strange kid who had come in. I never even saw him, the kid who stole my parents from me. I remember sitting in the corner of that room, feeling the whispers of something in my mind calling out to me. And then, the woman I had once called mom died. That night, I was thrown out. Left for dead in the woods. And then, in those woods, months later, I heard that bang. After that, it was all a blur. Until tonight.

Enough of that.

I'm in a fight, after all.

Snapping back to reality, I try to wake the boy.

Nothing.

One option left, I guess. I draw my arm, engage my shoulder and throw a straight right to the centre of his chest. Spit flies from his mouth as I connect, turning to steam the second it touches my skin.

For a second, he lies still. And then, suddenly, the base of his throat spasms–

A cough. A hacking, heavy cough, but still, he's alive.

After a moment more coughing.

I look straight at him, and attempt a real smile.

"You good?"

His eyes meet mine with a hint of humor.

"Do I look it?"

His voice is pained and weak. But he'll live.

"Just be thankful you're alive at all, the state you're in."

He smiles now, only to start hacking again. He doubles over for a moment, and his starkly blonde hair hangs in a matted curtain toward the floor.

He seems oddly familiar, like I've heard his voice some long time ago. And his manner, it seems like I know him. But I've never met him, at least not that I remember.

He straightens out again, and wipes the smears of crimson and spit from his mouth.

"Yeah, you're right. 'Fraid I'm in no position to fight, so do your worst solo."

Our gazes simultaneously wander to the devil-woman, watching as she slowly peels herself from the cracked crater in the wall–

And her face is starting to peel away?!

Oh for crying out loud.

Sighing, I stand up straight and stretch out my hands.

"Don't worry. I can handle them for a bit."

Where's this confidence come from?

I guess all that matters is that I win.

Standing and turning to the devil, now recovered from the flames, I look them up and down. Their once beautiful face is horrid, large pincers from their jaw, eight beady eyes, horrid musty brown hair all over them.

"What an idiot. Fell for the oldest trick in the book, works every time on men."

The devil's voice is deep and sounds like a thousand metal spiders crawling over rock. Suddenly it changes form again. Uncountable tiny spiders climbing each other, forming something. There it is, a beautiful woman all of a sudden.

"I wonder if you will too?" The voice is soft now, soothing. But it won't get me.

I grin in response, and raise my hands instinctively.

A wave of flame rushes forward, searing the air as it piles on and on like a supersized blowtorch–

How can I just do that all of a sudden? It feels so natural, like I've been doing it my whole life. Like gathering it in my hands and throwing water from a pond at somebody.

The devil jumps out the way nimbly and rushes towards me, mandibles clicking. They gnash rapidly, and a hiss escapes their V shaped mouth as pointed fangs click downward chillingly fast over and over again.

Everything slows, like a marble dropped in syrup.
The anticipation beneath my skin has reached a new level, practically demanding to be let out.
I don't know, I don't know if I can...
A sudden rush slams into my mind, and it all becomes too much to handle.
The pot boils over, and I black out.

***

–IKARI–

My head is still spinning, but I'm physically okay. I raise my head slowly, watching the battle around me. With my strength long gone I'm just an exhausted kid now. Helpless. But, this guy, something's up, like watching a creature...

The battle rages between the strange boy and the spider devil, but I think it's safe to say that the boy is more than human as well now. Hands filled with flame, searing orange eyes, an aura of heat so strong it melts the metal around him; but most of all, his expression is inhumanly blank.
Something happened a moment ago, when that devil was bearing down on him. Something changed. There was an explosion of flame, and when it died down–

He was different.

His hair is no longer black, now a cascade of reds and oranges. He turns to the other devil. And spears of fire surge from the air, whistling toward it–

But it lowers itself down, as the two human legs split into eight spindly ones–

Once again, it rushes forward, leaping at him. His hand curls around open air, as if grasping an invisible handle. He whips his arm around, like swinging a sword–

And a trail of fire cracks like a whip, drawing a line of searing hair and flesh across the torso of the spider. It scuttles back, hissing, and only now can I get a real look at its horrid appearance. Eight hairy legs twitch one by one, sharp spikes at the end of each tapping the floor. Its torso is entirely human, yet coated in a layer of that thick-yet-fine spider fur, and of course adorned with the wound it just received. As for its head, once again it seems completely arachnid. Those gnashing madibles, those fangs, that hissing V shaped opening coated with a sheen of saliva.

And the boy dashes back frantically, hands and fingers meshing rapidly to form a series of strange hand symbols, and with each one some new shape of blazing tendrils descend upon it–

Only for each one to be brushed away, and the spider bears down on him once again as it clicks away in glee–

He continues to back away, his expressionless face fixated on the horror of hair and legs that continues to advance. Raising his left hand in defence, a wall of fire springs from the ground. The spider is forced to slow–

He splays the fingers on his right hand, arm fully tensed. As it begins to glow white-hot, his palm shakes slightly, and then violently as a swirling globe of smouldering flame sparks to life in his hand–

Everything seems to slow as he steps forward, turning in a three-sixty and leaping into the air–

Like a baseballer throwing their pitch, he flings the inferno globe at the spider–

For a second, everything goes orange and red. And as the strangely warm flames wash off me and the air clears–

The body of the spider is slumped against the concrete, just like earlier. Except this time, a perfect sphere taken out of their torso, like an apple after being cored. Around the rim of the empty space in which their body should have been, embers smoulder aggressively. And as he looks toward the corpse, he still stands as stoic as ever, despite his rather heavy breathing.

Yet he shows one hint of emotion, as the corners of his mouth curl up.

Tasting the acrid tang of smoke reminds me of our situation as I recover from the shock of seeing whatever that was. The whole warehouse is burning now, flames rising up in every corner as the air becomes thick with haze and sparks

"We need to get out!"

My voice is as coarse as gravedigger's dirt, but this warehouse is about to go.

He looks at me.

"Can you hear me? We *need* to *go* now!"

Still he stares blankly.

"Can you hear–"

No emotion. His eyes are a flaming mirror, staring straight through me.

And something about that blank gaze–

A bead of sweat forms on my forehead, slowly trickling down. So this is how the helpless feel in the face of danger; deep rooted fear, complete, unbridled fear. We stare at each other, but I may as well have been looking at a blank wall. My breathing is out of control, my body shaking, my iris darting around the room. He steps towards me and I feel that scorching heat, if only for a few heartbeats. He raises his hand and–

Without warning, he drops to his knees and lets out a long, deep breath, like a sigh of final relief. His clouded eyes focus on me, becoming clear as crystal. The reds of his hair fade to black in an instant, like resetting him to default, or ripping threads from a frayed jumper. Instantly, he looks at his palm with an expression of pain.

"You okay?"

He sighs, and flexes his hand a few times.

"Yeah. But what just happened?-"

"Don't concern yourself with that. I'll explain later–"

I place a hand on his shoulder, guiding him to the wall.

"–But for now, sit."

Gratefully, he sinks to the floor, closing his eyes as he lets his hands fall to the floor, a sigh of exhaustion escaping him.

What should I say to him?

I mean, I can't even describe what just happened to myself. It was like one moment he was a boy, the next a creature. Like, how is that possible–

Hold on.

Actually, it doesn't sound too far off from–

He smiles weakly and opens his eyes again, but when he speaks it seems like he can barely form the words due to exhaustion.

"S-sorry… guess I never… needed to punch… you that hard."

I chuckle for a second, distracting myself from the reality of things.

"Don't worry. It wasn't that bad. Now rest. You need it."

Clearing some of the wreckage, I prop him against the wall and slump down next to him.
Breathe.

I glance at the boy, sleeping peacefully in a mess of fire and rubble and streaks of crimson. Looking away, I stare down the glassy eyes of the spider devil, trying not to look at the hole in its chest inflicted by my–
My what?
Friend?
Partner?
Enemy?
Saviour.
Yes. Whatever he may be, he still saved me. Someone saved me.
Saved *me*.
Someone cared enough to save me. After all these years…
Feeling something drip down my face, I glance at my hands. Splashes of crimson coat my palms.
But then, something else. A clear drop of liquid. Then another. And another. They pool together in my hands, like raindrops pooling in a divot. It's been a while, but… I know these…
Tears.

Am I… crying?

Yes. That's it. *Crying.* Something so alien to me, yet so wonderful. I wonder, how long has it been since I cried? I'm only sixteen– maybe seventeen?

Whatever I am, I know damn well enough that I'm not old enough to be emotionally stunted to the point where I can't cry. Good to see I still can.

Shutting my eyes, I relish the streams down my face. Sounds of sirens try to penetrate my bliss, but I shut them out. Nothing matters, not for now.

And in my bliss, I failed to properly register the men dressed in white who quietly sneak into the flaming mess, scooping the spider's body onto a stretcher, and vanishing into the shadows. In a daze, my mind wanders for a second–

Who were they…?

I guess…

But soon exhaustion takes over.

No matter.

Nothing matters for now.

***

–NAMELESS–

My eyes dart around the soft upholstered interior, the padded seats, the strange man behind the wheel. Every instinct is telling me to question, to find answers. But now doesn't feel like the time. I glance sideways. Phew... the boy is with me. Fine. I open my mouth to question the driver and–

***

A hospital. Why? How? Since when was I–?
Even more questions pile onto my consciousness, overpowering me. I feel less tired now, maybe even somewhat rested. That man. The driver.
Where am I?
Scanning the room I see almost nothing. Except hospital equipment of course, and on the table next to me a...
Painfully, I roll over and grab it.
A newspaper.
Odd. I lift it in front of me, taking a look at the date. The words hit me like a steam train ramming straight through my mind, brushing all other thoughts to the side.
September 7th? That means–
I was sleeping for... 5 days straight?
What happened to me?

The paper. On the front page...

The Supuritto incident?

As I prepare to read, the door bursts open. I jerk my neck
like it was electrocuted, eyes straining to see if it's...
Messy blonde hair. Piercing blue eyes. Katana by his side.
New clothes, yet the same person.
The boy from earlier.
The boy I saved.
There's someone with him. No, hold on. Two others. A
man and a woman, both sharply dressed. I can see it in
their eyes, they mean business. The boy leans against the
wall, the man and woman pull up chairs. All my questions
come flooding out, melding together into one phrase - one
word even.

"Why?"

And they begin to speak. Their words are a tornado in my
mind, swirling with oddities.
Spider devil... collapse from exhaustion... massive fire...
lifesaver... Ikari... national safety... devil hunting?
Devil hunting.
Huh?

But I'm one of the devils? That makes no sense. They speak again as their closing pitch cuts through my thoughts like a cleaver.

"So, will you join us? Use your power to save this nation. Be a national safety devil hunter. After all, Ikari here has already decided."

"What did he say?"

"First, answer my question. Will you?"

I look at Ikari. *Ikari*. A name, after all this madness. He's avoiding eye contact. Looking everywhere except for meeting my gaze. But I can see he wants to say something. He smiles, but it seems strained. He's worried. I know what he chose. But do I want that path? Maybe they retire, these devil hunters... if they survive. But if I do, and reach that point. My normal life. It would be mine to keep.

I keep my voice level–

Looking the man dead in the eye.

"When do I start?"

***

Ikari walks beside me down this strange corridor, but it will feel like home soon enough, I guess. I think back to what that man said.

4 weeks of training.

Simple enough, I suppose, even if I can't help but feel like it's a bit lacklustre. I glance back to Ikari, following his springy movements, his playful emotion. I know why he's happy. Apparently, we're going to have another team member. A girl.

I sigh. He really is quite simple, but considering my motivation I can't judge.

"You feeling okay?" His voice is some strange mix of soft and harsh.

"Yeah I'm fine. Just taking it all in…"

"Same here. Ain't it crazy? They made us devil hunters! I've heard this girl joining us is meant to 'keep us in check'. Hope she's *nice* though…"

"Keep us in check? They better send a jailer!"

Ikari's laugh is loud and grating, but it's good to have a normal conversation with him where we aren't soaked in blood. In fact, the standard issue clothes given to us are rather nice. A simple white shirt, black trousers, basic trainers. Far better than my old rags and ripped shirts.

He taps me on the shoulder.

"Hey, I don't know if this is sensitive to you but… I still never got your name"

That's a question that only now I realise I have no answer to.

What can I say?

The truth. I'll tell him the truth.

My name.

My name.

"To tell the truth, I– I don't know."

He raises his eyebrows.

"I, well, I was never named. I never knew my father, he abandoned me before he could give me a name."

"That's rough. Sorry, 'suppose the question was in bad taste."

His words are still pure, but the weight of that knowledge has changed him. His steps are less energetic, his demeanour more reserved. I can tell he's building up to saying something, to offer some words of healing. But what he says is completely different.

"Never knew my father. Filthy alcoholic, got himself killed and left me with a bunch of debt and no way to move forward in life. Really set me up for a crumpled future."

Hold on a minute. That sounds eerily similar to–

Thankfully Ikari interrupts my thoughts.

"United by oddball fathers huh? We might be quite the duo…"

"Maybe this girl will be the same. Now that would be crazy."

"Fatherless trio? Devils got no chance ay?"

We laugh together, realising we aren't so different at all.

"What's next?"

"Basic driving, apparently."

"Driving? Like, cars?"

"Yep."

"I'm so gonna crash."

***

26th September, August 2008

–NAMELESS–

There it is. Large oak double doors, hard varnish floors. A simple polished metal plaque, stamped with one word. I need answers, and if they'll be anywhere, they'll be here. A timeless vault of mental wealth, passed down by generations of hunters, so I'm told. The national safety HQ library.

Rows upon rows of books, seemingly endless, some not having seen human touch for decades. I stand, struck by awe in this treasure trove of ancient knowledge, surrounded by ornate gold and silver, deep mahogany shelves, and for the extra touch, the grandest chandeliers this side of the pacific. All spotless, of course.

What am I here for? Answers, but to what?

Stupid question. I already know, the truth is deep rooted in my subconscious. The rather grand index waits before me, pulling me in, daring me to find out. Running my finger frantically down the pages, I scan for any mention of that word I've heard far too much lately.

Devil, Devil, Devil, dev- ah! Devil contracts and merges. Aisle 37, section 5, shelf 6. I groan, and peer at the faded map.

The walk through the library is long and tiring, always fishing for those numbers in a sea of others. As I walk, I unwittingly recall the events of that night, casting my mind back, like I'm living the moment again. That feeling echoes in my head, the overwhelming sensation just before…

I didn't know, I didn't know if I could…

A sudden rush had slammed into my mind, and it all became too much to handle.

The pot had boiled over, and I blacked out.

Suddenly I had been watching my movements from some other place, some strange and dark landscape with a floor of reflective black. I saw what I should have seen, felt what I should have felt. And yet, it seemed… disconnected. Like

I was feeling and seeing somebody else's senses, as if I was only sensing the afterimage. And I felt nothing - no pain, no exhaustion. But there was one thing, one thing I'll never forget. I could feel its unbridled confidence, the way it knew it would never lose this. As if it was alive, and conscious. The devil that had waited too long, awake at last.

And that feeling, where my body was a puppet, strung only on strings of power, the true puppetmaster watching in horror from a cage of his own making. It still makes me shudder.

And when I, or it, turned to Ikari…

Thankfully, after a moment, the glass shattered, the true strings were reconnected, and I simply forgot. It's been coming back to me though, little snippets. Some in the hospital bed, some just in my day to day. During meals, during conversation, during sleep. And now I remember it for the most part. After all, it's what drove me here to find out more.

I peel the book away from the shelves - *Devil merging and contracts*. It's dusty, out of use for some time. As I carry the book to a chair, it feels far heavier than it should. Like the weight of the very words on its pages are weighing it down. Reaching a chair, I open it to a cloud of dust. A stack of warnings, and I flip right past them. I think it's safe to say I'm past the point of no return. Finally, the few pages of actual information. The answers I've been searching for.

Devil merging and contracting is an ancient process, often used by the devil hunters of the late Edo period to gain power. To begin, a brief definition of a devil:

Devil (devils,) [d-eh-v-i-l]
A devil is the fear of something personified. The greater the fear, the stronger the devil.
I.E The devil of something like sea cucumbers would be pretty useless, while the devils of things like knives, blood and loneliness would be a far greater foe.

With that established, let us turn to forms of drawing a devil's power for one's own. There is only one method to achieve this, with both advantages and drawbacks. It is as follows:

<u>*Contracting*</u>
To draw upon a devil's power, one must form a contract. This means summoning a suitable devil and offering them a suitable deal. Deals often go along the lines of the human gaining a large amount of power relevant to their devil,

while the devil resides in their body or spirit. Some devils prefer to inhabit an organ, but they do not physically affect it. A common place for contracted devils to reside is the eye. However, contracts vary wildly. The most risky place to contract or 'bind' a devil to is the deeper parts of one's mind. While this can give the user incredible amounts of power, it can strongly influence their emotions and psychological state. This can be extremely detrimental, especially if the user is already suffering. Contracts can be formed between devil and human by a third party if the human is incapable, with the third party choosing the terms of their contract for them. This third party is most commonly referred to as a 'devil speaker' and to tell the truth they are mostly all insane due to the prolonged contact with different devils. This can be terrible for the human they sign the contract for, as often they end up having no idea what the terms of their contract are. While most contracts are mundane in nature, some can have clauses such as complete body control for a period of time, or even manipulative clauses allowing the devil to bend the contracted to their will. While contracts can theoretically be changed, it is almost unheard of. It requires manifesting your devil and forcing them to change their hold over you. For obvious reasons, most devils will not like this. But, if desperate, the ritual is fairly simple. A circle of blood, a meditative state, and an object directly related to your devil is all you need. Oh, and an object imbued with emotion. I will however warn you, dear reader, that this ritual has not been successfully performed since the Heian[2] era.

Any devil bind, merge or contract will allow the devil to communicate directly with your mind. Depending on the devil's literacy, this can either be conversational or through common body signals such as blood rushes, ringing ears or headaches. Some devils choose not to speak however, particularly ancient ones such as the devil of noise, devil of conflict and even pain itself to name a few.

<u>*The 12 Fears*</u>
The twelve fears are the strongest of the common devils, due to them each being the strength of a widespread fear. For example, the 11th fear, fear of snakes. All of them are ranked from one to twelve, hence the name. We must clarify that these numbers are a ranking of more than just strength. It also takes into account strategic thinking and

---

[2] The heian period - Referring to 784 - 1185 japan, roughly 1000 years ago

experience. However, overwhelming strength can lead to a high rank. While this is the extent of our knowledge of these elite devils, we do know two things. Firstly, the 12 Fears are not strictly the strongest devils. As later stated, they are given their power by the first devil. For further information on the first devil and its council, please contact your local devil hunting HQ director. They are the only ones who are authorised to know, or tell people about it.

Secondly, all Fears are given a piece of the soul from the first devil, granting them immense power. The twelve fears are known for their ability to use the soul projection. This is a technique that projects the devil's soul, or put simply the fear felt toward them into the world in the form of pure energy. The effect of this varies, but it is powerful. And I mean powerful. In fact the true potential of this technique is lost to time. But, if you come face to face with one, run. And run fast.

I struggle to take in all the information, cherry picking only what truly matters. My father was a devil whisperer. He must have been. It's the only explanation. Is that why he was killed? Was he insane like they all are? So, my powers didn't awaken for so long because the contract was unreliable? And of course the only way to truly understand it is some ancient ritual. An object imbued with emotion? What even–

And the 12 Fears? Wait…

The spider devil. It's eye. It had something written on it. *The fifth.* One of the 12 Fears.

So, I beat one? One of the devil's elite? Or did it beat one– This is too much.

I need fresh air. Grabbing the book and sliding it into the waistband of my trousers, I run from the library.

I have my answers, but… I don't like the harsh truth. Well, who does, I suppose.

***

–IKARI–

I stare at the bottom of the bunk above me, listening to the subtle creaks as he moves about. What a strangely normal day. After he ran off to wherever he did, I just walked around the place. Not bad to be honest, they even gave us an apartment. And half decent clothes. And alright food. I call out softly.

"Hey, I've been thinking."

"Hmmm?"

His voice is kind, much kinder than when I first met him.

"Combat training finals start tomorrow and... I kind of need something to call you…"

"Yeah, I suppose. What are you thinking?"

"Something simple, but still memorable. Like… Tengen?"

"Tengen huh?"

He laughs gently.

"Yeah. I like that."

"So Tengen it is?"

"Tengen it is."

The conversion ends abruptly, but I could almost hear the smile in that last sentence.

Night Tengen. Sleep well, my friend.

***

"As your last companion is delayed, your finals training session will take place with just the two of you."

His voice booms, and his breath stinks of liquor. Messy hair, crooked glasses, broken nose.

For crying out loud, who is this guy?

I look at Tengen, kneeling beside me. I really wanna just say it outright - This instructor is off his head.

Knocking back whisky while introducing class?

"Your combat training is very simple." He tosses a large clear bag of what appears to be blood at Tengen, complete with a straw. "You need to beat me in a fight. Two on one."

Really? That'll be easy, so what's with the blood?

"If I *accidentally* kill *you,* inhuman one, simply drink up. You are a devil after all. And I'm sorry to say, I'm not the biggest fan of your kind. So apologies if I play a bit rough with you. But, before we begin, a quick quiz."

A quiz? After saying that? Could they have given us a sane instructor for once? And I'm not a devil, what on earth will I do?

"Only one question. If a man has eight screws, and his toaster breaks, how many ducks bombed Iraq?"

To my shock, Tengen responds instantly.

"Fish and chips."

Huh?

But when the instructor turns to me, I scramble for an answer, ending up with-

"Criss cross applesauce."

The instructor looks over us, scrutinising our physiques. He seems to ponder for a moment, and then smiles.

"You both pass."

We both look at him quizzically, expecting an explanation.

"After all, the best devil hunters are nuts."

You know what, I can't even be bothered to wonder what's going on anymore.

"Well. What are you waiting for? Attack me"

My focus snaps back to the instructor, rising to my feet and preparing to rush him. My footsteps blend with Tengen's as we move forward, I step in, ready to swing–

Crack.

***

My eyes flutter open, looking straight at that blue sky.

What happened? Why do I feel so groggy?

And who's this?

A figure is standing over me, looking down. I force my eyes to focus, squinting. A girl. That's it. Long cascading hair, the colour gently fading from red to orange. She's tall, I think. Or am I just really low? A leather jacket, ripped jeans. Concerned eyes, glints of concern trapped in amber, inspect my condition. Is this a hallucination, who is this?

Oh yeah.

This must be our new teammate. That's it. So where's Tengen? I strain my neck, sending waves of pain down my spine.

"Don't!"

The girl really does sound worried.

"He rocked you solid, and you hit the ground real hard!"

Huh? What is happening?

Of course, the training - that stupid instructor.

Great. He really landed one blow, and I was sleeping?

"You'll recover soon, but don't try to speak or move. You need to rest and relax as much as possible. Oh, and your friend is fine."

My gaze flits about as I search for his face.

"Afternoon Ikari." Tengen's voice is horribly rough, he sounds like someone with one foot in the grave.

"That didn't end well."

"Yeah. You can say that again."

Testing each limb slowly, I feel for anything majorly wrong, but I seem okay for the most part.

Very slowly, I start to rise.

"Wait, let me help!"

She puts a hand on my shoulder, guiding me to my feet.

"Thanks."

I look at her, and for a moment, just for a moment, our eyes lock. Quickly she pulls her hand away and turns to Tengen. I get a good look at Tengen as well. He looks to have lasted a moment longer than me, if only a fleeting one.

"How's my face looking?"

His voice has already improved a lot, devil healing really is amazing. Sometimes, I catch myself wishing…

"You won't be doing any photoshoots for a while, let's just say that."

The girl clears her throat, and looks back and forth between us.

"Names?"

"Ikari."

"Tengen. Nice to meet you."

"Shinobu. Nice to meet you both as well."

Tengen pulls himself up, and before staggering away he turns to me and Shinobu.

"Catch up over food later?"

"Sure. Our place?" I begin to follow Tengen, turning to Shinobu for her response.

"I'm down. Your flat is number 27 right?"

"Yeah, I think it is. Tengen! 27?"

He flashes a weak thumbs up, his thumb skewed toward his elbow.

"Uhh, catch you later!"

She waves, but her eyes are still on Tengen.

I run to him, almost falling a good few times. We walk in silence. And yet again, I find myself strangely jealous whenever I look over to him. I mean, it seems bad to desire something that is seen as such a curse, but regardless…

***

"So"

Tengen speaks through a bite of pizza, his mouth smeared with sauce.

"How'd they get you to join up?"

She looks up from her food.

"Well, I kinda didn't have a choice."

Shinobu goes back to eating, refusing to elaborate.

"Huh?" What does she mean?

"Well, my family tradition is to hunt devils. Those who don't are outcast and left for dead."

"Oh."

After a while, Tengen gets up for a drink.

"Care to join me?"

Me and Shinobu both stand as Tengen pours out a set of shots. I mean, I couldn't tell you what the shots actually are, but the bottle from the top of the dumpster must have a lovely flavour, right?

"Oh. Shinobu, are you 18?"

"Nope."

Me and Tengen laugh.

"Well neither are we."

Out on the balcony, the sun is a beautiful crimson as the landscape is bathed in the final light of the day. Some small talk is made, but we mostly just sit and watch. I meet Tengen's eye, and we smile, both of us knowing we made the right choice. And for a moment, even if it's a fleeting one, I can pretend none of this ever happened. All we are is three friends, watching the sun set over the hills.

The future looks bright for the first time in a while.

I wonder what the other me would think of this, if he was to emerge.

That doesn't matter now, I suppose.

Looks like I have found my people.

3: LET'S CALL IT A DATE

–IKARI–

She won't leave Tengen's side. I look at him, lifeless and slumped on the floor. He'll be back up once this is over, and then it'll start again. Their little inside jokes, subtle glances when the other isn't looking. I don't know why I find it so infuriating, but I just do. Am I just a petulant child–?

I need to breathe. Get in the game, Ikari.

Calm yourself. He's your friend - be happy for him. But I can't. I feel so much frustration for nothing and based on the way that jackass instructor is laughing at me, I probably look it.

"Something wrong, boy?"

He's jeering. He knows he's won. Smug fu–

Just stay calm. Quick breath out. Long breath in. Level his gaze. And charge.

Punch after punch, kick after kick, blows with enough force to smash concrete. Both of us unyielding, both of us amped up.

I and I step in, catching him off guard for a split second–

I rotate my shoulder in an arc, bringing my elbow crashing down on his skull–

Crack.

And I drop to my knees, panting. I actually landed a single blow.

That was all it took.

With any luck, she might look my way now.

***

Shinobu walks from the fallen instructor, waving a brief goodbye to the boys. Her mind wanders as the sun shines high in the sky, casting a comforting warmth onto the fields. She makes her way toward the canteen, enticed by the thought of lunch. A soft whirr accompanies the sliding of electric doors, giving way to the soft white halls of HQ.

She nods a greeting to a few passing staff, quickly reaching her goal. Hit by a wave of bustle and noise upon entry, she grabs a beat-up metal tray and approaches the serving area. The tray makes a dry scratching sound as it runs down the counter, finding itself pushed by slender hands toward the food station.

The red-faced dinner lady slams on a ladle of fluffy white rice, then another of creamy pork katsu, and finally a few biscuits. Nodding to the lady and taking her tray, she stops by the salad stand, scooping pickled vegetables onto it all. And, to top it off, a glass of lemon water.

The cream-coloured tables lined with blue plastic stools stretch down the expansive room, dotted with small groups of tired workers chatting about their afternoon duties. Sitting down by the window, away from it all, she languidly works her way through the meal. The breading of the katsu is soggy, and the biscuits seem to magically suck all the moisture out of her mouth. Almost gagging at the smell of the vegetables, she powers through it all in the name of hunger. A shame, considering how wonderful it all looked on her tray. Draining the cup of water with a sigh, she stands, making her way toward the back of the room. Dropping off the tray and glass, she thanks the dinner lady with a small bow and heads out. Sometimes, she really wishes they served something decent.

The door to her room swings open, the afternoon light streaming in. Her room is well kept, not a spot of dust. She heads to the washroom.

Looking into the mirror, she leans down and washes her face, cooling off. But, try as she might, she cannot keep her mind off them.

Ikari and Tengen.

What a strange pair.

But, she finds herself fixated on one in particular.

Tengen, the devil boy.

She can sense it, the ancient presence sharing his mind.

She knows it must be eradicated.

But, can she do it?

She stares herself down, circling the question through her mind. To kill the devil is what her father would do. What she should do, as a member of the Kusa clan.

But, whether she likes it or not, she knows.

She's fallen for him.

And he's fallen for her.

What should she do?

Perhaps a run would clear her head.

As she laces up her shoes, she makes a choice. Grabbing a piece of paper, she scribbles a note.

Folding it and slipping it into her pocket, she rises.

The door locks with a gentle click behind her, and she makes her way to the exit.

The sun is starting to approach the horizon now, amber rays thrown across the land.

Leaving the building, she begins to run.

No destination in mind, she runs.

Sound begins to fade, all thoughts taking a back seat.

All she hears is her breathing, all she thinks is to get one foot in front of the other.

Breath in, in, in, out.

Step, step, step, each time her foot falls it hits the ground with a soft thud.

Concrete soon turns to dirt underfoot, the flat ground starting to angle up into the hills.

Still she runs.

The sun dips fully beneath the horizon now, dusk turning to twilight.

Still she runs.

The peak of the hill looms, the incline getting harsher.

Still she runs.

Acid begins to well up in her legs as she drives each foot into the steep earth, dragging herself up the final parts of the incline–

Finally, she stops. Feet firmly planted into the dirt, she looks to the sky. The clear night allows the heavens to shine bright as ever, a swirling artwork of intricate shining points and splashes of ethereal colour.

Her mind wanders briefly, thinking back to all those times when she stood over Tengen while Ikari stood against the instructor. She sees it as odd, how the boy contracted to a devil is so much weaker than a regular human. Then again, it seems the boy is very new to his contract. And as for Ikari, calling him a *regular* human seems like somewhat of an injustice.

As she stands there, feeling the sweat slowly dry off, the sharp nocturnal air reminds her all too soon of where she is.

With the sight of her steaming breath, she decides to turn in.

The run down the hill is exhilarating, the steep ground and her dangerously fast pace combining into a rush of wind sending her hair wild. She smiles and laughs into the rushing air, her feet practically skimming the ground with each stride.

Here and now, flying across the ground like this–
She really does feel alive.

The lights of HQ come into view as she slows slightly, letting the rush of speed fade. She slows even more as dirt turns back to concrete, dropping into a walk. Clouds of smoke billow in her face with each breath as she nears the entrance, letting herself relax.

A short run, but she's now confident in her choice.

HQ is dark, the halls illuminated only by sporadically placed night lamps casting a soft glow. She takes a turn up the stairs, away from her room, toward the boys residential block.

Rounding a corner, she tiptoes down the hall, straining her eyes on the door numbers.

Almost missing it due to the darkness, she does a double take.

There.

27.

She crouches down and slips the note from her pocket, quickly scanning its message for the final time.

Tengen
Top of the highest peak, tomorrow at sunset.
There's something I must tell you.
Shall we call it a date?
Shinobu,
x

Satisfied, she slides it under the crack of the door, before creeping away down the hallways into the shadows.

***

"Ikari? Ikari?"

Urgh. That took it out of me. I peel my eyes open, and there he is. Alive and well, as always.

"You beat him! You knocked out the instructor! We all passed training thanks to you."

I did? Oh yeah. I did. And I only could because I was jealous of Tengen. Whatever makes me tick, I suppose.

"Morning Tengen."

My voice is horrendously gravely, like my throat was rubbed with sandpaper on the inside. Pushing away from my bed, the sheets sticking to my skin from sweat, I swing my legs over the side and rise. The sun shines bright, splintering through the blinds.

Rubbing my eyes, I only have one thought.

"Breakfast?"

He smiles.

"Yeah! I made beans on toast!"

Yeah. Shinobu's love for England got to him.

Hmph. Shinobu. Taking a seat at the table, I admire the light shining on the crimson leaves of the plant she gave him. Perhaps it isn't so bad. After all, ever since he came here and met her it's almost like that volatile, destructive part of him has melted away, revealing an honestly pretty golden core. Yeah. Maybe I should be happy for him.

"Ta-da!" He strides over, carrying two plates piled high with the finest western breakfast you can around these parts. Getting straight to stuffing my face, he rambles on and on about how cool I was yesterday. Apparently Shinobu told him everything. It would seem she might have over exaggerated it a bit though, as I don't remember anything about me flying. Ah well. Worse things to lie about, I guess. At least she mentioned me.

"Hey Ikari? I think me and Shinobu are gonna head out this evening, do you want to come?"

My knuckles are white with pressure, teeth grinding like some starving horse.

"I think I'll stay."

"You sure?"

"Yeah. Thanks though."

"Alright man."

We let the conversation die, admiring the sun's daily climb. Almost at the top of the sky now. Tengen will be going in a couple hours. God, how frustrating. I can try to be happy for him, but I can't control my subconscious. Me and me can enjoy a meal I suppose. Yeah. Just me and my desperate self. Great.

–TENGEN–

Pushing my hair into place, I smile as the fine mist of hairspray shoots toward my head. What a genius thing, this hairspray.

Saying goodbye to Ikari, I leave him watching the sunset. I do feel bad, but it's only today. Wonder what's up with him recently though. I feel like he's always frustrated, but I just can't put my finger on why. I'll talk to him when I'm back. Be nice to catch up properly, it feels like time has run away while training. That's over now, thanks to him. The sun falls in rays ahead of me, casting down the corridor. My footsteps seem to click with each bouncy step. Turning down the stairs, I switch my thoughts to Shinobu. I wonder what it is she wanted to talk about. To be fair, we have gotten pretty close recently. My heartrate has quietly increased, constantly checking my reflection on the polished walls. Being nervous is fair, right? Checking a map, I trace the route. Up to the peak of Kyoto mountains. Not a long walk, considering how high up in the hills HQ already is. The sun is turning that beautiful crimson again, akin to that day with the three of us on our little balcony. It seems things really are looking up, for all of us.

***

Shinobu looks out over the landscape, not really caring to take it all in. She fidgets nervously with her skirt, preparing herself.

Involuntarily, she finds her mind wandering to the past.

She thinks, what would my father do?

Her father.

Her family, the Kusa.

And her mother.

She scoffs–

And falls into a memory.

The grass and dirt beneath her turn to varnished wooden floors, the expansive view to a stark white wall. The family crest of the Kusa takes centre stage, ornately represented in the finest gold and silver. Beneath that, her mothers prized possession.

Her hunters whip.

Used to slay 1000 devils, she said.

What she ever followed up with, however, was that the strongest of them was the devil of gloves.

Shinobu chuckles.

What did she call herself again?

Humanity's greatest warrior?

What a joke.

Warrior? She was a fraud.

And an abusive one, with a harsh temper.

She was a sadistic, power hungry leader who led a clan under some grand delusion that she would bring peace to all the world.

She grabbed the Kusa by a chokehold, and forced them into her delusion.

And, in return, tainted thousands of years of rich familial history with her idiocrasy and violence.

She falls further into the past, and a figure stands before her.

It was her, and yet her face is coated in shadow.

How odd.

She has forgotten her mothers face.

And yet, her arms and hands are crystal clear. Her toned and scarred skin, those slender yet rough palms that bruised her cheek.

791 times.

She made her remember that.

Over a mere two years, 791 times.

And, if her mother ever asked her what the count was, and god forbid she had forgotten…

Her hand instinctively moves to protect her back, her mind dredging up forgotten experience. Her mother would hold that dark snaking tendril in a choking grip, and bring it down.

A sound like a gunshot, and a moment later, pain. Searing, acidic pain that tore her flesh asunder. Each strike compounding on the last, slowly ripping her back apart. Long lines of agony overlapping more and more, like hacking at clay with a bread knife.

But, left just intact enough that she could do it all again a month later.

She remembers the mornings after, her father tenderly massaging the mangled, lacerated flesh while slowly picking out shards of broken glass left behind by the strike. And the phrase her father would whisper to her, as she winced away tears, the phrase passed down for generations. Passed down by real, respectful hunters. The phrase to call upon when one is at their lowest. She remembers that.

And most of all, she remembers her words.

Disappointment.

Curse.

Rotten child.

Failure.

The way she would berate her, utterly unforgiving.

Why could she not just see her as different?

She didn't want to be a killer.

But she didn't care.

So she hit, so she yelled, so she lashed.

Two years.

She snaps open her eyes, the gentle sun bringing her back to reality.

Right now, she has a date to think about.

And after that, it's time.

Time to say goodbye.

And maybe, to pass something on.

Something to leave behind in this world.

***

Halfway round the world, a dark alley bears witness.

"Tell me, filthy devil. Of which origin do you reside?"

The man's words are confident, but his body betrays his true feelings. His voice shakes with every syllable, his knuckles are white on the handle of his sword. The tip of it, intended to be levelled threateningly at the figure's throat, shudders and sways like a flag in the wind.

The shadows of the alleyway seem to close in on him, a fly caught in a web.

The figure is but a smear of a slightly darker shade of black, barely noticeable. The clouds above part briefly, casting an eerie silvery light onto the scene. It shines off the blade, cutting away the shadow on the lower half of the figure's face.

A well defined jaw, smooth milky skin. A few loose strands of hair fall onto their rounded chin. They brush them aside, the cream colour of their nails matched flawlessly to the soft roses glimmering on the lower half of their face as they softly lay a perfectly manicured finger onto their pursed lips.

They part those same lips in a playful smile, and even with almost no light to speak of, their teeth almost glow with an unnerving whiteness.

In a soft, sultry voice barely above a whisper, they respond.

"Why should I tell you, hunter? What's in it for me, hmm?"

They step closer.

The man stammers horribly, the figure's sadistic allure snatching his breath by force.

"Tell me now, or d-die! And stay b-back!"

The figure's head tilts.

"Aww, what a shame."

They widen that provocative smile, layering their words with that same tone.

"And here I thought we could be friends…"

With a desperate cry, the man raises his sword to strike. The figure covers their mouth to suppress a yawn, still smiling. As the man brings his sword down, the figure's other hand twitches. They move their index finger left to right, barely two centimetres.

The sword clatters to the floor, the white of the man's knuckles dissipating as the pressure on the handle is released. His fingers remain wrapped around the handle, along with his calloused palm.

The sword lies on the floor, out of reach.

Wait, what?

The man's eyes move down shakily, to the sight of his... hands?

And his gaze is met by two stumps, cut so cleanly he barely noticed.

But now he notices.

A screams bubbles and rises in his throat, choking him. He opens his mouth, but no sound comes out.

The figure's finger twitches again.

He tries to scream again, but something is wrong. He feels himself moving, slowly tipping backward, but his feet are rooted firmly to the ground.

He spends his final moment in a swath of confusion and terror, unable to comprehend what has happened.

The figure smirks, as a thump rings out around the alley.

The man's glassy eyes meet the sky, looking up from the

ground. His body stands tall, swaying in the sudden wind as a few trails of crimson reach the base of his neck.

With a final playful giggle, the figure returns to shadow, and the alleyway is swathed in darkness.

The man once known as a devil hunter lies in the dark, yet another victim.

A sultry laugh rings out into the night, as the clouds coat the moon once again.

***

–TENGEN–

"Won't forget this view quickly." I murmur in her ear, not breaking the quiet whistle of wind. The expanse of greater Kyoto to our right, the beautiful rolling hills of the mountains to our left. All bathed in those beautiful godrays. I look to the right, watching as all the people miles below amble around their evening routines, the bustle of cars settling in place of conversation lost to the wind. Sun refracts off windows wet with the afternoon's rain, casting a rainbow hue over the city. Looking the other way, vibrant emerald greens juxtaposed with subtle crimson flowers of the sakura trees deep in bloom. They stretch till the sky meets the land, the slash of a heavenly knife across central Japan. And the sky. Oh the sky. Dusk is settling, the vermillion sun just a semi circle on the horizon. To the east, the night sky begins, a rolling black canvas sprinkled with dazzling stars, the same stars that had once seemed so dull. A long breath out. I feel as if I should stop everything here, cast this moment in amber. A memory to keep for all my life. One not spoiled by devils, not even by my own distracted mind. A truly golden memory.

"Tengen?"

The soft voice eases me out of trance, remembering I'm not alone. But I don't want to be alone. Not this time.

"Yeah?"

"Have you ever had someone special to you?"

The question catches me off guard, momentarily plunging me into memories of the past.

"I don't suppose so. Why?"

"Oh nothing, it's just that you seem so happy all of a sudden. I was wondering if you were remembering someone."

"No no, nothing like that. Just relishing the peace."

I see her bite her lip and turn away, a strange expression on her face, just for a heartbeat. What was it? Pity? Sorrow? Oh well. Think nothing of it. Just enjoy yourself.

The sun is almost gone now, the last breaths of golden light curling over the mountains. The night is high and clear, the grandeur of the sky once again taking my breath away. Is this how it feels? To live a normal life? With friends, beauty, housing? Have I done it? Have I truly accomplished my goal? If so, it feels every bit as freeing as I had hoped.

"Tengen. I want to say something. Something that I have to tell you."

I nod for her to continue; confused but intrigued. She takes a deep breath, gearing up. Her eyes brim with tears, her bottom lip shaking. She quietly turns something in her hands behind her back, evidently calming herself.

"I'm sorry that you've never found somebody. You deserve it, you really do. I can't offer any consolation for the losses and grief you've faced, but I can pass on the words of my family. So always remember Tengen. When in need, to protect what you truly care about, to pull out all the stops for them. To do what needs to be done. To scorch the earth, to give all which you have."

Tears are streaming down her face now, eyes full of sorrow. She's clutching something behind her back. Extending a hand, her fingers pull away to reveal a rose, its crimson petals akin to a soft fire as they rustle in the breeze. I take it, our fingers brushing gently. In these fleeting moments I notice she has a tattoo. How did I miss that? But then again, it's so small. And yet so eloquent, so pretty on her skin. A butterfly on a katana. And just like that, I snap back to reality as she continues to wrench my heart.

"I like you Tengen. I really do. And that's why I'm sorry. I truly am. But remember to always scorch the earth to help those you love. Those it would incur pain greater than death to lose. And so, for the final time, please believe me when I say, from the bottom of my heart,-

A final teardrop rolls off her cheek, her fingers like a gentle feather on my face. She closes her eyes, leaning in to me. I cup her face, brushing off moisture. I barely noticed it happened, just feeling the warmth of where her lips touched me.

- *I'm sorry"*

It all happened in just a flutter of the heart. A flutter of the heart, all the time it took.

For the world to become a jagged mess of red and orange.

4: UNTIL NEXT TIME

His eyes are so, so empty.

Crack. Crack. Crack.

The wooden sword on the wooden post.

Crack. Crack. Crack.

Staring with empty eyes, seeing a bygone moment. He feels nothing, his body is unresponsive to touch. His ears ignore sound, his empty eyes reject sight. He is a walking ghost, a man entranced, a man lost. A man clutching a single memory, but knows it can never be again.

Crack. Crack. Crack.

He trains all day, lies restlessly all night. He knows he is slipping away, but cares not. His golden moment shattered. His hopes crushed. He suffers in silence, wallowing away in his own little void.

Crack. Crack. Crack.

He is a broken man.

***

–IKARI–

There he is again. Tengen, out on his own, rain pouring down, is training. The same place he always is. The same expression he always shows. And, after all, I would as well. I too have lived as a reject, a failed experiment. I too found sanctuary here, with these people. But I never felt for them. And I cannot emphasise fully. But I understand. He tried to open up, and he got burnt. Perhaps it was immature, or foolish, to become deeply attached so quickly. I remember finding him on that mountain. He was kneeling aside a crater, a blaze engulfing everything. Tears running dry, hair matted with blood whipping in the night wind. Clutching that rose. And then, even then, he had those empty eyes. All the life I had once seen from him snatched away. I don't know completely what his intentions are now, what his reason is to keep going. But I can assume it's revenge. Even after he was provided irrefutable proof that it was an assassination attempt, irrefutable proof that Shinobu was a devil, he believes that the first devil is at fault. I think that now, he will stop at nothing to hunt it down. If only to find a reason to keep living, but he will nonetheless.

"Hey Tengen." Nothing. As expected. I keep talking, knowing that he won't respond.

"I think I might take a trip. Nothing big, just to get away from all of this. I know you're knee deep in training, but I thought you might want to join me. So?

Crack. Crack. Crack.

As expected. Fine. Time for my trump card.

"And Tengen."

Crack. Crack. Crack.

"I didn't know her as well as you, but I know you want to avenge her. And you want to get stronger.

Crack. Crack. Crack.

"But you and I both know you've reached the limit on your current training. I found that book you took from the library. Before all of this. When we first got here. Quite the read, I must say. And so we both know what you must do to get stronger. Strong enough to do what I know you want to do."

The cracking stops. He turns to look at me. I didn't notice because of the rain, but he is crying. His grip on the sword loosens. Thunder drums aloof; our own little musical ensemble to play to this moment.

"So take that rose. And tell the son of a bitch in your head what you want. What you *truly* want."
There. My cards are laid flat, I've given my ultimatum. I see the gears in his head turn, but I know him. I could've walked away now and I know what he would choose.
He walks towards me, rain cascading off his clothes. He rubs his throat, preparing. When he speaks his voice is soft yet croaky, a feather door swinging on rusted hinges.

"I know."

The tears have stopped now, a steely expression taking its place.

"I will. I will."

His words are flowing now, he knows what to say. To tell the truth, I almost forgot what his voice sounded like.

"I know she would have wanted it. For us."

As expected, he has not let go yet. He must let go, or this will never work. But can he? Only time will tell. I snap back to the moment, as he once again continues.

"But what will you do? Is this trip going to be long?"

"Perhaps. I need to train. And I know just the place."

"I see. When do you leave?"

"Tonight."

As for myself, I also must reach my goal. I yearn for a life different to this, but I realise that revenge is on the cards. The first devil is also what has held me from my goal too, and it will die for that.

So I too must get stronger.

And really, there's only one place for me to go.

The liminal mountain.

He speaks again.

"Thanks, for all of this. You pulled me from that rut, showed me what the right thing to do is. You've shone the light of strength into my eyes. And we can do this."

I grin at him.

"Yes we can."

"Thanks again. Let's stop at nothing. Yeah?"

My grin drops into a subtle smile.

"Yeah."

"I know you won't stop, not for the whole world."

Time for one final goodbye, I suppose.

"And thanks to you too, Tegen."

He extends a fist, and I bump mine into his.

"Until next time, Ikari."

We turn apart and begin to walk, glaring at the task ahead with steely determination. A small smile. Feet splashing. The rain tumbles down where we stood, filling those footprints with water. Still the thunder rumbles, still the world bears witness. Time had once seemed so slow, but now it begins to race. You can't expect it to stand still for goodbyes. Things must go on. And they will.

Until next time, Tengen.

PART TWO;
WHAT WE MUST
DO, ABOVE ALL

5: SELFISH THOUGHTS

"It's evident that our little academy is failing us then."
"You're quite right. Perhaps we should, ahem, spur them on?"
"Quite the illustrious idea. I like it."
The room is vast, shadow crawling in every corner. The walls are plastered with uncanny art, with an odd piece in which a butterfly rests upon a katana taking centre stage. A once intricately carved table takes centre place, now a patchwork of poker chips and burn marks left by the rather boisterous regulars. A cavernous ceiling curls high above, the rafters of ivory and steel a distant, unreachable ceiling. The air is thick with smoke, clouds of white constantly curling from cigarettes lounging on calloused, torn lips.

The room is raucous yet royal, inviting yet uncanny. The men jest and shout, but soon they're cut short by a shout–
"Enough."
The voice is booming, echoing around; a blitz of command. The table members snap to attention, cards thrown to the side as pints are smashed in haste. Its source is hard to find, but a perceptive one may see the silhouette of a towering man in the smoke.
"The assassin may have failed, but we can see to that later. We are keeping tight tabs on *him*, he will not prevail."
The certainty in his words quells the unrest around the table, but the talk about him is enough to cause vicious whispers amongst them.
"AS for now…"
The burst in volume cuts away the chatter as a cleaver does through butter. "We have fallen comrades. The fifth has fallen. The 6th Fear has not been seen for years now, as such we can assume she too is gone. And many others. The ninth. The eleventh. Powerful, powerful devils."
The room is stunned into silence, memories of the aforementioned slashing through the listeners minds. Memories good and bad, but most all that really matters to these men is the strength they lost as such.
"Face it gentlemen. The 12 Fears are no more. We are only a few now, myself included."
An instant uproar.

"How could the great devils of our group fall to insufferable humans?"

"Are you sure so many are gone?"

"What will we do now?"

"What will happen-"

"When wil-"

"How can we sit and wait whil-"

One man raises his voice, drowning out the others. He slams his palm to the table like a thunderclap, his words once slurred now perfectly clear.

"What will become of Azoth?

Silence. All eyes turn to him, daggers flying towards their mark. He has overstepped his line, and even a newborn child would be able to perceive the change in atmosphere. That name is taboo, no one wishes to remember the one and only known traitor in the history of devils. Eyes bore into him, knuckles turn white round the table. Faces are tense, time is half frozen in shock. That name is the Achilles heel of their resolve, the only thing to put them off. And then, as a stone crashes through glass windows, that same voice brings it all to a stop.

"He raises a good point."

Stunned faces, pure disbelief. Cigarettes fall from their mouths with a soft tap.

"To tell the truth, I do not know. He has been a constant thorn in our side, always stunting our moves. I believe it was he who took down the fifth after all. I do not think he would be such an imbecile to sign an equal contract, but if he does…"

The words hang like a noose on everyone's neck. They all know what that would mean. Disaster in the form of a soul projection. With all of Azoth's fiery calm, it would probably rival that of the leader. The soul projection. The pinnacle of strength, in which the fear felt toward a devil is turned into something unique to each devil. But, despite each projections differences, one thing is constant.

Their pure, unrivalled power.

The man continues.

"No matter. For now, keep moving forward. Kill Ikari Uzumaki and Azoth, along with his host. The one they call Tengen."

Nods all around. Their goal does not waver, not even for the greatest of storms.

"I shall go alone. I have work to do, and a friend to meet."

Disconcerted murmurs. That's unusual.

They watch as the man rubs his wiry grey beard, and dons a long knitted trench coat over a perfectly fitted tweed suit, then cushions an almost comically large cigarette in between his lips. He nods his goodbye, and the smoke billows up. When it settles, he is gone.

***

–TENGEN–

The night is all engulfing, the darkness blinding. The conversation with Ikari still rings in my head, the words echo around and around.

Until next time.

I barely remember the time between now and the incident. It was like living life through a pinhole, only seeing one route.

I'm still on that route, and sometimes I wonder if I will ever leave it. And now, it's time to get going down the only path that leads to the strength I need for what's to come. The path that begins with an enormous task, something I had previously thought insurmountable. A redo of my contract, a second chance for us all. I realise now what the item imbued with emotion is, an item gifted with true intent. And I have that, thanks to her.

Her.

The pain is great, greater than any before. I feel lost in a void, being dragged around by a rope around my neck. My mistake was great, and almost cost me my life.

Blind trust, attachment after one day. They lead to nothing but sorrow.

I know that now, but knowledge does nothing to dull pain.
To live you must treat trust like a terrible law system.
Always guilty until proven innocent. Yeah. Don't trust until you know.
And with that final thought, I murmur to myself.
"Let's get this ritual over with, shall we?"

***

–IKARI–

The mist coils like a looming python, the thin air bites with frosted teeth, the cold clamps inwards tight as a fist. I take one step after another, pushing through the barrage on my body. Being here strips me of all other thoughts, except for the reason I'm here. My one simple goal. Simple perhaps, but another realm from easy. But all I can do now is keep moving. Don't even think about stopping, don't let your resolve waver. Keep moving.
I won't be broken, not here, not now.

***

–TENGEN–

A dark room, a single candlelight. The mirror wanes, yearning for the usurping gaze of the human eye. Circles of incantation round the floor, shadows piercing the corners. A single breath in. A single breath out. The slowing of a heartbeat, the hardening of a resolve. Footsteps echo among empty thoughts, reaching for a single goal as a moth strives for the flame of fire in the dark. I stand, ready. Waiting. I clutch the rose till my knuckles turn white as protruding bone, the thorns drawing pinpricks of blood like nails driven in plaster. Another breath, the heart now the living juxtaposition of softly flowing water splashed on a roaring flame. The steam curling away the thoughts out of my mind. I'm ready. More ready than anything. I begin to chant, a grating hymn spoken of words otherworldly. The beat of a drum reckons in my words as the tempo creeps up, my breath shortening as the words are forced out like a cascade of water through a pinhole. My voice is thunderous now, on the knife's edge of screaming those strange, strange words.. Sweat trickles down my face, my iron fist beginning to shake, my blood pumping in overdrive. But still, I'm calm. More calm than ever. Mind and soul, flesh and blood, tears and sweat, all come together as layers of steel in a finely honed blade. A sharp breath, my throat a tunnel of gravel by now. I spit the final words, all too aware of who I'm about to come face to face with. I'm ready. At least, I think I am.

***

–IKARI–

Another step. One after the other, and as I walk the mist still beckons with looming figures. I'm not really thinking now. I walk as tempered iron crashes on the anvil, the past footsteps echoing all that has been left behind. When will this end? He does not know, nor does he care for an answer. All that matters now is to move forward. Blonde hair thrashes in the wind, my mouth beckoning into a grimace as the frigid air rushes through my smiling teeth. I take a deep breath, focusing myself.
This mist will not end, not till I've conquered myself. But how?

***

A raven carves its way through ashen skies; fire crackles across the ground as flames walk the path of dry tinder; the light fades to dusk as the sun cowers from the rising night;

sprinkles of disfigured plants repeatedly ripped from their hold by screaming wind fly through the air as the strange plane stands before two silhouettes. One seems to reach for the sky, one remains rather grounded. A human and a beast. The human rubs his wiry beard, the beast clanks along as a ball and chain drags the ground asunder. A tweed suit so perfectly tailored it seems as if the wind is still; walking alongside nightmare black armour so large two grown men could stand inside the chest plate. A rather strange duo.

The man speaks, his words cast by the wind to what he considers to be deaf ears.

"Come, First fear. I have a job for you."

Flames part for them as they keep moving, the ground shaking with every step the beast takes. Strangely, the beast stops moving but as the man walks the shaking continues. He yanks the chain, and off they go, marching to the point where gunmetal grey skies greet scorched earth with open arms.

***

–TENGEN–

I'm watching myself fall? Falling, falling, falling.

Falling, falling, falling. Up and down, left and right blend into one as I fall. I open my mouth to cry out, but my throat is still desiccated by the chanting. All I can manage is a sharp exhale. The ground rushes up to me, a cat pouncing on an unsuspecting bird.

And then, nothing.

Opening my eyes, I feel almost blinded by the heat. Raising my head induces a horrible pounding behind my eyes and a terrible rush of blood in my ears, but I will live. I think.

Air ripples up from the ground as a crimson sky fills my sight. The pain is falling by the wayside, giving room to thoughts. Most pointedly, where am I?

That same crimson sky grasps at the ground. As for the ground... a smooth, abyssal black pane of what appears to be perfect glass. As I stare into it, it stares back. Of course. Everyone knows what happens if you stare into the abyss long enough. And right now, it is most definitely staring back at me. In the distance there's a strange structure, eerily close in appearance to a supersized ribcage. Against my better judgement, I realise there is only one place to go. The footsteps echo so perfectly it feels like this whole space isn't real, like a room full of pictures. It feels like I'm in someone's head. And considering how I got here, I suppose that isn't too far from the truth. And I guess if I'm here, it must have worked. But that means that… the only thing I had left of her.

Gone.

So be it, if that is what it takes. I have to let go, and this is just the first step.

The wind rustles softly as if breathing down my neck, the air stands still as I walk. This plane seems to stretch so endlessly that it's hard to even comprehend.

No, not hard, impossible.

I was just subconsciously shutting out the possibility of trying to understand it.

The thought that she is truly gone encircles my thoughts, but I suppose there really is nothing I can do about it. No point crying over spilled milk so out of your control it could have been divine intervention. Or maybe, hellish intervention. Yeah.

I like that more than trying to put faith in some unknown heavenly entity. Devils however, I can see, I can know, and understand and, in a place like this, I should imagine meet. Shutting out the still perfect and uncanny echo of my every move, the fact that I can hear my hair sway by my ear; I see if the alien place has got any closer. To be honest, I don't know what would be worse. If it has, or if it hasn't. Just before I find out, I allow one rogue thought.

What has become of Ikari?

***

–IKARI–

A cacophony of nightmares assaults my weakened mind as I stagger through the dark. But still, I remain on the knife's edge of sanity. I find myself slipping with every moment, however for now I can still form thoughts. And a few of said thoughts are taking centre stage. I should not have come to this place, should I have realised what it means to truly conquer yourself. My worst nightmares, memories, realisations and failures bombard me. The most monumental challenge is simply to put one foot in front of the other, fighting through the moments that make up my way of being.

But something *is* happening.

I feel myself changing. Evolving. But what way? Will I walk out a hideous creature, or a perfect life form? I suppose that depends on what lies within. I need to prove that what lies within is human, that should be the ultimate goal. Because I don't care what everyone will say about my past, about my friend. I am just as human as them, that will not be changed by who I choose to spend time with, or what I may have been labelled as a child.

Then again–
What does it mean to be,
human?

Is it sadness? Or even emotion at all? Is it self-consciousness? Shame? Is it just chemicals in the strange lump of meat we call the brain? What does it mean to be alive? What does it mean to be an individual, or to be social? Can we call ourselves unique, when we all feel the same pain?
Or is it to be successful? But what is success?
A family, a strong bond. Money, a 'high lifestyle'.
What is it?
Why do some pray and some curse? When one stands alone, their body telling them to release salty water from what they need to see, why do others group together while their body tells them to bare their way of eating and create strange sounds that only paint them as a target for predators?
Why do some see themselves as superior, tearing into each other's flesh or boasting the size of reproductive organs?
Is that what makes us human; a sense of competition?
But then why do some lack that competitive drive?

So perhaps it is individuality.

But then why do some try so hard to be like others?

Do they feel a sense of inferiority? But surely that should just lead to individuality? Or is individuality only what makes us human if paired with what we see as success? After all, the most unique of us is the homeless man around the corner. But no one calls him empowering. No one stops and listens to his tales, no matter how great.

Why?

Are we driven away by a sense of disgust, or perhaps a sense of self preservation? To be truly human, must you be attractive? Or must you be yourself? Why when a man in green patchy clothes holds up a gun, people rejoice; and yet when a man in orange clothes does it people make noises of terror like wounded animals?

Is it because of the fact they love the man in green, yet feel great animosity toward the man in orange simply because they have a different sense of individuality? Both of these men have killed, both have maimed and struck terror. Yet one is celebrated. Are we such sheep that we turn bipolar just for the way the barrel of a gun may point?

If it's away, celebrate,

and if it's toward, cry?

But what of the thoughts for the people across the ocean who face the barrel of the man in green? Should we not feel anything for them?

Should we not love them, as fellow members of the 'human race'?

So is it love?

Is that what makes us 'human'?

But the baby left in a cardboard box in the pouring rain in a back alleyway never felt love.

Are they human?

Or just another lost animal?

The dog on the lead of a joyous child splashing in the same puddles the baby soaks in unconsciously feels an immense amount of love.

So are they human now?

Or just a dog?

Think for a moment. And consider, if it is love that makes us human.

Person A is buried at a wonderful funeral, tears spilled and hundreds stunned by their death. A cake is cut, an afterparty is held and people come to terms with their death. Even in death, they feel love. Person A has always felt love.

Person B is chucked into a grave by their killer. They had no family. No friends. No funeral, just a hooded person stubbing out a cigarette on the pavement slab they chucked onto the dirt just inches above the still warm skin of the person no one cared for. Person B was never loved.

And we eat animals.

We eat creatures we deem as not human.

So, you would eat person B then, with no qualms, wouldn't you?

If love makes us human, and they have never felt love, they are not human.

Right?

An animal. And we eat animals.

Right?

So, you would eat person B with no worries then.

Right?

Or would you be scared to?

Scared.

Perhaps that's it. We all feel fear. Uncertainty.

Embarrassment.

And yet we award the 'fearless'? We award someone dehumanising themselves? But I thought dehumanisation was torture? Is it torture to be truly fearless?

And to be truly fearless, must you:

Not know pain?

Not know embarrassment?

Not know when to stop?

Not know *how* to stop?

Is that fearless? Is that 'human'?

Perhaps that is fearless, and thus is not human?

What is to be feared?

What is it, to fear?

Do we fear our loss of life or love, or do we fear dehumanisation brought about by the idea of being 'fearless'?

So, if I remain fearless - Would you eat me?

Like the man who felt no love, or would you applaud me - Like the man in patchy green who points the gun at the people across the sea whose deaths you cheer when you hear about loss of life through ink on paper?

What would you do, with a man who calls himself 'fearless'?

Or maybe, we require 'self' to be human.

But 'self' of what kind?

Perhaps it is the bygone self. The self that will always be forgotten in the passage of time, the self that cannot see through the visage of the present moment. The self we all possess, the self we seem scared to show by way of thus imagining scars on it for when it is finally brought to the light of the future?

The insignificant self.

The unknowing self.

That self is so social with the ideas that find themselves wallowing in loneliness.

That self.

When everything we are too scared to do, everything we do, everything we think of doing. All the conversations we have, all the muscles we move and all the strange thoughts that relentlessly plague a sleep deprived mind. All the lovers and family and friends and foes, all the spilled blood or torn clothes.

The horrid claws of war.

The people who walked out the door.

All the money raised, all the money spent. All the warming moments of love at first sight and all the coldness of sleeping alone in a bed once for two. All the touch and smell, all the unforgettable sights and blaring sounds that shake your brain within its skull and spasm your body. All the kindness, all the sorrow. All the gentle touch, all the thrown punch.

All of it.

Every last drop or crumb or flickering flame.

At some point, it will be gone.

The last thought cast back to this time, to these lives, will be thought.

And that's it.

Gone.

A race united by the feeling of being small. Every man and woman, child or baby has felt it. That nothing matters in the end. Nothing at all.

Insignificance.

It truly is what we all feel in the end.

A small speck on such a large canvas it feels as if it flows between realities. And for all we know, it does.

Of course.

All we know, forgotten just like that bygone self.

But none of this matters.

Because maybe we will all be gone. Maybe we will all be forgotten. Maybe we are just born to be insignificant.

Maybe we will all end up dead.

Maybe we won't.

But that's okay.

Because it makes us human.

To get up and keep going, even if all that has been said comes to truth before the eyes of our fate.

We are insignificant.

But we don't care.

And that makes us human.

And I know that.
And I accept that.
And I am now,
Human.

Or perhaps, I'm just going mad.
Perhaps, I'm just rambling internally.
Perhaps, perhaps, perhaps…
Ah damn.
Being human is weird.
After all, I just said so much. But in reality, did I say anything at all?

6: FLAMES OF TRUTH

–TENGEN–

Dread creeps through my bones. To my horror, as I stand amongst the structure, I realise I was right. Before me that black plane stretches, but now accompanied by something rather chilling. Ribs so large it seems hard to think they were once part of a creature curl over me, creating a tunnel of bones toward a roaring flame just a few heartbeats away. The heat is immense, bombarding my skin to the point it has turned utterly crimson. I look to the sky once more and see just how high this fire reaches, a beacon of uncanny light in this dark world. And through this wall of flame, I see something. The sky above me has darkened, and a strange storm-like formation is spiralling into something on the other side of this flame. I lean in closer, and suddenly it becomes obvious.

The silhouette.

A pile of something towering above the ground, topped by some kind of throne. And on it sits a figure. Even if he is nothing but a shadow cast through fire, I could swear on all that I love, he smiles. A cold, emotionless smile, and a silent challenge.

He beckons me to come. To walk through the flames.

A baptism by fire; a test to see if I am worth his time.

Fine. I'll play his game.

Another deep breath, and I step in.

The pain is great. Oh so great. A thousand needles pierce my every blood vessel, a thousand hammers pound my every bone. And my eyes. They feel as if dipped in lava whilst simultaneously frozen in the harshest of winter. It is all so bright I lose bearing, stumbling blindly through the agony.

But, above all, I must put one foot in front of the other.

Like I always have.

And after what feels like an eternity, the pain stops.

I'm through.

The first step is done.

A nightmare black throne perched atop a mountain of bones and skulls, a wall of empty eye sockets that stare back as I gaze upon this surreal horrorscape. That strange storm is in full force, creating this flame cyclone in which I now find myself the eye of. The raw heat has barely subsided, but I have borne it now at its worst. I stand in an inch of viscous crimson, and suddenly I'm that child in the woods, reaching out for that wooden door. But a realisation brings me back; this horrid land of crimson and void; flame and storm; unknown and fear stems from one person.
The man atop the throne grins, and let me tell you it was not a friendly one. Such a cold smile, even among all this scorching heat.

His hair is a wild mix of reds and oranges whipping in his own storm.
Just like hers–
His skin is charred and scarred, but he bears the marks of a warrior in every way. A vermillion cloak, streaked with black, cascades down his slim yet undoubtedly muscled figure. He sits almost still, simply checking for any dirt beneath his fingernails, but with the subtle move of his arm the flash of a metal emblem is revealed. A butterfly, split in half, and the shattered edge of a katana resting in pieces beside it.

Just like fire, he oozes confidence and natural, rugged, haunting beauty.

As for eyes–

Wells of power and superiority, garnished with two mini suns that pass as irises. Staring into them triggers something primal, as if my subconscious instincts are telling me to fear him. Once again his lips peel back from their uncannily white teeth, the movement casting a shadow over his rugged face. A devilish smile.

Fit for a devil.

I call out to my feet to move, for my body to do anything. But I'm frozen. Frozen in fear and anger. This is the man. The man who has done all this to me. To my friends. The man who I know knew what she was, and said nothing. The man who let her die on that mountain side beneath the stars. The fear subsides, but still I am frozen by rage. All the anger and hatred spirals through my head so fast it clouds my every sense, there's so many things I want to do I end up with nothing. And just when it couldn't get any worse, he speaks.

"Oh come on…"

That voice. Smooth, utterly confident. *Come on. Come on. Come on.* Don't you dare tell me to come on, after all you are responsible for–

"Are you so blinded by childish rage you can't even move?"

Childish.

Am I being childish? I have to get a grip, to say something or do anything. But I can't. All my senses are collapsing, overloading me. I feel as if all the knowledge of everything is at my fingertips, as if I can see, hear, touch, smell and taste all there is.

But it's too much. I have so much information, and I can't process any of it. A broken computer. A child.

"If you can't even handle my presence, how on earth will you make me accept your terms?"

He's right. Too right. It's like I just forgot how to live. But I really wish he would stop smiling. Mocking me. It's like he stares right through me, into my very soul.

He sees it all. And he just laughs. The icy sound of it only drives my despair deeper. So this is what it's like, to be in the presence of true power. That feeling of utter inadequacy, utter hopelessness.

But still my rage swirls within, pushing back that feeling. Enough.

This ends now.

Everything I have done to get here, I will not allow myself to lose before speaking a word. I owe it to everyone who got me here, and most of all, to her. One foot infront of the other. Like always. Just move that foot. Shut out the overload. Close your senses. My muscles are spasming, the flames around me pushed away by some invisible force.

This.

Ends.

Now.

And it shatters. I don't know what, but something does. A crack rings through the plane, the snap of some deity's fingers. And my senses are mine again. My body will obey me.

Raising my neck, I meet his eyes.

And, just for a heartbeat, his grin falters. His eyes narrow. And he rises from his throne.

Casually, showing no exertion whatsoever, he leaps down from the pillar of bones, and his impact with the ground is no more than that of a feather. He casually rests his hands in his pockets, his fiery hair flopping like a blaze hopping between treetops.

And he walks.

Each footstep leaving a pool of molten glass, the sound of it ringing all around.

His cloak billows in the smoke like the flag of a fallen nation, and he's smiling again now.

I see my silhouette against a backdrop of roaring flame reflected in his eyes, and I feel his gaze.

Like two harsh points pressing against my own eyes, the points of two knives gently pressed against skin.

He walks, closer and closer.

***

The little girl watches with wide eyes as it settles on a flower mere inches from her nose. A butterfly. Beautiful shades of turquoise and supple blues streak its fragile yet reassuring frame. The girl creeps closer, leaving muddy swipes where her knees pull through the moist grass. Dewdrops adorn the petals of the butterfly's perch, vibrating softly as the girl's tiny fingers curl around the stem of the flower. Her breath steams in the air, clouding around her face. She pulls it closer, the butterfly now but a hair's breadth from her eye. The shades of colour shine bright within her mahogany iris, her pupils dilate as she grins with what few teeth she has.

"Wonderful, aren't they?"

She falls back on her behind, startled. Her eyes grow somehow wider as she sees a kind faced man in a tweed suit crouching before her, his eyes crinkled in a soft smile. He reaches out a finger, and on it perches that same butterfly.

The girl meets his eyes, wide irises roaming among his wiry beard and strangely dark eyes. Her mother always told her to be wary of strangers, but this one was just too nice. How could she resist the offering of a butterfly?

Reaching out a delightfully pudgy finger to the flying bundle of stunning colours, she begins to widen that same almost toothless grin. The man retains his smile, still that warm appearance.

Out of nowhere, the butterfly springs to the girl's nose. And stays there. Too shocked to move, the girl simply tries and fails to see the bridge of her own nose. And then begins to laugh. A raucous, joyous sound rings through the park. It really was quite funny, the man supposes. Still chuckling with the girl, he subtly checks a rather antique pocket watch. And then quietly moves as to block the path of sight which may lead the girls eyes to the walking mass of nightmare black armour that thunders past them both, that same ball and chain dutifully carried against its huge chest by arms so large they could probably crush a building. But the girl sees none of that, only the parting smile the man gives her before pressing the pocket watch into her rosy palm. She looks down at it, the butterfly seemingly having parted ways with her by now, and as soon as she turns her eyes away he vanishes. Like dust blown by the wind. And as little children often can, she forgets all about it. And him. All she does now is run off to her mum to show her what she just found.

A rose gold pocket watch, the back engraved with a rather eloquent insignia.

Nothing but an elegant butterfly resting on a well polished katana.

***

The question I've been meaning to ask is on the tip of my tongue, and I need to ask it. All this, this could have been prevented, if only…

"Why?"

My voice comes across in a strange tone, some mix of anger and sadness accompanied by a heavy exhale. He looks at me, and still he smiles.

"Why what, Tengen?"

"Why would you leave it so late? Why would you refuse to show yourself until *after* he died?"

My voice cracks, but still I continue.

"You killed him, *you* let him die!"

I sweep my arms out in front of me, practically yelling now.

"All you had to do was help, all you had to do was to do *anything*, *anything* to show you were there!"

Tears well in my eyes, my voice is now barely a whisper.

"But you didn't. And he's dead."

His expression is unchanged.

"Tell me Tengen. Do you believe in such a thing as evolution?"

Huh? He is still smiling, that devilish grin as he bears too-white teeth and deep crimson gums. But his eyes remain that of a cold killer. A business smile. That's all this is to him. Politics. Business.

Except, here we deal not with money, but with the lives of innocent humans. How can he stand there, after all he's done.

"What, what are you talking about? You killed him–"

"Tell me, do you believe in evolution?

I guess I have to play along. Gathering breath, I answer his stupid question.

"Yeah, how a species adapts and changes over time."

A sharp, razor's edge laugh. It cuts the air and assaults my ears. It echoes all around, bouncing off these towering walls of flame.

He gets even closer now, close enough to reach out his arm and touch the tip of my nose.

"Evolution, Tengen, is indistinguishable from progress. It is but steps any self respecting being takes to power. It is the path away from weakness."

His breath is clawing its way down my neck now, curling away as it reaches my spine.

"Now, do you think humanity is evolving?"

Is humanity evolving? We must be, to have lived so long. We have taken steps away from weakness, taken steps from the dark to the light. We are getting stronger. Right?

But then, we are still so powerless against the devils. Have we even evolved at all since sticks and stones, fire and caves? We must have.

Otherwise, what was the point of it all?

To help others. The strong help the weak. And yet, if evolving is taking steps away from the weak, are we cursed to forever remain unchanged by that ideal?

No, we can't be.

I thought that was the whole point.

To get stronger, to protect those who cannot.

"You wish for a normal life, do you not?"

How does he know that? I hate the way he talks, as if I am an open book left out in the street. Like he knows everything about me, and the way he brings up my greatest ambition for nothing but an example. I grit my teeth.

"And so what if I do?"

"How can you live a truly normal life, if you are constantly reminded of how weak you all are?"

"We are not weak. We will never be weak."

That laugh again.

"Humanity cannot progress as you are. That is final."

"As we are? What do you mean devil?"

"You are caught in a cycle. And seem to have no desire to break it."

"Cycle?"

"Allow me to explain. You are such simple creatures, you do not see the trap you goad yourselves into every time."

I can tell how much he is enjoying this. That cold, calculating air is gone. Now, nothing but malice. I feel the crushing weight of liberation as I am free to move once more. But I do not. The smile finally reaches his eyes. The truth of it all, told by a being as old as fear itself.

I wonder if I will see it as he does.

"The cycle of humanity, what keeps you from evolving. The problem with your species, unbeknownst to all of you. You depend on hope. You love it. You live on hope, let yourself be controlled by hope. And yet, you do not understand what hope does.

Hope leads to desire.

Desire leads to striving.

Striving leads to power.

Power leads to corruption.

Corruption leads to dictatorship.

Dictatorship leads to suppression.

Suppression leads to oppression.

Oppression leads to rebellion.

And rebellion leads to hope.

Rinse,

And repeat.

Over,

And over.

You lead yourself back into the cycle every time. You expect to break it? When you relish such menial strife as war, or such childish pleasure as love? Hope is what traps you. What makes you weak. Stop depending on hope. To do that, I shall let you go your own way to reach that goal. Hope changes nothing. Strength changes everything.

Your weakness disgusts me.

Change it, Tengen.

Be the one who pries open the eyelids of humanity and shines the light of the strong into their eyes.

Be the one who ends the era of cowering in fear of the first devil. Be the one who goes against it all. Be it alone, or with your family. Be the one brave enough to leave the weak behind, in the name of progress. Of evolution. The way you all giddy get back up after everything, without thinking *why*.

Blinded by hope, all you see is a chance.

You need absolutes, Tengen.

Make it happen.

If you truly believe you can, I shall grant you the strength that which you came to my land to strive for." –

His breath is cold against me, breaking through the wall of heat. His left ear brushes my right as he moves to stand next to me. I feel the sideways gaze of those piercing eyes as they run up and down my skin.

–"Only a fool does not know how hard something is. That is not bravery. Bravery is knowing exactly how hard something is, and doing it anyway. I don't need to tell you how hard it will be. Are you a fool, who has come here with the elementary illusion of gaining flash power to use toward some noble goal with no real hardship?
Or, are you brave?"

He rests a calloused hand on my shoulder. I can almost feel that smile. At this moment, he might be acting like an inspiring friend, but really all I am is another way for him to enter the real world. To him, this is like a theatre, and he just happens to be one of the characters. Despite that, the things he's saying...
"Can you do it, Tengen Uzumaki?"

***

–IKARI–

Sometimes, the truth can burn as frost bites. Sometimes, it can be as cruel as the greatest lie.

But sometimes, it can be so warm. It can wrap around you, soft as a dove quilt, and bring peace to that moment.

This is one of those truths.

And, as that truth wraps around me, my eyes bask in the glory of the peak. The peak of the mountain, and to say stunning would be a disrespectfully gross understatement. Simply breathtaking, heartstopping and surreal in the best sense of it all. The gentle rays of an early dawn sun rest upon a rolling tundra of sparkling lakes rimmed with the frost-capped rings of lesser heights. A kaleidoscope of intoxicating colour shimmers moments from the ground's surface as the mornings dew splits the light; a herd of deer not two seasons old frolic with utmost leisure; a drowsy eagle takes flight, throwing the silhouette of a bird across the land; a rustle of wind playfully tugs the strands of my hair all over.

It's… beautiful.

My eyes so wide they could be mistaken for that of a lemur, the ethereal scene shines in my iris.

What absolute bliss.

However, time is up. I can feel it.

He's waiting for me to return.

But I must learn to make the most of fleeting moments like these.

I fear that soon they may be my only source of joy.

***

"You two are quite something, you know."
I can barely see the man's face due to the almost incomprehensible amount of paperwork stacked on his imposing desk. The half I can see reveals black hair pushed skyward like grass in the wind sat atop a face deeply etched with lines gifted by age. Thick metal framed glasses rest crookedly on his weathered and evidently bashed up nose, while the tip of a scraggly moustache peaks above the piles of paper.

"After all, I couldn't tell you the last time a pair with your joint accomplishments sat before me. Redoing a contract, and conquering the liminal mountain? Simply spectacular."
His voice is croaky, yet unmistakable in its authority. Is this old man really the head of our devil hunting association? He seems so frail and, based on the amount of unfinished work before me, rather useless. So why is he at the top of the food chain here?

"I appreciate it, director."

I look at Tengen, fiddling with his tie. It is rather itchy I guess. There doesn't seem to be any immediate change in him, not that I can see. But, when we were talking earlier, I could have sworn to see something in his right eye. Like a burning figure, inside his pupil. I'll have to brush it off for now, this conversation should be my priority.

"As do I, director."

"Well, I suppose you may be wondering why I called you before me."

I can see the edges of a smile above the beige stacks.

"It's because I have a task for you. A quite unsavoury devil has been going around pretending to be the leader of the Yakuza, and appears to be the current chosen of the first devil. He has been placed in charge of the ancient devil force known by us as the 12 Fears."

Wait, not that Yakuza man right? Not the one my father was indebted to, right–

"You may have encountered him, or one of his devils. As a matter of a fact, I know you both have. You may recall the spider devil. We knew that devil as the fifth.. So you see–"

"Wait."

Come on man! You can't cut him off like that!

"I thought the leader of the 12 Fears *was* the first devil. Why do you say he is only claiming to be so?"

"I see you have been led astray by the book you stole from my library."

"Lead astray?"

"You see, the power hierarchy of devils is not quite so simple. You will know that the 12 Fears gain their power through slivers of the first devil's soul, and that it is thought the 12's leader is the first devil. A common misconception."

"Commoner? Now just who are you call-"

"Please, settle yourself. After all Tengen, it may well be you that topples the very system I am currently explaining. Every millennia, the first devil will choose an individual to lead the 12, and gifts them a larger portion of soul. Usually, this leader will simply make sure nothing goes astray, and that devils keep fighting as much as needed."

"Why don't they just order them to kill us?"

"That would be the same as a constantly starving person burning all of the food offered to him. Devils need our fear to live, and as such, their goal is not an annihilation, but a cull. They wish to keep us under their thumb, living in the fear they find so nourishing. However, the past leader of the 12 made a mistake. Under his rule, a member of the 12 turned their backs and went AWOL. The first traitor in history. As such, the leader was executed. This new leader was brought forth with a new goal.

Find, and kill the traitor.

And, that traitor is in your head Tengen."

An ominous grin creeps upon his wrinkled face.

"The one the devils want, is…–"

No, no, no. This can't be right. He can't finish the sentence like I think he will. It's just not possible, just not possible for Tengen to be some central player in this madness. And yet…

His unbelievable power. The fact that despair seems to follow him, no matter what walk of life he tries. His almost bipolar behaviour, his seemingly contrasting persona.

Some days frantic, some days calm and calculated.

Is that all just the work of some exiled high-ranking devil?

"–You. They want you, Tengen. And especially now that you have reaffirmed your contract–"

"How do you know about that?"

So he managed to do it? Unbelievable. And I guess, all along, it was. It was all just the cause and effect of some exiled high ranking devil.

"I know lots of things. The grapevine in institutes such as this would make for some fine wine, if you know what I mean."

So that's it then. This whole time, he lied.

Lied.

And kept one of the greatest devils in the world right in his head, right under my nose, and never said a word.

I suppose it's my fault for trusting a devil.

No more.

I won't make that mistake again.

7: PATHETIC, DEVIL

–IKARI–

The meeting passes in blur, I can barely focus on what this old bag is spewing.

Because what does it matter anyway?

He lied. He kept it from me, the thing most important above all. I thought we were friends? Friends don't lie, not about something this big. One of the 12 fears.

Tengen.

One of the most powerful devils in existence, and my only friend.

What do I do?

What can I do?

A devil. My friend.

Or is he?

Did he save me as a gesture of kindness, or simply to prevent another insignificant civilian death? Or even to use me for some devilish scheme?

Devil.

My only friend, a devil.

He is my friend, right?

So why would he abandon me for Shinobu so quickly?

Did he ever really care?

Liar. Devil.

Devil.

How was I so blind?

They're all the same, aren't they? At the end of the day, a devil is a devil. Maybe it doesn't matter who it might possess. He never cared; he can't care.

Devils can't care for people.

Devil. Liar. Devil.

The words loop in my mind, over and over.

I wonder what that old bag is talking about now.

–"So you see, I need you two to fight back."

Fight back? Against what?

As if reading my mind, he continues.

"Against the first devil. Wage war. Show them humanity has had enough of being trampled on. Attack them, starting with the current leader of the 12. What do you say?"

Wage war?

Yeah, I can get behind that.

"You will work toget-"

"No."

Silence. The room falls still, recoiling from my words.

"Ikari? What are you saying?"

Tengen finally speaks up.

"No. I won't be working with *him*."

He sits there, his face a mask of confusion and shock, along with one other thing I can't quite recognise.

"I'll do it, that's for sure. You can count on me."

And I stand, then walk. Away from that room. Away from *him*. That lying devil. To think I saw us as friends. What I fool I was, to blindly trust someone who clearly showed no trust back.

"Wait! Ikari!" His voice rings down the hallway, grating my ears.

Just keep walking.

"IKARI!"

I can't do this, why can't he just-

"Shut up." I speak softly, but the message reaches him.

I continue, finally speaking my mind.

"You're all the same, aren't you?"

His response sounds desperate. Confused.

"Ikari? What are you talking about?"

"I'm talking about Devils. How did I not realise? It doesn't matter who they might use as a face, they are *devils*. Liars. Murderers. Inhuman psychos. That's *you*, Tengen."

I can see him change, see his expression morph. Finally he shows his true colours, his anger.

"How can you say that? I thought you were better than this, Ikari. I thought we were friends?"

He scoffs. And continues, his tone getting harsher and harsher.

"Maybe I was the fool, to save the pathetic boy who froze the instant they saw a pretty girl. Maybe I was the fool, to think you might amount to anything."

"Pathetic?" I spit the word back. "Pathetic?"

"Yeah. That's *you*, Ikari. Pathetic."

Our voices are rising, a crescendo of anger. I can see him grinding his teeth, and I didn't even realise how hard I was clenching my fist.

"You're calling me pathetic? Did you see yourself after you blindly trusted some random girl, and it literally all blew up in your face?"

That hit a nerve. His voice changes, becoming quieter. But unmistakably threatening.

"You, leave her out of this."

"Aw, I guess that's still a rough topic, huh?"

He looks straight at me, and there it is. His left eye is gone, replaced by a black void surrounding a harsh star of reds and oranges, as if his iris was reflecting the sun in perfect detail.

"I said, leave her *out* of this, *pathetic boy*."

Flames begin to gather in hands, and as he clenches his fist, arcs of red scorching fire bend out from between his now blackened knuckles, like solar flares on a dying star.

"Looking for a fight, devil boy? Or maybe you just can't control your emotions… Perhaps you should run off home and join the other psychos in hell."

That was the final straw.

Flames flare around his feet, and the ground shatters as he breaks into a sprint. The flames between his fingers envelop his fist fully, like a boxer's hand wrap of pure heat. No time to enter the stance for a quick draw.

I flick the blade out of the saya slightly, before fully drawing it and levelling it at him. He bears down on me, leading with a left handed jab. I slip the punch, but the immense heat blisters the back of my neck. He follows with a right hook, and I meet his fist with the katana directly.

The sound of it rings out, like metal on metal.

I stop thinking about each move, letting instinct take over, as we fight on.

Slash, stab, slip, feint…

Watch his shoulders, predict each punch.

Spotting a twitch in his arm, I swing for the head. His guard is down, his neck wide open.

I win.

Tensing my arms and slashing directly into his-

Huh?

My blade whistles through thin air, and I realise.

Instinctively looking down, I see him bending backward, his spine parallel to the ground, left hand supporting him. I see his quads tense, and his lower body springs into the air. His heel rushes toward my jaw, and I feel the heat getting closer.

My sword is out of position to block, and I can't dodge to the side because of the wide flames.

Only one way to go.

I launch myself backward, seeing him complete the cartwheel and landing back on his feet.

Hitting the ground hard, the breath is knocked out of me-

No time to recover, I see him raising his foot for a curbstomp-

I slam my left shoulder into the ground and roll to the side, the floor imploding where my head was a second ago. I see him go to strike again-

In a desperate rush, I spring to my feet, slashing down with all my force-

A clang of metal on metal.

My sword presses against the cross of his blackened forearms, forcing the blade closer to his face.

I want to beat him. To end him, this damned devil.

Wait. I don't have to kill him.

He called me pathetic?

Let's see, how about I bait him, and crush him in competition?

I would say that showing I'm the superior hunter will do the job.

Yeah. A competition.

"Hey devil boy." My gritted teeth reflect in the polished blade, along with his searing flame.

"Yeah?" Such a thick sarcastic tone, dripping with malice and calm anger.

"You call me pathetic."

"You are."

"How about some nice unfriendly competition?"

"Competition?"

He laughs, and continues condescendingly.

"Sure, but why would you? You simply can't beat me."

"We can see about that, *devil*."

He smiles, baring sharp canines.

"So Ikari, what are the rules?" He spits my name with such acidity, like it pains him just to say it. Good.

"We both accept the old bag's challenge, and whoever can bring back the head of the 12's leader to him wins."

"I like that. Any other conditions you want to make, maybe to give you a chance?"

"No chance. I can beat you without them."

We both step back, and his laugh rings out over the clink of my katana returning to the saya. It's a cold laugh, sharp on the ears. The flames subside around him, and the blackened skin returns to normal. He takes a long blink, and his left eye is also human again.

"See you on the battlefield, *Ikari*."

"You'll be dead long before we cross paths, hopeless *devil*."

We turn and walk, just like that time in the rain. But this is very different.

You're a dead creature walking, devil boy.

The hallway goes quiet, as a horrified janitor rounds the corner to the sight of pure destruction.

It'll be a long evening for him.

He should be more paid for this.

***

–TENGEN–

Tch. What a fool.

Why, why would he see it that way? How can someone be so blind?

Of course.

By being pathetic. A pathetic, weak fool.

To think I ever called him a friend.

And to be so stupid as to challenge me to a competition?

Maybe he might finally see things the right way when I crush his every hope of winning.

But how?

By getting to the target.

That's right, I have to be the first one to reach that damned representative.

Now, where would it be?

Where do devils love to be the most?

Places they can feed. Places of despair and fear, places of death and destruction.

A battlefield?

Too far away from the city.

A homeless shelter?

Such an important devil would be too proud to lurk around those.

Think, think.

Where do people fear visiting, where do people fear losing all they love?

A hospital?

Yeah. A hospital. A place people hate to be, a place of death and despair, a place of lost hope and crushed aspirations.

But which one?

I need information, and I can think of only one place to get it.

***

The towering mahogany doors beckon, those intricate details shining in the light of a grand chandelier. They swing open softly, barely a whisper from their hinges. A catacomb of knowledge is revealed, one of mind-bending proportion. I find myself back at the index of HQ's library, flicking through pages till the section on geography. Aisle 23, section 8, shelf 2. Emergency services of Kyoto. Compared to the area where I found the book on devils, this section of the library is much newer, with the soft crackles of traditional candles and wax lamps replaced by the hum of a warm white ceiling light, and the creaking of wooden planks underfoot replaced by an echoing thump of shoes on concrete. Strange bubbles of colour and abstract design litter the walls and floor, some corporate graffiti.

I find my eyes wandering about, and almost missing the book I was searching for.

Emergency services in Kyoto - How have things changed since the beginning?

Bit of an overly lengthy title. Reminds me of a certain author I know.

Regardless, it should have what I need. A list of all Kyoto hospitals.

I flip through the book, searching for a map.

Got it.

So, 24 hospitals in the city centre.

Which one?

Which one would hold the most negativity?

Hospitals that treat severe cases.

So how many of those 24 have intensive care for life threatening cases?

I look further into the book, searching for answers. 7 of them.

7 possible places, and no way to know which one the devil favours.

I check my watch. Two minutes to 12. Sleep, or start the hunt?

What a stupid question. No time to rest, crushing Ikari should be my utmost priority. That look on his face, when he realises how blind he's been.

I let the book fall to the floor, and head back toward those grand doors.

***

The car park.

Yet another place I never thought I would end up, let alone at midnight by myself.

Now, which car to take…

A sea of drab hatchbacks and saloons fill the lot, nothing catching my eye in the slightest. An ocean of gray and silver bathed in harsh electric light.

I jog among the cars, searching desperately for anything at all with the power I need to do this *fast*. I round the corner, and there it is. Tucked away in a far corner, surrounded by yet more boring salaryman wheels.

A beauty.

An Aston Martin vantage, in a stunning purple and chrome wrap. I remember seeing this car in the trampled magazines on the edge of the woods, and thinking it was from a Sci-Fi film. Something like this, to my mind back then, simply wasn't possible in this reality.

And yet, staring before me, here it is.

Now, how to take it quietly?

I walk to the driver side window and peer inside. The black upholstery is spotless, and the chrome elements around the dash are passable as mirrors.

I check my watch.

12.15 A.M

No time for finesse now. I run to the front and send a blast of flame into the horn output. Black plastic drips out of the grill as it melts, soon joined by the metal inside the housing.

No horn, no alarm.

Returning to the driver side, I draw my arm back. Feeling the heat surge through my bicep, I push one knuckle forward and slam it into the window.

The concentrated pressure practically evaporates the tempered glass, as a cascade of tiny particles shower the interior.

Reaching through the smashed window, I pull the door. A satisfying click rewards my efforts, and the butterfly door raises silently. The lights flash, but the melted alarm produces no sound.

12.20

I need to move fast, and this next stage needs to work. I sweep the glass off the driver seat, and press my index finger to the ignition keyhole.

Here goes nothing.

Closing my eyes–

Small tendrils of flame emerge from my finger, filling the keyhole. When the flames have filled it completely, I begin to compact them. The metal in the hole is glowing now, signaling my need for haste. If that melts, this will all be for nothing and I'll have to go back to square one.

The keyhole is filled with compacted flame, the searing block pressing all the lock pins to the right height.

Deep breath.

And turn.

I flick my wrist, twisting the flames in the lock.

Please, please pl-

The soft purr as the engine wakes is like a sweet song to my ears. Recalling the flames and thanking no one in particular, I settle down, and try to recall as much as possible from my HQ driving lessons.

Left foot on the clutch, right foot between the accelerator and brake.

Left hand on the gearshift, right hand on top of the wheel. Slowly raising my left foot, I feel the biting point. The engine cogs click, and I get ready to go.

I clutch the shifter and gently ease it into reverse. A dab on the gas is met with the soft growl of the engine, and a controlled roll into the road. I take my hand off the stick and bring it to the wheel, locking it to the left. The car turns out of the space, facing the exit.

Alright, time to speed things up.

I let my muscle memory take over, and shift it into first.

And roll out.

8: UNFRIENDLY COMPETITION

I tear through the empty roads, cutting across every lane in sight.
The engine hangs below me, and it feels as if the car is begging me to properly put my foot down.
I swing around a huge roundabout, almost missing my exit and having to swerve to make it.
A cloud of tire smoke rises in my rear mirror, as I pull out my phone.

Checking the map while driving causes me to drive like a drunkard, but no one is around to see it.

There. My first stop.

Kyoto city hospital, the largest in town.

The Nakagyo ward huh? Never been to that part of town before, HQ only took us to the places they saw fit.

Putting my phone away, I yank the wheel and the car flicks toward the slip road. A sign flashes past, indicating the expressway. I rest my hand on the shifter and get ready to really pick up the speed. A quick check of the watch.

12.37

Should be there by one, if I can average 120 Km/h.

Currently, I'm going at 40.

Average 120?

Doable, considering my ride.

The merge with the expressway nears, and I begin to shift up into 3rd.

Then 4th, then 5th.

The expressway hits, and I press my foot down.

All the way till the pedal hits the floor.

3.72 seconds.

That's all it takes, to hit 160 kph.

The roar of the engine as the combustion hits at full force is like some ancient dragon being released, the sound of it rumbling and screaming through the night air. I'm pressed right to my chair, as the speedometer slowly climbs. What can this thing do again?

180.

190.

200.

210.

The road carves through valleys and forest as I descend toward Kyoto. I can feel the power surging through the metal underfoot, feel the unbridled *speed*.

230.

240.

250.

260.

I'm in 6th gear now, with one shift to go. Only 50 Km from the end of this road in central Kyoto.

If I can get to 300, I'll be there in 9 and a half minutes. 9? Seems a bit long. I reckon 6. I narrow my eyes, and slam it into the final gear. 7th gear, something most cars won't even have.

270.

280.

290.

300.

300 kilometres per hour. Insane, truly insane. But I want more.

310.

320.

The engine is shrieking now, the tires screaming against the tarmac.

325.

There goes the rated top speed. But I want more, on this downhill, with all the momentum, not a whisper of the brake–

330.

332.

333.

334.

335.

Come on, come on. I'm pressing the pedal so hard it's scraping the floor, the cries of metal on metal drowned out by the insanity of the engine. The frame is groaning now, this car is being pushed to its limit– no, beyond its limit.

336.

337.

The neon lights of the city are streaking by now, and looking straight ahead causes everything to merge and blend into one. All I know for certain now is speed.

338.

339.

The city is almost deserted, but the few cars and pedestrians cry out in horror as the purple blur passes them by.

340.

There it is, central Kyoto.

Now, a fun quirk of this road is that it ends in an elevated T junction. And at the top of that T, is Kyoto general hospital.

This car is my way in, a wrecking ball through the side.

I can see the hospital, a hulking concrete mass surrounded by ambulance parking. The road begins to ramp upward, toward the intersection.

341.

342.

I clench my hands around the wheel as tight as I can, and strain to cast a small wall of fire in front of the car as it practically skims the tarmac–

343.

345.

I can feel it begging me to slow down, but I keep on pushing.

Wait. What if the devil isn't here, and I'm about to demolish an innocent hospital?

No time for doubt now.

The devil is here.

He has to be.

346.

347.

I reach the top of the ramp, and time seems to slow. First the front wheels lift into open air, then the back.

The car is flying through the air now, wrapped in flame. To any bystander, nothing but a flaming blur seen for a split second–

Heading straight toward the concrete side of a hospital. The wall fills my vision, and the car is mere inches from impact.

I better be right about this.

And if I'm not, then–

***

The man rests his feet on the desk, leaning back in a dusty office chair. He strokes his wiry beard like a lion stroking its mane, thinking. Clouds of smoke rise into the dark room surrounding him, emanating from a hefty cigar lounging on licked lips. An aging stack of monitors stares him down, choppy CCTV footage taking the stage for all of them. He watches lazily as the smoke rises from the hole in the wall, the explosion having rattled the building mere moments prior. The crumpled nose of a once hypercar is barely in shot, and flames crackle around it. Piles of stone and glass litter the floor, and cold air rushes in through the crater. A silhouette stumbles from the scene, shrouded in smoke.

The man smiles, and plucks the cigar from his lips with two calloused fingers. He speaks with a drunken tone, but undoubtedly authority.

"Run wild, first fear. Keep him busy, get him to the town centre. Halfway toward the fourth fear."

He takes a long puff, relishing the cloud of smoke billowing before him.

Suddenly, shadows in the room seem to move, to take form. A hulking mass of darkness rises from the corner, an enormous ball and chain dulled by the elements dragged behind it. As it moves, each footstep booms with the sound of cascading water breaking free from a dam.

Pulling his feet from the desk before him, he leans forward in his chair.

He makes a gesture, and a clanging sound rings out. The chain restraining the shadow is released, hitting the floor loudly.

He takes another puff, resting his head on a lazy fist.

"Let's see how time has treated you, old comrade…"

***

–IKARI–

Liar. Traitor. Damn you, Tengen.

I'll beat you, even if it takes all I have to do so.

After storming away from him, I just walked.

And walked. I had snuck onto a bus, and swayed back and forth while staring at the run down ceiling for what could've been for hours. I then snuck off, and kept walking until…

Looking around, I find myself in a quaint alleyway scattered with small family shops. I can barely remember getting here, all I remember is that anger.

That rage, directed toward him. And, as for how I can beat him…

The first devil representative. If I find him, and kill him before Tengen, that's it. Now, where would that bastard hide?

Where do devils, strong devils, thrive?

Places of fear, places of disgust. Like what?

As I walk the moon shines dimly amongst shadowy clouds, watching ominously. The darkness in every corner seems to lurch out at me, reaching for me.

Think Ikari, think.

My finger taps my leg in a rhythm, drumming a beat I heard long ago. The austere lights of the main street nears as the alleyway comes to an end, their harsh brightness forcing a squint. A faint memory calls out to me, from a time long gone. I was freshly 6 years old, my birthday just past.

And, in classic six year old fashion, I wanted a pool party. I remember this one kid, I didn't know him that well. He would always sit in the back of class, knees tucked to his chest, staring at the floor.

I'm not sure why I invited him, I think it was more my mum's doing.

The main thing I recall though, was what he did at the party.

He stood in the corner, nibbling on a cheap sashimi platter like some timid mouse. I tried and tried to get him to the water, but he just refused. It was like talking to a brick wall, he just wouldn't. Eventually, I gave up, but I remember someone didn't - this other kid. I had always hated him, but my dad played golf with his. I don't remember much about him, except he *never* took no for an answer.

So, this kid smacked the other's food away, and he pushed him into the pool. And the sound that came from that kid's mouth the instant he surfaced again, was like nothing I have ever heard. A raw, guttural scream.

Time seemed to freeze as my blood curdled just from the sound, that haunting scream. A sound of pure terror, emanated from some lonely kid.

Safe to say, that party got called off. Wait–
That's it.

It might not be the most common fear, but when it hits it hits hard. I pull out my phone and scan the map. Not three blocks away, a public pool. Closed for the past few years. And by the looks of it: rated one star, all reviews absolutely scathing - Even when it was open, it wasn't great. On top of that, all the reviews are talking about safety.

In the absence of safety, fear thrives. Oh yes.

This will do nicely.

***

–TENGEN–

My head rings from the impact as I stumble around, desperately trying to get my bearings.

The smoke fills the room as I trip over fallen rubble constantly, staggering like a drunkard.

Deep breathing, get yourself together.

Looking around, I find myself in a dingy hospital ward, still hazy from the lingering smoke. A small red light blinks in the corner of the ceiling, but apart from that and the eerie glow of the burning car behind me, the room is dark. That same glow casts long shadows over the dusty equipment; a bed that hasn't seen human touch for years, and aging monitoring gear that would be more use as a comical paperweight by now.

Of course, Kyoto general is split into four wings.
This must be the east wing, the abandoned one. Urban
myth tells of people losing their grasp on reality here. And
sadly, in this world, myth often stems from forgotten truth.
I strain my ears for anything, but–
Silence.

***

–IKARI–

The whining hum of an electric light pierces my ears, its
weak glow cast across the concrete poolside. The sad,
stained slab of stone is surrounded by a rickety wooden
fence that would've barely been an obstacle, even when it
wasn't rotten inside and out. Stepping away from the
mouldy overhang of the musty changing rooms, I near the
water.
As the weak light hits the stagnant pool, it seems to be
completely absorbed into nothingness. The surface of the
water is coated in a strange, grimy film that remains so still
it might've been mistaken for solid ground.
A rat scurries past, sniffing around a crystallised towel left
by the last poor sod who took a dip here.
So, any devils?

Or perhaps my train of thought was completely off the rails.

I bend down, scooping a largish rock from the ground.

Egged on by my frustration, I lob it high into the air above the pool.

I watch as it reaches the peak of its flight, and starts to fall again, slowly gathering speed. As it rushes toward the water, I realise just how desperate I actually am. I can't lose to him.

To it.

I, I just can't.

I refuse.

The rock nears the water at an even greater rate.

After all we've been through, all the blood we spilled together, all the miles we walked side by side. The first person who cared for me, and the first friend I ever had. All for nothing, I guess.

The rock impacts the water with a crash, sending swampy droplets flying all directions. Ripples undulate outward from the now slowly sinking projectile, washing over the edge and brushing the ends of my trainers. The once still water scrambles to fill the dent in its surface, the rebounding waves surging toward their origin.

Dammit Tengen.

That lying bastard.

I open my mouth to sigh, as the water folds in on itself.

I watch as the returning waves crash back down, rushing over each other-

Darkness. Cold, cold darkness.

What?

Where is the pool? Where is the ground?

What happened?

I was at the pool, in the dim nighttime.

Cursing my rival.

So then-

Then-

WHERE IS THE LIGHT?

Panic seizes hold of me, as I open my mouth to scream-

Only for lame bubbles to float up in front of my face.

Raging water cascades down my throat, into my lungs, pooling in my stomach.

Cloaked by this inky blackness, I thrash aimlessly in the dark as my throat is flooded with more and more water. Only now does my body register this icy cold that wraps around me, and I feel my temperature plummeting.

A sinking feeling overwhelms me as I desperately try to draw breath, only to be met with empty choking as my body frantically attempts to get rid of this water flooding my insides. My body gets ever colder, and despite my raw panic, my heart begins to slow.

I try to grab at something with dulled fingers, but nothing comes to my aid.

Shadows overlap darkness as my vision fades, slowly
taking away what little I could make out.
This is it.
Trapped in this inky abyss–
I'm going to die.

**

–TENGEN–

I tread carefully, each step feeling like a mile.
Uneasiness lurks around every dusty corner, the strange
haze that fills these halls broken only by pinpricks of red
light that appear sporadically.
I head in the direction I think the centre is in, the direction
that will take me out of this wing. Does a devil really lurk
here–
Or did I assume something utterly wrong?
Well, there's no going back now. I have to be right.
Or else, I might lose to him. And that's unbearable to think
about.
How could he do it, how could he just turn on me like it
was nothing? Like we had met yesterday? I saved his life, I
acknowledged his aspirations, he gave me my name, he got

my helpless self through training. We bonded over our crappy childhood, we looked back and laughed.

Together.

All for what?

Just for him to come at my throat the moment I take my time before telling him something?

How pathetic, to be consumed by anger at such an insignificant thing.

In a way, I feel bad.

But this is what he deserves, the consequences he must face. This competition, it serves only one purpose.

To crush Ikari.

Bringing myself out of those dark clouds, I survey my surroundings once more. The haze is like an impenetrable bank of fog here, and that coat of dust seems even thicker.

But how? I should be headed for the newer part of the hospital, the non-abandoned part.

Unless I got my directions wrong?

But this wing is straight, and I crashed into its end.

Walking this way can only go to the centre. Or, that's how it should be. As I lose myself in thought, a sound echoes.

Almost jumping out of my skin, I look around with a panic infused vigour.

The sound echoes again.

Then another.

Then another.

Something eerie, akin to footsteps. But their pattern is random, sporadic.

And each sound rings from a different direction, each one emanating from someplace else. They get louder, each random beat more aggressive than the last. I look up and down the hall, desperately searching for the source of this noise. The beats get closer and closer together, the tempo rising. But they remain random, nonsensical.

The beats meld into a drone, now a steady and deafening sound shaking the halls. The dust that once coated everything is flung into the air, mixing with the haze to form something completely impenetrable.

The thick air, the noise, the shaking building, the impossible layout of the wing. None of this makes sense, this shouldn't be happening.

Something flashes in the corner of my eye, a blade arcing toward me.

Too late, I go to move, but it hits me.

And passes through me.

What?

Instinctively, I raise my hand in the direction it came and push forth my flame-

A trickle of water drips to the floor.

Looking at my hand in horrific confusion, I turn to run, raising my leg and pushing off the solid ground-

As if it weren't there, my foot falls through. The ground is there, but...

But not there.

My body follows my foot, pulling me through the concrete. The floor of the corridor below looms, and I brace for impact-

Only to pass through it again.

Okay, I see how it is–

As the next floor looms, I get ready for what's below it-

A sickening crunch meets me as I slam onto the hard concrete, a cloud of dust billowing around my fallen body. The dust settles, giving way to those same halls.

Dull pain shrouds my entire body, but as I tenderly test each limb, there appears to be no breaks. Rising shakily to my feet, I try to call out confidently.

"Wh-Whos there?"

My voice comes out timid. Afraid. And I find myself met with silence.

It's like everything I ever knew has changed.

And now, I don't know anything about this place, or even myself.

Just what the hell is happening?

***

"So, all is going to plan, I assume?"

"Yes. First and fourth have begun their assault. They are instructed to lead the targets to my new location during the encounter, as a failsafe in case they lose."

"Oh, you really think the targets would have a chance of overcoming them?"

"No, but, better safe than sorry."

"A wise decision, my precious underling…"

"I am unworthy of such praise, great first one."

"Oh, it makes me feel so happy to hear that."

"I'm glad. I must go now, I bid you farewell."

"Good luck, my precious little disease."

Satisfied, the figure flips their phone closed.

Resting their smooth cheek on their palm, they sigh and run a manicured pinkie finger over shaped eyebrows. Lounging on a crimson sofa, they stretch out and assume a languid pose. Still fully relaxed, they call out.

"Bring me my target at once."

Head bowed, a young woman scurries from the shadows, dragging something behind her. A wooden cart, with a post reaching from its centre. Bound to it by thick rope is a man, dressed in nothing but a rag over his crotch. His body shakes in fear as he stares with wide, terrified eyes at the figure. He clearly wishes to scream, and he would, if not for the tape restraining his lips.

"You feel such fear, don't you."

The figure intensifies their gaze, as they rest their other hand on their outstretched leg.

"After all, you just can't help fearing death…"

Each word is dragged on for longer than the last, their smile stretching wider. The man stares, frozen in terror. If he looked close enough, he might have seen his mortified face reflected in the figure's perfect teeth. The figure locks eyes with him, and curls one of their fingers inwards. The last thing the man knows is the sight of them smirking, followed by the soft pat as their finger falls back to their skin.

From shoulder to hip, drawn both ways.

A cross drawn across his body.

His left side falls first, then his right.

Lastly, his head rolls down his carved midriff to the floor. The figure rolls to face the ceiling, adjusting their position. They now lean their head all the way back, one hand cushioning the back of their scalp as the other rests on the abdomen, rising and falling with their relaxed breath.

Timidly, the girl wheels away what is left on the cart, before returning to collect his other bits and pieces.

"Come here."

She shuffles over, focusing intently on her own feet.

"Raise that head, twelfth fear."

The girl obeys stiffly, looking gingerly through overgrown hair cast across her face.

"So timid, but I suppose that makes sense."

The figure rolls their head to look at the girl.

"What a strange world we live in, where I can casually chat to the embodiment of social anxiety."

The figure chuckles.

"And I guess I was the one that started it all, many thousands of years ago. The day the first human as we know them was born, so was I. We go way back, me and humanity. I guess you could say, without me, they would be extinct. Without me, they would be far too reckless, too confident. I stand at the end of it all, even after they may overcome all my comrades, it is in their innate nature - they can never, never truly overcome me."

They laugh, a loud, proper laugh this time.

"It's funny really. Y'know, younglings like you missed so much! You missed the first generation of devil hunters! You missed Arthur's crusade to take me out! But, I guess you didn't miss much. After all, it took until the fourth generation for someone to finally even see my power. That was Arthur, the closest humans have ever gotten."

They sigh.

"Even so, all of them, they are all so weak. They carry no conviction, no resolution to follow through with their goal."

They meet eyes with the girl, the figure's eyes lighting up as they see something the girl can't.

"That, young one, is what I envision. A courageous human, ready to give everything to overcome me. Someone who will not stop, in the face of my power. Someone with *power*. Power to rival my own even."

Finally, the girl speaks in a mouse-like whisper.

"Is-is this what you want?"

The figure smiles once again.

"Indeed, I wish for that to be the case. It gets so, so boring at the top. I want another brilliant warrior to rise, maybe more than one. And I want them to come, and give me a real fight. Then, I might start appreciating humanity."

The joy melts from their face, and their eyes are now lit with a different energy. A grin once again appears, but this one is different.

This, this is malice.

"But, until that day comes, I'll relish their death."

The little girl's eyes widen as she looks at the figure. And just like before, as if a switch was flicked, the figure's menace melts away. They lift the girl's chin up, angling her face toward their own.

"And as for you, I want you to leave. You're far too precious to be caught up in what's about to come. So go to this address. Now."

The figure hands them a slip of paper, and the girl looks shocked as she reads it.

"But– this is- in a different country–"

"Shhh."

The figure removes the finger they placed on the girl's lips, and whispers to them.

"Just go. What *this* country will soon become is no place for a little girl like you."

***

–IKARI–

I guess it was all for nothing.

Blackness has almost completely taken my vision, and what I can see bears no hope.

Maybe I should have just died in that shed. But, I thought I had come so far? Just like in the barn, it all floods before my eyes.

Dad.

Mum.

That doctor, that boxing ring, the wiry-bearded yakuza man.

The fight with the Spider devil, the first words exchanged with Tengen.

Tengen, our arrival at the HQ. Shinobu, our combat final training.

Watching the sunset, all three of us. Tengen, returning from the mountain.

My time on the liminal mountain, his time with his devil. Our meeting with the director.

Our fight.

That bastard.

Damned devils, all of them.

As my final throes of life are seconds from being snatched away, I realise.

I'm not scared anymore.

With that, I say my final goodbye–

The water floods my body fully, and I feel my lungs fill completely. My already slowed heartbeat comes to a stop with one final, weak pulse. But I'm not scared anymore–

I feel rough, hard ground beneath my knees. Light jams its way through my pinpricks of vision, and cold *air* rushes around my soaking body. Before I can even think about what just happened, my body takes over, and I throw up. Litres of darkish green water spill from my mouth, pooling on the pavement before me.

Pavement?

The creeping shadow resides as my vision is returned to me, granting me sight of my new surroundings. A stark streetlight casts harsh white light around me, shining on the water pouring off of me.

But, I just died?

Right?

"Hmph. He broke my hold."

What? Who said that? I cast my head from side to side frantically, water sloshing around my eardrums.

There.

A figure stands just out of the light, not five metres away. A tall man, dressed in ripped clothing and ropes of sodden kelp thrown over him. He steps into the light, allowing me a full look. His tattered clothes look decayed and ancient, and those strands of kelp drip with a grotesque murky liquid. He scratches aggressively at the side of his neck, his skin flaking away in dry, wrinkled clumps. Like a corpse dragged from the sea.

He speaks absently, as if I wasn't here.

"No good, I can't trap them if they don't fear it…"

His voice is a chilling, raspy sound.

I go to move, but my body has not recovered from the shock. It refuses to move, my mind unable to recover so quickly from the doorstep of death.

Come on, move.

My finger twitches in response.

"I guess I'll just kill him now, this is close enough to where the boss wanted…"

No, this can't happen.

He raises his hand, and water gathers in that half rotted palm. It begins to take shape, to form into something.

I still don't understand what that drowning thing was, but I just escaped death.

I won't stop going here.

Move, move, MOVE. The water shoots from his hand, rushing toward me.

This won't end here. I won't allow it. And at the last moment, my body returns to me.

In a desperate roll I evade his attack–

And rising shakily to my feet, I turn to face him.

Only to find myself looking into a swirling whirlpool.

He lacks facial features, or even a human face at all.

Spitting the last dregs of water from my mouth, I stare down his whirling face, and draw my sword. Water drips from the handle wrap and the tip of the blade, but the edge still shines true.

I level it toward my opponent, throwing him a challenge.

A strange sound, as if towering waves were crashing down on shingle and scattering it about.

"Fine, I'll play by your rules. Considering you overcame my fear, I think you deserve something.

A jet of water hardens in his hand, forming a lethal looking edge.

His rasping voice holds a touch of amusement.

"Shall we begin?"

I smile, masking my complete confusion and fear, and settle into a fighting stance, clasping my sword. My voice comes across ragged, but nonetheless–

"Let's go, devil."

9: SOULFELT DECAY

–TENGEN–

The walls are turning in every direction, things once solid now as firm as running water.
I stumble blindly, a strange fog beginning to enclose me.
My senses refuse to be themselves, telling me things that make no sense.
What is this?
How can it be that my body, my mind, how can it be that they know nothing?
Of course, this is the work of a devil. But which one?
A hospital, a strange sound, an odd mist.

Everything I knew being flipped on its head, and now a complete loss of what's real and what's not. What I know being wrong, not being able to gather any new information. Knowledge, knowledge, knowledge. Everything is about knowledge.

So, what is this fear? Knowledge, understanding. The known, the...

The unknown. Fear of the unknown.

That's it.

The fog still looms, and the corridor I once thought to be solid is nowhere to be seen. Asphalt runs underfoot, the occasional marking on the ground looming from the fog.

Asphalt, markings–

A road.

There, something I know for sure.

This is a road.

Or is the devil just playing with my mind?

What if this is nothing but an illusion, something to trick me?

No.

This has to be real, I know it is. If I don't believe anything, if I let myself know nothing, I'll die here.

And that can't happen, not before I beat him.

Gaining some confidence, I manage a somewhat steady walk down the road, each step recoiling into my battered body.

Focus on what you know.

Come on Tengen, don't fall now.

What I know.

Strange silhouettes creep into the corners of my vision, barely visible through the mist. They seem to move with me, akin to a hunter encroaching on its prey. Flames. I need flames.

I will with all my might, I will for that burning rush.

But nothing comes.

Am I still scared, still scared that I don't know what will happen?

Focus on what I know. And I know that my flames exist, that those searing crimson arcs can spill from my palms once more. I have to believe, to will it to be true, to find what I know.

And to clutch it, to bring it close, hold it close to my soul. I can't be scared, not now. Not here, in this devil's grasp.

One foot in front of the other, over and over again.

That pain that comes with each one, I know that pain exists.

The sound of my footfall on the road, I know that exists.

This heat that now brims beneath my skin, I know that exists.

I know.

Time to show this devil the one thing I've always known how to do.

It's time for a baptism by fire. I don't fear you, devil.
Not anymore.

***

–IKARI–

Each clash of our blades sends waves of pain down my
arms, each movement met with laboured breath.
But I can see it, the devil is tiring.
Compared to when we started, his movements are sloppy.
Unrefined.
He swings wildly, each blow delivered with nothing but
anger.
When he speaks, that raspy voice is charged with primal
anger.
"Why, why don't you fear?"
Our blades clash again, each time more ferocious.
My actions ooze confidence, but in reality, I've never been
more scared in my life.
Faced with this *thing* dripped in water and coated in
seaweed.
This thing that has witnessed so much death to the point
that it enjoys it.

This thing that terrorises so many innocent children, this thing that stops people even stepping foot into water from the moment they can walk.

All this fear, all this rage, all this confusion. Turn it into strength.

Muscles burning, I keep crossing swords with it, desperate for an opening.

I fight on, ignoring my body screaming at me.

Something is nagging at me, not letting me fully focus on this fight.

Without warning, my mind is snatched into a memory, leaving my instincts to fend for themselves.

Earlier this month, before my fight with Tengen, I felt him.

Tugging at the back of my brain, scrambling for control.

Wait.

I… I didn't take one this month.

No, no this can't happen.

That can't be right.

If that's true, then…

No.

He can't take over, not now.

No one can tell him what to do, no one can stop him doing what he wants.

I snap back to the fight, barely slipping away from each attack.

My swings get weaker and weaker, each strike being parried easily.

Sensing my growing weakness, it presses on. Attacks begin to rain down on me, a constant barrage from what seems like every direction. Small cuts begin to appear as its blade slips past my weak excuse for a guard, and before long I look like I've walked through a hurricane of razor blades. Blood flows from a cut above my eyebrow, blinding me in one eye.

I can't keep up with it now, my body has failed me.

That nagging fear of him torments me, even as I face defeat.

My sword begins to slip from my hand as it gears up for the finishing blow–

I open my mouth, ready to speak some final words of defiance.

And, previously unnoticed until this very moment, a drop of blood runs down my cheek.

And up, onto my top lip.

Too late, I go to brush it off.

It wobbles slightly, as if choosing a path.

And it rolls, agonisingly slowly, over my lip.

It hits my front teeth, running down the groove between them.

After what felt like forever, a single drop of blood, hits my tongue.

I have time to think one thought, time for one goal to flash through my mind.

I must win this fight.

I must win this fight.

I must win this fight.

And everything in my mind cuts to black.

***

The man claps slowly, a begrudging smile on his face. Clouds of smoke still billow from his lips.

"Most impressive…"

He talks in solitude, his own ears the only thing to hear his voice. Rising from a battered leather chair, he shrugs on a black jacket over a cream coloured shirt. With a sigh, he blows another cloud of blue tinted haze.

"Kids these days, eh?"

He reaches into his jacket pocket, pulling out a dozen small vials. Under the flickering light of the displays behind him, he admires the deep red colour of the liquid that flows inside each one.

"Let's see…"

He turns each vial one by one, as if seeing them as something different entirely to glass containers. The way he looks at them, they seem akin to weapons, or perhaps old friends.

"I reckon... 6, 7, 10, 12."

Smiling happily as he holds the four chosen vials, he opens each one.

And then, raising them up and tipping his head back, he pours the liquid down his throat. In this light, it's all too clear what it is.

"Lovely and fresh, brimming with the cells of my wonderful playthings."

He wipes a few loose droplets from his wiry beard, and slides a white surgeon's mask over the lower half of his face. Speaking through the fabric, his voice picks up an excited tone.

"It's starting to look like this might be rather fun."

***

–TENGEN–

Around me, sirens of parked cars scream as orange tendrils flare around them. The mist that had once blinded me has been burned away, and those strange silhouettes were scorched away with it. Looking down to my hands, my vision is filled with angry reds and subtle oranges spilling from my palms.

Eventually, the sirens burn themselves out, and I find myself in the silence of the night. Was that it? Or will that devil return?

I guess I'll never truly know.

How ironic.

Walking away from the scene, I notice the plumes of smoke rising from somewhere not too far off. They don't appear to be those of a fire, more like dust thrown into the air by a falling building. I break into a jog, flames still licking the road underfoot.

As I run, I recall what happened in that hospital.

When I had tried to use my fire, and no heat had answered my call. It made me realise, I rely far too much on this power I barely understand. I mean, even after changing my contract, it still feels like all I can do is borrow power from Azoth. Like scooping water from a lake just to put it into a bucket, and then only using what's in that bucket.

How can I access that lake, and use as much as I want?

A painful rush of blood to the ears answers my question.

Of course there's that option, but I can't do that. Just like in the fight against the Fifth, when I let it take over completely.

Is that really the only way to gain the full power that lies within my devil?

No, it isn't – My fight with Ikari.

What did I do there, to gain so much more strength and yet keep my mind in full control?

It was like, when I saw him and heard him say those things, I stopped thinking about anything else. I wasn't thinking about calling forth those flames, they simply answered the call of my emotion.

Like, I was punching with the arms of Azoth, and yet thinking with my own mind.

That's it. Like a sort of unity, a perfect combination.

Halfway between scooping handfuls of water from the lake, and drowning in it. That's what I need to be able to do at a moment's notice, not just in a fit of anger.

I let my flames die away, and instantly my body is hit with a rush of pain from every step. But, I've arrived.

Peering into the clouds of dust and smoke, I try to make out anything tangible. For a moment, I could have sworn there's a group of men clad in white, hauling something onto a stretcher– but it seems too outlandish to investigate. This reminds me all too much of that mist back there, but at least this time there's no silhouettes except those men that aren't real–

A shadow looms in the dust, barely noticeable at first.

It takes on a vaguely human form, something clutched at its side.

And it's definitely getting clearer.

Something is coming.

Almost subconsciously, small tendrils of fire form around my arms, almost like gauntlets.

"Who's there?"

I call out in a steady voice, masking my unease. Still the figure approaches, getting clearer by the step.

Wait.

Even through the smoke, something becomes clear. Well, two things.

Messy blonde hair.

A katana by his side.

And, with the final step, my gaze meets those piercing blue eyes.

His face is covered in scratches and cuts, but there's no doubt about it.

"So Ikari, looks like we've met on the battlefield, just like I said."

I meet his eyes once again, glaring at him.

Here he is.

The boy that turned against me so easily, the boy who threw away everything we had for some stupid reason. And yet, something seems off.

He holds the katana in his left hand. Ikari's not left-handed. And he holds it in reverse grip, the tip of the blade pointed behind him.

Ikari never did that.

It's like, I'm looking at Ikari's face, but behind those eyes is someone, or something, entirely different.

"I must win this fight."

Finally, he breaks his silence.

And what an opening that is. But, he's not Ikari, there's no way. Who is that?

"What do you mean? Who are you?"

I speak cautiously, my instincts on edge.

"I must win this fight."

He smiles, and it isn't Ikari's smile. His eyes snap onto me, and something blooms behind them.

"You seem confused. So, for your information, I am an honored guest in the body of the one you call Ikari."

The edge of the katana glints in the moonlight.

"Call me Kur–"

BANG!

I'm thrown off my feet by the force of the explosion, sent skidding across the ground. Smoke billows en masse from the side of a building just across the road as my ears ring from the sound.

Looking to my right, I see not-Ikari digging the point of the sword into the asphalt to hold him in place.

Wait, did he just pierce solid ground with a regular steel katana–?

My attention is snapped back to the place of the explosion, but all I can see is fallen rubble amongst a cloud of thick blueish smoke.

But then, just like a moment ago, when I saw not-Ikari.

A figure in the smoke.

No. Two figures in the smoke. They get clearer as they near the open air, slowly revealing their appearance. One of them is average height, with short gray hair and from beneath a white surgeon's mask I can see the edges of a wiry beard that covers a face wrinkled by age. The other is tall, inhumanly so, and yet its limbs seem to be so incredibly thin. Almost akin to a scarecrow.

Finally they enter the clear air, and the full details of their appearances are revealed. The man wears maroon suit trousers above polished leather loafers, and a cream coloured shirt half covered by a tailored black jacket.

The other has milky, chalk like skin stretched over lengthy bones. Its face is featureless, nothing but that haunting milky skin pulled taut around an inhuman skull. Its arms hang limply at its side, and it hunches over the same way a person does when completely exhausted. Around where its joints should be is a collection of odd lumps, like blood is swelling up and causing the skin to bulge out.

So, a well dressed grandpa and an exhausted monster.

A voice rings out, tinged with age and yet undeniably excited.

"Greetings, my friends. It is your lucky day, for you two will bear witness to my presence!"

"Any just who the hell are you? You know I'll kill you, because I must win this fight!"

The response is angry, spoken in a disinterested tone.

How could I forget?

Having been so caught up in those two, I had forgotten all about Ikari.

No, the one who resides in Ikari's body, not Ikari.

"I am the almighty representative, the man chosen by our gracious leader to carry out her wishes."

He bows as he speaks, like he expects us to clap for him simply being here.

So, this is him. The one the director wants dead. I should make a move now, while he's still bowing. Scrambling from the ground, I gather flames in my fist and charge–

Like a light switch flicked the other way, my muscles lose all energy. I collapse to the floor, waves of exhaustion rolling over me, and it feels as if my body is simply too tired to obey. With a struggle, I raise my head, only to see the lanky arm of that thing extended in my direction.

"So aggressive, so passionate. The boss would like you…"

I can hear the smile in his voice, and can almost feel the pleasure he takes in doing this.

"So young man, what do you think of my number 6?"

Number 6?

What the hell is he on about?

He continues, talking like a proud dad telling the other parents what his son did.

"He's quite a rare one, only about 8 million have him in the world. But those that do, they have no choice in the matter. Forced to carry his burden, all their miserable life."

"Shut up. I don't know who you are, or what the hell you're on about, but something about you infuriates me."

And with those bold words, not-Ikari yanks his sword from the road and begins to advance, his bloody face adorned with a grim smile. He walks faster, closing distance rapidly, soon breaking into a run.

And then, just like with me, he collapses as if his muscles just gave up.

Wait.

Like that same lightswitch has been flicked back, energy floods into my muscles. Once again rising to my feet, I advance on the pair. The tall one's hand is extended toward not-Ikari now, those grotesque limbs even worse the closer I get.

Another step, and I'll be in the range of my flames–

Collapsing to the floor, once again my energy abandons me But, I still hear the sound of footfall on asphalt.

Not-Ikari is moving again. That's it. I understand.

"It can only get one of us at a time!"

"That's obvious, but we need to get closer!"

Rude.

But, he's close. We both are.

That thing can't get us both, and if it stops Ikari I'll be able to reach it.

Ikari's advance continues, one more step and he'll be in striking distance–

Hold on, where's the old man?

Straining my empty muscles to look around, I see him.

Roughly a hundred metres down the road, watching with a lazy smile.

How can he move so fast?

But, that monster he seemed so proud of can't do a two versus one, that's the worst possible scenario for it.

Which means...

"GET BACK!"

"What?"

"GET BACK!"

After a split second, he too realises what is going on.

Something beneath the stark skin of the monster is bubbling, a pot of water on the stove right on the edge of overboiling.

And, just like that pot of water, all that energy is about to overflow.

The bubbling gets worse, and the slender limbs begin to convulse and flail wildly–

Its hold on me releases, and I scramble back the second I can.

Not-Ikari watches on beside me, the almost surreal scene before us about to reach its final moment. And then, it happens.

Like a balloon struck with a pin, it bursts.

The resulting shockwave causes us to stagger, but we remain on our feet.

Where the monster once stood, a crater maybe five metres wide takes its place. The scorched rim of it is thick with strange, blue blood.

Hold on a minute.

Blue blood?

I remember that diagram, the one they showed us back in class at HQ. What was blue blood again? That's it.

Deoxygenated.

A monster that bleeds deoxygenated blood, a monster that saps all the energy from a person. A monster that has blood bumps on its joints, a monster who affected 8 million people from birth.

A disease.

That monster was–

"Thanks."

The sudden sound snaps me out of my thoughts.

The word is mumbled by not-Ikari, as if he isn't used to saying it.

"Huh?"

He turns to me, his expression unreadable.

"I said thanks."

"Oh, uh sure."

Who is this?

Just what the hell happened to Ikari?

"And, by the way, who *are* you? 'Cause you're definitely not Ikari."

"Don't call me that."

A smile once again blooms on his face.

"Call me Kurayami."

"Kurayami? Like, you're a completely different person?"

"I suppose you could put it that way."

"So you're like–"

My words are interrupted by the sound of a slow clap ringing out through the night. Our attention is drawn to that same old man, now walking toward us. Maybe fifty metres away, and yet his voice is clear as ever.

"Perhaps it was poor planning, to bring one so inept at two on one combat. That said, the way you both managed to realise the self-destruct and get out of the way was *most* impressive."

Kurayami snorts.

"Yeah, *thanks*."

He tightens his grip on the katana. I turn to the man, meeting his eyes.

"So, you're the representative of the first devil?"

I raise my fist in front of my face, knuckles pointed towards him. Flames burst out from between my fingers, enveloping my fist in blue flame.

"Tell us where they are, and we might let you live."

A croaky laugh echoes around us, emanating from the man.

"Being threatened by kids. What's it come to, eh?"

He snaps his fingers, and a strange murky liquid gathers before him. It writhes and bubbles as if it was alive, before slowly taking shape. Puddles of the stuff form limbs, and harden in place. Then it crawls up those limbs, forming more. Like a terrible tree sprouting from the ground, that liquid slowly shapes into something humanoid.

The man laughs, a more sinister tone to it this time.

"If you can beat my toys, perhaps I'll take you seriously. Behold, my number 7."

The liquid has fully formed now, and before us stands another grotesque monster. Its body is a mass of limbs, each of them shuffling around like branches in the wind. This one's skin is a pale green, the colour of a cartoon zombie.

"This one is even rarer, only 10 people in every 100,000. Lets see how you do, children"

The man turns and walks, tauntingly slowly, away from us. With a growl, Kurayami starts to run after him, only to trip over his own feet after five steps.

"The hell?"

He rises again, only to stumble. He puts an arm down to catch himself, but his elbow bends slower than it should, and he hits the floor again.

What happened to him?

I turn to the thing, my eyes searching for any evidence of tampering. It looks as disgusting as it did before, but...

Nothing stands out, but this has to be its ability.

The last one could sap our energy, so what's this one doing?

I take a step toward it, and nothing seems amiss. I take another, and it's fine.

I break into a walk, cautiously approaching the thing.

Just as I'm about to get close, my next step falls short. I stumble, and try to get up. But my muscles overcorrect, and I stumble the other way.

I manage to stay somewhat on course, staggering like a drunkard towards it. Straightening up, I throw a punch.

And it careens completely the other way. I try to throw another one, but I overcorrect and it goes flying past my target. Stepping back, I gather myself only to clumsily trip over my own feet when standing still.

Kurayami rises to his feet, speaking gruffly.

"Your muscles, idiot!"

"What?"

What does he mean, my muscles?

"The thing messes with your muscles!"

Messing with muscles?

Is that why we can't walk properly, or throw a punch?

Out of the corner of my eye, I see Kurayami swing his blade wildly toward it, but his shoulder tenses out of nowhere and the blade sails over its head.

He's right. Whether it's Kurayami or Ikari, he would never miss a target from that close.

"We need to attack without using our muscles!"

Saying that, I realise how impossible that sounds.

"And how the hell do you suppose we do that?!"

"Just trust me! I have a plan, I think…"

"Oh great. What are you gonna do, ask it to leave?"

Deep breath.

Think about the lake, the way the flames flow through my body. When I use more flames, or when my emotions take over, the fire spills out of my body uncontrollably.

If I can do that, and direct it toward that thing, we can do this.

Come on Tengen, gain control. The lake. Scooping water into my own bucket. Gather the water, and spray it.

Like partially covering a tap.

Gather the water, and spray it.

Focus on the flow of the heat, bring it all to one point.

The tips of my fingers. Concentrate the heat. Compact it, just like when I stole that car.

Build that pressure, form it into something. An elastic band, right on the edge of snapping.

Gather the water, and spray it.

Focus Tengen. Don't fail to save them this time.

Gather the water, and spray it.

Gather the fire, and–

A column of swirling flames erupts from my fingers, but this isn't like before when I was running on pure emotion. This is calculated, controlled–

The flames spiral into the sky, and slowly, carefully, I lower my hand until the tips of my fingers face that thing. And that scorching, crimson whirlpool that extends from them follows suit.

I see Kurayami watching it all unfold, an expression of begrudging respect on his face.

Fire now engulfs the road before us, fanning out in a great cone and incinerating everything before it. The black surface of the road begins to turn slick, trails of tar running like spilled water.

Now, stop the flow.

Like turning a valve, bring the water back under control.

The tips of my fingers are blackening now, they're not meant to channel this heat.

Come on, you did the hard bit.

Stop the damn flow, Tengen, get it under control.

I grind my teeth, my free hand turning white as I clasp my outstretched wrist.

Windows on the side of the road are starting to turn orange, the glass becoming almost like a thick syrup. Car tires are melting, the metal on their doors turning white hot. The tips of my fingers are scorching now, the pain racking my body.

Come on Tengen.

Stop the rush of water from the lake. Like a dam, hold it back.

Build a dam between you and that lake, only let through what you can handle.

Build a dam.

My vision is cloudy on the edges, shadows sneaking in toward the centre, and I see nothing but swirling reds and oranges.

"Snap out of it!"

Huh? Kurayami? Is that you?

"Snap out of it!"

Build a dam. Cut off the water. Stop this.

I fall to one knee, and it happens. It all stops.

The fire vanishes, the burning in my fingers resides.

And I look at what I have just done.

A small pile of ash lies in place of that thing, the surface of the road for the nearest twenty metres is nothing but viscous black tar, the cars that lined the road are slanted since one of their sides has been completely melted.

All done at my hands.

"Hey fire boy, pull yourself together. That grand show you just put on did the job, but we still got that grandpa to worry about."

He's right.

Things aren't over yet.

That same slow clap rings out once more.

"Once again, most impressive. Such spectacular firepower, for such a young man."

The wrinkles around his face deepen as he narrows his eyes at me.

"Though, that is to be expected for the boy who harbours the traitor."

Kurayami interjects, speaking with a tone of amped up disdain.

"Stop hiding behind these things, fight us yourself!"

The old man laughs, and readjusts the mask on his face.

"My boy, I am simply seeing if you are worth my full effort. And, having put on that display–"

His tone switches, becoming something much more threatening.

"I'd say you are."

The air around us seems to thicken, and begins to swirl around a point next to the man. The wind picks up speed, sending fragments of rock and small bits of grit flying toward us. It speeds up even more, and the man tosses something into the middle. In an instant, the wind picks up a deep red colour.

I tentatively reach my hand out into the edge of the red swirl, and it comes back sticky with blood.

The crimson colour obscures all vision of the man, but I can hear his laugh. I look at Kurayami, who is staring grimly at the sight. But, I see something in his eyes. Some small sparkle of joy. I remember what he said earlier, the first thing he said to me. Perhaps this is what he wants.

Or maybe not.

All he said was that he must win this fight.

The sound of the man's words drag my attention back to the storm.

"Behold, one of the strongest fighters in my arsenal."

The wind begins to fade, and in what was the eye of the storm, a man kneels. His skin is a deep crimson, and as he raises his head blood drips from his chin. I can hear his breath, a gravelly, wheezy sound that emanates from a pair of blue lips. It gnashes its teeth in a series of bites, like a feral animal.

The man sounds elated when he speaks, like a mad scientist showing off his latest breakthrough.

"By combining numbers 10 and 12, we create this. Born from the red gale, he carries the power of the most common chronic disease, and the most deadly disease there is. He affects millions every day, and kills hundreds of thousands a year. If you can beat him, I shall attack you with everything I have."

Combining the most common chronic disease, and the most deadly?

This is bad. Really bad.

"So, kill this thing then I can have at you? I'll do just that. Listen to me you damned idiot. I must win this fight, and I will."

Kurayami sounds almost excited.

The man laughs, and ignores everything he said except his first question.

"That's right, so try your best. Good luck children!"

And, just like last time, he walks slowly away.

Those deep, laboured breaths fill my ears as I focus on this thing that he brought before us. It's clearly struggling to breathe, and yet there's something about it.

Like looking at a serial killer who's oblivious to what they've done.

It rises, and a cascade of red falls from it. Stangly, the moment those crimson drops hit the scarred road, they crystallise into something solid. It takes a step, leaving a deep red rock formation where its foot was.

Then another step, then another.

It walks toward us, each breath a suffocated scream.

Come on Tengen, do it again.

Gather the water, as much as you can handle, and spray it.

Just one fingertip this time, levelled at this fresh abomination.

A swirl of seething reds and oranges rush to meet it, spiraling toward–

It waves a dripping red hand, and the flames dissipate.

What?

Another spiral, faster and stronger–

Gone.

How, how can it completely nullify my fire?

Think Tengen, think.

The most common chronic disease, combined with the most deadly one.

That means that blood must be from one of those two. The most deadly one?

That's it. Heart disease. The blood in the arteries cannot get through to the heart, and the person dies.

So if the blood comes from the most deadly one, then what is the most common chronic one? And what power could it have to completely nullify fire?

It takes the final step, and raises a fist surrounded by rock-like blood over Kurayami's head.

It brings it down in a flash, and the sound of stone on metal cries out.

Kurayami's katana, the flat of the blade holding off the strike. He slips from the attack, and the fist continues its path, shattering the asphalt. He arcs his sword toward its head, but the creature ducks before countering with a kick to the side of his ribs–

In a split second, he gets his sword down to his side and that screeching sound rings out again as the steel of the blade collides with its shin.

I watch as the fight speeds up, each side putting in more and more effort.

It's almost mesmerising, watching them exchange blows. Kurayami's sword flashes around like a wild snake, and the creature contorts inhumanly to avoid almost every strike.

Slash, dodge, block, slash, punch–

I have to help, but if I can't use my fire then what do I have?

Without my power, I'm useless.

I look down at the flames spluttering from my palms.

No, there has to be something.

That fight with Ikari, when I was using Azoth's arms, they were blackened, almost rock-like. That's it. Just like how I managed to make a ranged attack from my fire, I can do that reinforcement again!

Back to the lake, visualise it.

Like dipping my arms into the water, letting it coat them.

Dip your arms in, feel it flow over your skin.

Feel the heat brush across your forearms, let it envelop them.

Exactly the same as against the green one. Envision it, then do it.

The water, running over my arms. The heat, brimming beneath the surface. Combine them, make it happen.

Heat erupts from my skin, swirling around my arms like a sleeve. I can see it charring my skin, changing it from something human to something rock solid.

This is it.

The second way to use my fire that I've learnt today.

Time to test it out.

Sounds of rock on metal are still being flung around, and the fight between Kurayami and that thing has reached new heights. Moving almost too fast to see, they exchange blow after blow. Somehow, that things breathing has become even more horrific, and it appears to slowly be running out of that crystallising blood.

This is our chance to end this.

I can see Kurayami is starting to tire as well, each exchange sending waves of pain into his grim expression. But still, that grimacing smile remains firmly in place.

Each step takes me closer, and I quickly break into a run. Almost there, a few steps away–

It makes a clumsy swing for him and I manage to land a strike square in its back, the sound of the impact like boulders smashing into each other.

The creature turns and lashes out at me, a kick aimed straight to my head. Instinctively, I snap my head back and the rock-like shin whistles past my face. It follows up again, but more sluggish this time. As it gears up to strike again, Kurayami manages to slash it where it hasn't had the chance to crystallise, causing it to stagger and let out a warbled, choking sound.

It redoubles its effort, the blood spilling from its wound being used as a shield against my next attacks. Kurayami lands another strike, then another, each one hacking more and more away from this thing.

The creature doubles over, and I land a series of strikes square on its face.

Blood like rocks begin to shatter all over its body, the once so great power fading from it.

To be honest, it was kind of underwhelming.

Is this really one of his strongest warriors?

It lets out a final strangled sound, before collapsing fully. All around us, shards of those crimson crystals lay in pools of deep red. And then, before our very eyes, the thing slowly melts back into nothingness, a swirl of wind emanating from where it lay, before every trace of it has faded.

Rising slowly, Kurayami calls out in that same spiteful tone.

"Show yourself, old man. You promised me a fight, against *you*. So let's go, but be warned– I must win."

"I like your tenacity, young man. Don't fret, you shall get a fight."

There he is. Stepping out from the shadows of a building, he pulls the straps of his mask tighter and shrugs his jacket higher on his shoulders.

"That was a most spectacular show from you two. I commend your strength and level-headedness."

He raises an open hand before him, palm facing the sky.

"I don't suppose you've figured me out yet? My power? My fear?"

My voice comes across flat.

"Yeah. For the most part."

"Good, good. So, you understand that you have been fighting the embodiment of different diseases this whole time? First, you fought a nasty thing called sickle cell anemia. After that, a rare yet devastating issue with the nervous system known as ataxia. And, as for that last one–"

"Asthma and coronary heart disease."

Huh? I mean, I had guessed about the heart disease thing but how did Kurayami manage to get such an exact read on it while locked in that fight?

"Very good, your observation is astute. Now, do you know the one property shared by all those nasty diseases you just fought?"

"Just get to the point already, old man. You promised me a fight."

"Very well. All those diseases were natural, with real, evolutionary origins. Now, imagine a non natural disease. A bio-weapon, built to infect and destroy until all that remains is dust. Could such a thing even exist? What do you reckon?"

What is he talking about? A bio-weapon? All that remains is dust?

Kurayami snarls in response, and the man continues.

"Such an infection's existence would cause untamed panic, to think there is something out there that could turn the human body to dust with a touch. Or perhaps, more than just the human body. Something that could turn anything to dust."

I hate this, listening to him talk and talk.

"What are you saying? Quit rambling and get to the point before we just kill you!"

He laughs again, and for some reason it sends waves of anger through me.

"So be it. My point is, there will always be a more deadly infection. And, as the devil of plague and disease, it is the duty that resides within my *soul* to *show* you that. So be glad, for it is time to do just that."

He raises his right hand to the sky, his left hand covering the top half of his face. Ash coloured roots begin to sprout from the road beneath him, encircling his legs and raising him upward.

The black night sky fades to a lifeless grey, and small flakes of something slowly fall from the sky.

One of them lands on the tip of my finger, resting there.

It feels like a patch of dead skin, and the moment I touch it with another finger it crumbles to dust. Those roots are growing faster and faster now, the tip of his skyward hand at least fifteen metres above the ground.

And, as I watch this unreal sight unfold before me, I can't help but feel a sense of finality.

The grey flaky snow, this pillar of ashen roots, the lifeless sky above it all.

It feels like the thing that comes at the end.

Having brought him level with the rooftops, the roots stop growing.

And before me lies a tower of anemic roots holding up a devil, a devil who is now laughing maniacally.

This sight, it reminds me of Azoth's realm.

Of him sitting upon that pillar of bones.

That too had this sense of finality.

The man's laugh subsides, and he speaks once more.

"This, this is the artful annihilation I wish for! The beautiful infection that will turn everything this world knows to dust!"

He brings his skyward hand in front of him, sweeping it in an arc like a performer greeting a crowd.

"Now fear me, for this world shall know the terror of my existence!"

Still that other hand covers his eyes, and now the hand he just used to address us covers the lower half of his face.

But those words, they triggered something. The roots are shaking, as if they are under incredible tension, and the colourless flaky snow turns into a washed out flurry that forces me to squint to see him, to see his hands wrapped over his face as he tips his head back toward the sky.

Everything seems so quiet, so dead.

His next words are but a whisper, yet they are as clear as if he was yelling.

"Soul projection–"

The pallid flakes now stop falling, and those that hang in the air rush toward him as if about to implode. So, this is it. This is the power of the soul projection.

A man atop a throne of ashen roots, a flurry of pallid flakes swirling around him, the slate-grey sky watching on sadly.

He speaks again, and as he does, he tips his head forward, slowly coming to face us.

"–Embodiment of flawless decay"

And on the final word, the middle and ring fingers of his left hand snap apart, revealing a singular eye.

And the moment that eye's revealed, it begins.

I fall to my knees in the face of total annihilation.

An avalanche of lifeless roots, turning the ground to dust wherever they fall.

A cascade of that flaky snow, filling the air with the stench of putrescence.

And a lifeless sky that feels as if it's collapsing, denying dead men a final glimpse of the sun.

It seems almost, peaceful.

To fall at the hands of something so unstoppable.

I look at Kurayami, and smile.

I see him mouth one thing, one thing only. Sorry Kurayami, but you can't win this one.

I look at Ikari, and smile.

And they stare back, undecided about me.

I sigh.

Fair enough.

With that, it all turns grey.

***

"They have been far too bold. We must remind them of how this world works."

"Yes, we cannot allow the deaths of the first and the fourth, along with an attack on the second in command, to go unpunished."

"They must feel the fear that they have always felt, we cannot allow such an uprising to slide."

Four shadowy figures sit in the dark corner of the room, a dingy candle throwing flickering light across the table.

The three who have just spoken look anxiously to the head of the table, awaiting a response.

The figure at the head places a delicate finger on pursed lips, and watches the changing light as a cat watches its prey, ready to pounce.

The figure smiles, and speaks softly.

"Gather our forces. I say we stop sitting in the shadows and go on the offensive."

Their smile widens, the table before them reflected in their teeth.

"Let's remind them what fear feels like."

And, with a lazy breath, the hopeful light of the candle is extinguished.

PART THREE;
YOU CAN'T DO IT
ALONE

1 YEAR LATER

10: SURVIVALISTS

–IKARI–

Grey skies look down upon empty streets, each drop of
rain echoing through the silence. A soft breeze curves
amongst the weathered buildings, lazily pushing frail
weeds that sprout from the cracked roads. Shattered glass
and strewn litter coat the sidewalks, occasionally sliding a
few feet at the hands of the wind. Despite the distinct lack
of colour in the sky, the faint signs of a fading sun reach
desperately through the cloud.
Night is fast approaching.
I should get going.

As I stand, my eyes flicker about instinctively. My hand waits impatient at the hilt of my blade, anxious to draw the blade.

Annoyed at the incessant itching, I pull the tattered remains of a scarf from my neck. It falls as if in slow motion, slowly tumbling toward the surface of the road.

Small wisps of smoke rising into the frigid air remind me to stamp out what remains of my fire, sweeping the grey ash into the open air.

For some reason, the sight of that grey ash falling slowly through the air strikes a chord in my subconscious, like a sense of deja vu.

Choosing to think nothing of it, I turn from the ledge and set out. Each footfall sends splatters of rain through my ragged shoes, spilling onto filthy socks.

The darkness sets in, and light drizzle soon turns to a downpour. Entering the stairwell of the aging apartment block, I get flashbacks of the flat back at HQ.

It seems like so long ago, that we all lived under one roof. Squinting my way through dingy light, descending down in choppy spirals, I try to shake the growing sense of unease that crawls beneath my skin. Drumming rain beats on the filthy windows, shaking them in their frames.

I need to get outside, and fast.

Breaking into a jog, my feet throw up a cloud of dust with each step down, filling the stale air with a definite scent of damp mold.

At last, the final spiral is finished and I find myself thrown into an almost fossilised lobby area. A thick layer of grime and dust hugs everything, and a flickering electric light emits a droning buzz.

How could this happen, in only a year?

It seems ludicrous how quickly everything fell into disarray.

Picking my way through the almost haunting scene, I pass by the front desk and notice something glinting, even in this dull light. Taking a step closer, the source of the sparkle is revealed.

A picture frame, the front glass shattered, shards spilled all around it.

Resting within the rotten wooden boundaries of the frame, a faded picture.

It depicts a man and a woman, standing together in front of the setting sun. Based on the surroundings, it was probably taken abroad. My best guess, one of those two was the person that worked behind this desk.

I can't imagine them smiling on holiday now.

The image, once vibrant, has faded to a mix of dull and whitewashed colour. To fade so quickly, it can't have been natural. If I had to guess, a burst of unnaturally bright light.

And that means they've been here.

And he's been here.

Hurrying from the lobby, I burst through the grimy double doors into the night. The crumbled remains of an overhang lie around my feet, and almost immediately I find myself soaked. With the sky fully opened up and rain cascading down, water crashes in waves onto the city. What remains of the drainage system always struggles to control the downpour, and the roads begin to transition into canals. After a few moments, the banks burst and water rushes over the curbs, turning the sidewalk slick with rain.

Clambering onto the rubble, I reach into my pack and pull out a pair of plastic bags. Stepping into each one, I tie the handles in a makeshift knot around my ankle.

Inching carefully back down the fallen rocks, I land on the flooded pavement. Dragging my makeshift waterproof shoes through the two, maybe even three inches of rainwater, I head away from the apartment block.

Looking around, the darkness and the pouring rain limit my vision to nothing but imposing silhouettes, the shadowy faces of the buildings even darker than the night sky. Even with nothing but their faint shape, the destruction and scars they all bear is clear for the eye to see. Craters in their sides, imploded windows on all floors, scorch marks turning their walls into a series of black spots.

To think that less than a year ago this was the bustling centre of Japan's eighth largest city.

I walk briskly on the edge of breaking into a run. My eyes start to flicker again, anxiously checking every inch of my surroundings. Resting my hand on the hilt of my sword for comfort, I peer ahead.

Without thinking, I realise what direction I'm headed.

The same way I seem to always end up going, regardless of whether I want to or not. As if I know that something lies in wait for me, but I don't know what.

Or do I?

No, this direction leads to the edge of the Nakagyo ward, where it transitions to the Sakyo ward. I've never been to either of them.

So why, why does my subconscious drag me toward this place every single time I start walking?

Everytime this happens I force myself to turn around, to head back to the areas of Kyoto I normally hunt in.

But maybe... maybe the best thing to do is to go with it. To see what the corners of my mind want me to see.

Trudging through the flooded streets, I find myself thinking back.

Hunting devils for the marketman, living out of a trash heap, nothing but pills and a sword to my name.

Almost instinctively, I touch the side pocket of my pack.

Good, the bottle is still there. There's no reason it wouldn't be, but I can't bear the thought of what happened that time. It was a year ago now, just before all this madness kicked off. Not long after my fight with Tengen, when we were in competition to kill the representative. I had just broken free of the ocean devil, and was fighting him head on. I was getting exhausted, and the devil was closing in for the kill. And I remember that moment of realisation, the way that fear had coursed through my body.

When I realised I hadn't taken one that month.

I grab the bottle from the side of my pack and shake it. The rattling can barely be heard over the thunderous rain, but I can tell. 5 left.

Time has gone so quickly, so quickly that it's beginning to feel like a countdown.

As for what it's counting down to, I almost don't want to know.

Re-focusing on my surroundings, I realise how completely unfamiliar this area is. In all my time working alone, hunting those horrid creatures of fear, I've never ventured from the places I know.

Until now.

Battered signs for the Sakyo ward begin to appear, and I draw ever closer to where my mind wants to go.

The rain eases off, slowing to a heavy drizzle. Clouds begin to disperse, the dull stars looking down upon the city with a forlorn gaze.

And I round the final corner, taking the final steps toward this mysterious location.

Oh god. This- how can this be–?

Where is the city?

Before me, nothing lies in wait. No buildings, no lights. A crater, the edge barely visible in the dark.

A gaping hole of nothingness, stretching as far as the eye can see in this darkness.

And a missing city.

Small fragments of rock crumble idly from the edge, as rain streams down into the abyssal darkness. Thousands of buildings, hundreds of roads, countless lives. Reduced to nothing.

As the rain floods through my hair, plastering it to my forehead, I can't help but feel that same sense of deja vu that I felt watching those ashy flakes swirl through the air earlier. Is this it?

Is this what I subconsciously wanted to see, this utter destruction?

It's as if the city just crumbled to dust, and was blown away in the wind.

***

–TENGEN–

Scurrying to the overhang to escape the downpour, I check my watch.
Dead on midnight.
Heading toward the rusted door, I check my shoulders nervously. I don't know why I do it, there never is anything to see bar the usual decrepit alleyway. To think that here, hidden away in the poorest area of the Minami ward, resides the only group of people that have a chance to return things to how they were.
Well, except him of course.
Checking my surroundings for the final time, I drop my hood and stand before the door.
Knock, pause, knock knock, pause, knock.
The sound of my fist on the rusted door rings out through the alleyway, and I anxiously look around again. After a few moments, I hear muffled footsteps from the other side of the door.
It swings open on rusty hinges, and there he is. Just like last night, and the night before. And every night since this whole thing began.
My eyes are met with a beaming smile, a well tanned face bursting with joy and hope. He stands tall as ever, maybe

even encroaching on six feet now. His clothes are the same as always, that tattered old costume his parents got him for his sixteenth birthday. Despite the once vibrant magenta, blue and yellow now being barely visible thanks to smears of dirt and grime, its charm is not lost on me. I meet his eyes, wells of warm brown, and his fair hair falls messily around his crinkled face. The excess of his power spills from his skin, giving him an almost ethereal glow that illuminates his dingy surroundings.

As I speak, I find myself smiling at his infectious unspoken optimism.

"Raito, my man, how are you?"

His ear to ear grin settles into a confident smile, the corners of his mouth curling up.

"I'm doing well, thanks for asking."

He guides me inside, leading me down the shadowy corridor as the door swings shut behind us.

"How have you been, boss?"

The shadows dissipate as Raito passes them, and we take a left deeper into the building.

How have I been? I guess…

"Same old, same old, I suppose. Today was rather uneventful, it's been almost a month since something came up worth chasing."

"Tough work, but we keep on pushing. Right boss?"

"Yeah."

I pause.

"I appreciate the support, as always."

We round the final corner, and there they are.

I wish they all saw things as Raito did, but sadly not all of us are quite so hopeful. As I enter the room, six sets of weary eyes meet mine. The eight of us move almost robotically, taking our normal seats. Settling down in the ever-uncomfortable chair at the head of the table, I address each of them with a nod. A long rectangular panel of wood stretches out in front of me, lined on each side with tattered office chairs, populated by slumped shoulders and tattered clothes. A disgruntled coffee machine that spits out nothing but burnt plastic sits in the corner of the square room, and the previously artistic wallpaper has peeled until it curls back in on itself.

This is it, pretty much.

A shoddy room. And a table with six boys and one girl. Mustering what little faux confidence I can manage, I attempt to kick off the conversation.

"How are we all?"

The usual chorus of muttered words, ranging in their tone from slightly happy to utterly exhausted. Silence falls once again on the table, the room completely quiet except the soft whirr of an overhead light.

"How did it go today, everyone?"

Damn it, was that the right thing to say? I glance to Raito for support, and he gives me a subtle nod. Thank god he's here, because I sure as hell can't handle this alone.

Still, the table drowns in silence. I try again.

"Would you mind starting us off, Yasei?"

She leans forward, slumping down as if too exhausted to even straighten her back. Long, unwashed hair spills onto the desk, and she manages a lazy smile.

"Nothing abnormal. Gave a brief chase to some kind of rodent devil, but it was illiterate. After that, the downpour made it almost impossible to do anything else."

I nod my response and shift my gaze to the man next to her, Yuno. He scratches at unkempt facial hair and rubs at the baggy circles beneath his tired eyes.

"Managed to catch one, I think it was something ridiculous like going bald. It was barely literate, only managed to repeat 'the phrase' no matter how many limbs it lost."

Damn. That makes the third devil that said nothing except those words.

'Memento mori' - 'Remember, you will die'

Damn it, why won't it make sense?

They've been saying that for months now, but nothing has happened. Is it just an empty threat, or is there something far more sinister behind it?

"Hey boss, I got something you might want to hear."

I flick my gaze to Shoto, the sinewy man who sits at the far end of the table. He looks somewhat well rested, but still he has those almost dead eyes.

"I was poking about the Nakagyo ward, not too far from the crater. Top of an apartment block, the one we went into and Raito flash banged the lobby by accident? Yeah, the roof of that building."

"What did you see, Shoto?"

That's his area, his hunting ground.

"It looked like the marks of a fire, but the ash had been swept away. Based on the colour, I would say a small one was burning until about twenty minutes before I got there."

He looks me dead in the eyes.

"If I had to guess, it was him."

Argh, why now.

This is the worst time for him to show his head again.

What should I do?

What should I say, to lead the room?

Just make them stop thinking about that.

"Right now, our priority should be gathering information on what the devils are planning, and figuring out the meaning behind the phrase. Dealing with him is not what we should be focused on right now."

Murmurs of agreement round the table.

"Now, does anyone have any ideas about the phrase?"

Yuno drums the table with his fingers.

"I think it's pretty obviously a threat."

One of the most level headed people here, a boy named Kiaran, counters quickly.

"If that's the case, why have they been saying it and yet not acting on it for months?"

Yasei jumps back in, sweeping her matted hair out of her eyes.

"Perhaps they're planning something big, and need time to work on it?"

Shoto pipes up again, his eyes sweeping around the table.

"Then why would they be telling us about it in such excessive advance?"

Everyone's making valid points, and I'm just sitting here in silence. Dammit, what kind of leader sits in silence?

"Now, I understand that you all, for the most part, know how this began?."

Collective nods of agreement.

"May I?"

They indicate their approval, Raito gives me the perfect opener.

"The stage is yours, take it away."

So, I take a deep breath, and begin to recite the story we've been living for these past months.

"So, immediately after the attack on the representative, they made a move. In a single sweeping attack, they struck major social and technological infrastructure. Not long after this, they began to infiltrate key organisations and spread distrust, aggression and tension between important public figures, primarily politicians."

I pause, gathering breath, before continuing.

"This meant that the public began to turn on each other, and since no important figureheads or leaders could see eye to eye, they turned whatever jurisdiction they had power over into a tight knit community. Before long, major cities turned into cesspits of political tension and minor turf squabbles. And then, with fear running deeper than ever, those squabbles turned to wars. And after that..."

I let myself trail off, the rest of the story not needing to be told.

"I know that you knew all this already, but if there is anything you can think of with it fresh in your mind, please say it. I don't nee–"

A quiet voice sounds toward the back of the table, originating from the youngest member of our group. We all simply call him the silent one, but his real name is Kuro. The first thing anyone would notice about him was his hair, such a striking red colour.

"This feels like a cull."

"What was that?

Yuno sounds almost shocked that Kuro actually spoke, and based on the looks of the others we all feel the same.

"It was in this wildlife book I used to read as a kid, I was always a fan of animals–"

He glances down nervously and quickly continues.

"Anyway, I read about this thing they did in England, a badger cull. I didn't know what that was, so I looked it up. It's like, when you k-"

He chokes on his words, before gathering himself up again.

"When you kill a certain amount of a species's population to keep them and their effects on the environment under control. After I read about it, I found out that they used to cull dangerous bees and ants by hitting the nest until the queen was drawn out, and then killing it to force the hive to disperse, so they could kill as many as they needed."

A wave of stunned silence washes over the table.

Is that really what's going on? They want to control us by systematically killing a certain amount of us? Treating people like livestock.

"So you mean to say–"

Shoto's voice is dangerously low.

"That all of this-"

He gestures around us, to the dimly lit room and ravaged city outside.

Yasei finishes his sentence, speaking our collective train of thought in a grim tone.

–"Was to lure out the strongest in society, and kill us off."

Once again, we sit in silence.

Was the banding together of this group exactly what they wanted?

"Remember, it goes both ways."

Huh? I turn to Raito, and unsurprisingly find myself met with that same old smile.

"While yes, maybe they have got the strongest fighters left in one place…"

He clenches a fist.

"That means nothing if they can't beat us head on."

He's gathering momentum now, each word piling onto the last.

"We can beat them, head to head, and tear this carefully crafted plan right from their hands!"

He slams his fist on the table, and rises to his feet, bearing an even wider grin as he speaks.

"We'll be the heroes of the story, dammit! When the dust settles and the sun rises with refreshed hope, we'll be the ones who usher in a new dawn!"

His speech reaches its highest point, his voice like a drumming beat that you just can't resist bobbing along too.

"We may be called survivalists, but is that all you people want to do!? Survive!?"

His question rings out, a challenge that goes unanswered.

"We can do more, there is a path we take in which we walk out into a new world at the end of this! So will you walk to the light, or wallow in the darkness!?"

He sits back down with a heavy exhale, and is met with a round of applause.

Now, it's my turn.

"I won't even try and match that, but I will say this."

I meet eyes with every last one of them, exchanging determined looks.

"I've had enough of hiding in the shadows, being trampled on by fear. Let's show them, show them what the best of humanity can do. For the next week, I want everyone working at their best, tracking down every last one of those things you can. This may only be a fleeting, or foolish hope that we feel, but let's take it for everything it's worth. Fight with all you have, and don't let your fires burn out."

They all rise to their feet, tightening straps on packs, fastening masks around faces, cracking knuckles.

Rain still falls in crashing beats outside, but none of us care about that now. For the first time in a long time, we feel ready to fight. Because we *want* to.

"And one final thing."

I smile grimly.

"From now on, Nakagayo ward is *my* jurisdiction."

***

"You intend to bring the final date forward?"

He stares out over the city, not a single light visible. Rain runs in swaths down the windows as he admires his own reflection, smiling thoughtfully. He risks a glance at the figure beside him, equally enjoying the view.

After some time, they respond in a mildly bored voice.

"Yes, I think it would be wise too."

"And what makes you say that?"

"We must give enough time for some kind of resistance to form, but not enough for them to become an actual problem for us. I fear that the window of time in which both are true is rapidly shrinking."

Placing a thoughtful finger on their lips for a moment, they shift their gaze to the man beside them. A small inflection of joy creeps into their next words, as they look the man up and down.

"That said, if a pair of them forced you into using *that*, perhaps they are already a tangible threat."

The man scoffs.

"I admit, they gave me far more trouble than expected. And, the fact they survived flawless decay shows they're not just glass cannons."

The figure smiles, interjecting playfully.

"But you and I both know how they managed that."

His voice is taught with frustration as he responds.

"Yeah."

"Ah, try and loosen up."

They tilt their head thoughtfully and return their gaze to the outside world before continuing.

"Admittedly, his presence in this whole situation *is* annoying, but it's not the end of the world. Besides, you believe you can beat him, don't you?"

The man turns away and looks to the floor.

Laughing, the figure backs away from the window, sweeping long black hair over one shoulder. They stroll over to a long mahogany table, sweeping their hand over countless burn marks before sitting down. Just as they settle down, a knocking sound rings out from the door. After a moment, it bursts open despite the lack of response. Within a moment of the door opening, the air becomes almost dry, and a distinct smell floods the room. A sharp, fresh scent, with a definite after scent of pool water. A lone fork resting on a countertop begins to buzz sharply, and a few strands of the seated figure's hair are drawn toward the ceiling. With expressions akin to tired parents, the man and the figure turn to the intruder.

A young man, perhaps around twenty. He drops to one knee, and looks to the floor, his shaggy black and blonde hair spilling over his eyes. As he talks, he raises his head in acknowledgement of the room's two occupants.

"May I?"

After receiving a pair of begrudging nods, he once again rises to his feet, dusting off his white cargos. Pushing his hair back into shape, and walking to a seat at the table, he clears his throat to speak.

"So, here is the breakdown of what's been going on."

Two pairs of eyes settle on him, and he continues.

"As per your instruction, all devils have been told to resist any attempts at interrogation, and have been saying nothing except the memento. Myself and the rest of the field unit now believe that there is no doubt about the existence of a resistance force. Thanks to this force, we have lost roughly eighty devils since the operation began. Irritatingly, every devil that has been sent has been killed before it could report back to me. As such, we have no idea who the members of the group are, or what they number in total."

"That's not strictly true."

The young man turns to the older man, looking at him questioningly.

"Do you mean to say that you know who may be in this group?"

"I know two of them. Both teenagers, one contracted to the traitor, one with no contract."

"Teenagers huh? And you're sure that they both are a part of this group?"

The older man nods.

Clearing his throat once more, the young man continues.

"Okay, so we know two of their members. However, the issue of a total number still stands. Moving at our current pace, I think we can–"

"There's been a change in plan."

The young man snaps his attention to the seated figure, watching himself in their teeth as they smile. Laughing at his confused expression, the seated figure explains.

"We have decided to shorten the window of this operation."

They lean forward in their seat, switching to a more serious tone.

"I want two high ranking fighters sent at first dawn, with the goal of gathering as much information as possible. The moment they return, prepare for the final stage."

The young man responds, his voice full with shock as his hair stands straight up.

"You mean to move to the final phase so early?! But we can't possibly–"

"That's enough."

It's the older man interjecting now, warning him to stay in line.

The seated figure continues.

"So, two spies at first dawn. After their return, we allow for two days of preparation. Then we move in. Understood?"

The young man nods nervously.

"And two final things."

The seated figure rises to their feet, casually pacing around the room as they speak in a low voice.

"Number one: I want you to tell the spies that if they fail, don't bother coming back."

They smile, and raise two fingers. A series of deep gashes appear on the wall, only an inch above the young man's hair. A few strands of it fall to the floor, cut from the rest.

"And number two: From this point on, the final goal has changed. It's no longer just the weakest, or the weakest plus half, or even plus three quarters."

The young man is almost a statue, listening in excitement.

"From now on, the final goal is to reach zero percent. Got that?"

They wave him out, and just before the door is slammed in his face, they say one final thing in a sultry tone.

"So pass on the message. When it's all said and done, zero percent remains."

II: HUNTERS, PART TWO

–IKARI–

A washed out sun casts bleak rays over the crumbled rooftops as dawn creeps into day. Clouds flood the sky, a blanket of rough greys and whites. A chill rests in the air, and there's a crispness to it only found on these winter mornings. Not fully recovered from last night's storm, large puddles adorn the roads below, and what little bright light can reach the street level shines dully from their surface. Briefly checking my shoulders with a glance, I pull up my hood and stretch the mask over my face, leaving only my eyes exposed.

Crouching down, a series of footprints left on the concrete roof by a set of wet feet leads me toward the edge of the building.

Approaching the sheer drop onto the street some 30 metres below, I peer out across the neighbouring buildings for any sign of it.

Damned devil, scared to face me.

As I unclench a fist I didn't even realise I had clenched, the faint sound of metal hinges shoots through the air.

Snapping toward the direction it came from in an instant, my ears strain for anything else.

Nothing.

Fine then.

At least I have a direction now.

Setting out across the rooftops, making constant leaps and bounds over chasms leading to alleyways flooded with rubble, always keeping crouched behind what little cover remains when crossing open spaces, always scanning back and forth.

Every sound, no matter how insignificant, causes me to clutch the handle of the sword that hangs temptingly at my side, and every minute movement I see sends a pang of adrenaline driven excitement down my spine.

A raindrop falling from a broken gutter, a pebble rolling a few inches, a few flakes of rust peeling away from a twisted antenna.

In this state of hyper-alertness, every one of those things sets my senses alight as if doused in fuel and tossed into a fire.

The sound of shifting winds, the sound of creaking rebar, the sound of footfall–

Wait.

The sound of footfall.

As all thoughts of subtlety vanish from my mind, I break cover and launch into a sprint, practically throwing myself from building to building in a mindless pursuit of that sound.

And there, maybe three buildings away, I see it.

The shape of a human scrambling over pipes and rubble, a mess of black hair whipping around with each jerky movement. They glance back, and even at this distance, it's clear what they are.

In a surge of energy, I give chase.

The faint rumbling of a train rings through the air, and some part of me realises how rare that is, but my conscience decides almost unanimously that the chase takes precedence. Watery light spills through the now patchy cloud, revealing the sun as it rests just above the horizon, climbing ever so slowly.

The groan of that train has faded into the distance, and bar the two sets of pounding feet, a blanketing silence falls over the Nakagayo ward.

I can see its breath curling out before it, clouds of steam that billow up in front of it only to be dispersed in a heartbeat as its head bursts back into open air.

Still the distance between us remains unchanged, and as I follow in its footsteps I see the trail of destruction a devil like that leaves. Solid steel railings crumpled where it grabbed them, spiderwebs of cracks emanating from where they land after each jump.

As the chase gradually takes us further and further from the city centre, the rooftops get closer and closer to the pockmarked streets, and the chasms that once threatened forty metre drops can now only offer some twenty metres. Still enough to keep my heartrate up, but something tells me this chase won't be on the rooftops forever.

Slowly, the distance between us inches ever smaller, to the point its steaming breath is rattling in my ears. Instinctively, one hand begins to reach for the handle of my sword, as my body waits with bated breath to draw its lethal edge. Our two sets of footsteps have now blended into one, a drumming beat that echoes through the alleyways and streets, piercing the blanket of silence. Only two rooftops away now, its features begin to gain detail. That long black hair that whips around behind it is streaked with blonde, like the stripes on a beach hut. A tattered leather belt strangles the waistband of its oversized trousers, the belt itself adorned with a whole host of knives. It wears a single black glove on one hand, and it only covers its pinkie and ring fingers.

And now, as the distance encroaches on one rooftop, the final and most unsettling detail comes to light.

A handle; the metal, shaped handle of a small kitchen knife, sprouts from the side of its neck. As it runs and jumps, the handle moves perfectly in sync with its body, as if it's lodged solidly through its entire neck.

One rooftop away now, it checks its shoulders frantically, seemingly distraught.

But then, it does it again, it checks its shoulders.

And as it locks eyes with me, even though it's only for a fraction of a moment, an unmistakable smile reaches at the corners of its mouth. This panic, those frantic movements, the seemingly excessive force it's been using all this time. It's acting, making it seem like it's running on adrenaline and instinct.

But in reality, it's planning something.

As we near the end of this block, it launches onto the last rooftop before swinging a sharp left, heading back south toward Kyoto station.

With no choice but to follow suit, the chase begins to speed up as the buildings once again climb above from the streets.

I suppose this chase won't be reaching the streets any time soon.

A burning begins to creep up my calves, gentle at first but soon blossoming into a stabbing sensation with every step. I can feel the sweat from beneath my hair rolling down my forehead and running through my eyebrows, and there's a distinct dampness on the portion of my mask where my mouth is.

Without warning, its arm jerks outward, coming straight out before bending the elbow inward.

Despite it only being maybe twenty meters away, I can barely see what it's doing in front of its chest. And thanks to that, I almost missed it.

A momentary glint of light as the faded sun catches the edge of something grasped in his hand, as it checks its shoulder once again. Its arm snaps out, and another glint of light shines in my eye for a moment. A strange whistling sounds out, and there's a rush of air as something passes by my face.

What the hell was that?

At the very bottom of my vision, a small piece of black fabric waves in the wind just below my eye. Reaching a hand to my cheekbone, my fingers feel a long slit in my mask just below the cheekbone, and as they press against the now exposed skin, I feel a damp warmness.

Risking a glance down at my fingers, that harsh redness is all too clear.

Whatever that was, it cut me. And, it cut me so finely, I barely noticed.

Damn.

Looking back to it, I barely catch the sight of another glint, and its arm once again snapping outward. Another whistle, and this time I feel a slight pressure for a moment on the outside of my shin.

Glancing down again, it's the same as before. A thin slice through the fabric of my trousers, and beneath that a fine red line that is beginning to sprout red beads.

What is it doing?

Snapping your forearm outward, away from your chest, as if hitting somebody standing at your side with the back of your fist.

Or, as if… That's it.

It's throwing something. But what?

Wait.

I'm being stupid. The handle sprouting from its neck, the belt of knives at its side, and now this. I'm being hit with throwing knives.

And they're being thrown by the knife devil.

With that realisation, I pour on speed, giving all I have to close the distance. This is not a small fry, some insignificant player in the great scheme of things.

No, this is a devil that wreaks havoc on countless lives, ruining them, snatching them away, dooming them to fail.

Every stabbing, every cut, every innocent life lost at the hands of a misplaced blade.

It all comes back to the figure running across the rooftops in front of me.

The distance closes evermore, not even ten metres now. We're having to haul ourselves up ledges, leap over ever deepening gaps between buildings. In the distance, but fast approaching, Kyoto tower stands lazily as it watches over the city. When it all went to hell, that tower was one of the first targets for the anarchists and desperate people trying to be heard by the government. Now, it stands crookedly, for about halfway up, an explosion from a suicide bomber ate away at the supporting column on one side, causing it to lean horribly. Before the city was left to rot, the people that lived near it said it used to groan in the wind, as if every second was torture for it to stay standing. In the end, the tower became somewhat of a symbol for the people, a symbol of how even an inanimate object can stand tall throughout hardship. But now, it's neither a symbol nor a source of haunting urban tales.

Now, it's a hulking mass of concrete that's threatening to collapse, while towering over a neighbourhood of utter disrepair.

It's sad, really.

Hauling myself up another ledge, I realise just how high we have gotten. Now we're running across the highest buildings Kyoto has to offer, some fifty metres from the street far below. And now I'm close, almost in range for a thrust of the sword.

Taking my eyes off of him for a moment, I see the all too famous curved glass that adorns Kyoto station just a few buildings ahead. Despite the disrepair that has overcome the whole city, this particular marvel has withstood not only time, but the countless bombings and attacks that it suffered. In fact, I'm so enticed by the sight of it, that I don't even notice how quickly this block is running out until far too late, and after three more jumps, the nice flat roofs come to a stop.

In their place, a sheer drop down onto the roof of Kyoto station.

Looking ahead at the knife devil, it seems completely unbothered by this, and is still taking confident strides across the final few roofs.

Another jump and scramble, another glance down to the weathered streets far below, and that's it.

We've run out of buildings.

It takes a final few steps toward the ledge, and with a burst of speed, I find myself only an arms length away. I see it reaching for a knife, as my hand clasps around my sword handle.

And, almost in perfect sync, we take the final step, out into the open air.

Time slows to a crawl, as if everything is happening while submerged in syrup.

He turns, coming to face me with a smile.

A horrid scar parts his face from left to right, cutting in a diagonal across it.

A knife arcs toward my chest, as I bring my sword down toward its head. A faint screech from a bullet train rings in my ears as we approach the glass.

Sparks fly as our blades clash, grating against each other. The glass crawls toward us, only an inch away. And, in a shower of sparkling fragments, it disintegrates beneath its body. Shards of glass whirl past us, opening countless cuts. There's a yell from a voice that seems vaguely familiar, and the screech of that train is deafening now.

The tracks scream;

That voice yells again,

The devil before me grins.

Here we are.

Falling through the air, trailed by blood and glass.

Blades crossed, locked in some god awful dance.

***

–TENGEN–

Sometime before

Darkness.

A sea of inky black closes in on all sides around me, and a heavy silence fills my ears. Underfoot, train tracks and gravel. With a click of my fingers, a small flame sputters to life at my fingertips. It casts an eerie spill of dim light, revealing the curved ceiling above me, and the flat walls to my sides.

Creeping down the tunnel, a zone of light moves with me as the darkness swallows up everything beyond my few metres of vision. Stopping, I listen.

Nothing.

Curling my fingers into a fist, the flame is snuffed out and the tunnel is once again plunged into darkness. Deciding to take a risk, I call out.

"I know you're here, you can't hide forever."

My voice seems intrusive, alien to this dark quietness. It echoes down the tunnel, gradually fading to a distorted mumble. Memories of my time in the Kyoto hospital, at the mercy of that devil, surface one again. So much has happened since then.

So, so much.

At that moment, a deafening bang rings out through the tunnel, emanating from someplace far ahead of me. I break into a sprint, charging through as the darkness shrinks away from the flame cradled within my palm.

Another bang, then another. A sharp whistling sound passes by my ear for a moment, before the silence returns.

Slowing to a walk, then to a stop, I gather breath.
Crouching down, inspecting the ground for any trace of the damned thing that I know made that noise. The ground seems mostly untouched, barring a small portion of gravel pressed further into the ground than its surroundings. The depression takes the vague shape of a foot, and not too far in front of it, another similar mark is visible. A set of footprints, each far enough from the other to assume it's moving fast.

Setting off at a brisk walk, and once again allowing my flame to flicker out, I give chase. But this chase is slow, methodical. Not like in action films; bursting through alleyways, clattering innocent fruit stalls.

No, this is more like stalking.

And now, trailing this devil like an obsessed fan desperate for a mere glimpse of their idol, I'm the stalker for once. Padding along in this tunnel, a sense I should imagine to be akin to sensory deprivation sets in. When all you feel is the musty air on your skin, and the rough gravel and steel rail underfoot. An almost trance like state, in which one sense is so far deprived the others amplify to an unbelievable level.

But despite that, not even a whisper from a mouse is heard. Not even a slight breeze is felt. The damp, musty smell bears no variation whatsoever.

This tunnel could be another world entirely, a different dimension to the abandoned city not twenty metres above. A different world, that right now, has only two inhabitants. Briefly flicking a fire to life, the previously unknown changes in my surroundings are revealed. What was once a more rounded, old brick affair has morphed into something squared off, with painted concrete walls bearing lifeless electric lights.

Deciding to keep the light for a little while, I keep on moving through what is now clearly a subway tunnel. Calling out again, almost shouting now, I make myself known.

"Just give up, this is futile!"

Still nothing in response.

That's until another ear splitting bang shatters the now untrustworthy silence, and a moment later a more muffled one followed by the sound of pebbles falling.

Whipping my head back and forth, I see it.

A blackened spot on the wall, not a metre from me. A notch rests in the middle of the charcoal halo, and below it a small pile of concrete chips.

Snapping to high alert, my flames rush outward, and an almost blindingly bright light rushes through the tunnel. And, with the sudden rush of light, I catch it off guard. The corner of a foot flashes in my peripheral vision for a moment, before vanishing.

Instantly breaking into a sprint, leaping over each strut of the tracks before each foot comes crashing down on the rough gravel, I dash through the tunnel.

But the light of my flames can only stretch so far, and soon the faint edges of a figure right on the edge of my light once again melds into the darkness.

Dammit, it can't keep getting away with this.

Refusing to drop back into a walk, the walls still rush by as I run on.

And on,

and on.

But to no avail, as the shadowy outline never again slips out of the darkness. As my frustration grows, my flames become almost angry, lashing out and flaring up almost against my control; a worrying sign, but in my anger I dismiss it.

And now, as my target once again slips away, something other than anger rises up. Something that I've chosen to ignore, to forget about as I focus on more important things. I've hidden it behind laughs, behind swearing, behind anger. Most of all, behind silence.

But, to tell myself the truth for once.

I'm nervous, I'm stressed.

I'm worried, I don't know what will happen.

And I'm scared.

Not scared of death, or devils, or pain. But I'm scared that I'm letting those around me down.

I've slowly been torn apart by so many emotions, holding myself together with solitude and adrenaline.

The survivalist force entrusted me to be their leader, and yet it seems I can't make a single decision that really benefits them. It feels as if all eyes are on me, inspecting the way I move, the way I think.

And it feels like I just don't meet their standards.

It feels like I'll never live up to what they want, and they'll always see me as inadequate. Everyday I face that meeting room, and it takes everything I have to hold brief conversations without freezing up.

And what am I meant to do, as leader?

Every day, the hardest fight is the one to get out of bed. The one to keep moving, despite the sinking feeling that none of this matters, that I haven't taken a meaningful step in any direction since the fight with the representative.

In limbo, caught between determination and giving up, caught between confidence and crushing anxiety. A year, that was what life was like for a year.

And on top of all that, all that *human* struggle, was Azoth. Waking up in cold sweats, his icy laugh and fiery eyes plaguing my dreams. A devil, in every sense of the word.

His cold, calculating malice seems to seep into my bones, and sometimes it feels like he's taking parts of me away.

Swapping out little fragments of me, for fragments of *him*.

What if I just, I just become him?

Is that possible?

And on top of even *that*, is me.

Like, *me*.

The nameless boy born to the Uzumaki family, given the name Tengen.

And it feels like everything is piling up on top of me, driving me further and further down.

Stress;

time.

Confusion;

responsibility.

Anger;

Ikari.

Survivalists;

inadequacy.

Azoth;

fear.

And there's no escape from this, no way out.

As if all I can do is leave myself in the hands of fate.

As if I've unknowingly leapt off a cliff, and now all I can do is to wait and see where I land.

Another ear-splitting bang, closer this time, brings me back to the moment at hand. That same whistling sound, and a sharp pain flares up at my side. Instinctively clutching my side, I can feel the tender bloodied flesh, torn by some invisible force.

Well, invisible to my eye.

Despite the endless burn in my legs, the walls rush by faster and faster. The tunnel begins to curve into a bend, and the unmistakable seeping light of an exit comes into view. In this newfound light, the outline of its figure is once again revealed; a tallish woman, with short cropped hair that falls neatly around her neck in a bob, dressed all in black, and hips complemented by an assortment of ugly grey objects. The same things I've seen in so many movies, and yet never managed to learn the name of.

I remember though, that book I read in the library all those months ago, mentioned a knife devil and a…

What was it?

A *gun* devil.

That was it.

So those ugly, stubby chunks of dull metal hugged against her by some kind of holder are guns? Those sounds in the tunnel, that burn mark, was the work of these things? Something so small, yet so much power at the fingertips of its wielder. No surprise it's a great enough fear to constitute a devil of this calibre.

We've fully exited the tunnel by now, and before me lies the hyper-modern spiel of glass and escalators of Kyoto station. Far above, that statement curved glass ceiling still looks down on the station, as weak sunlight streams through. Platforms appear on each side of the tracks, walkways lined with yellow paint and vague signage. Lifeless arrival boards hang limply from their brackets; the power long gone. Dust gathers on the floors, the lack of footfall for months clear to see.

Almost halfway into the main complex, the gun devil makes a sudden leap from the tracks up onto the platform on the left side. The abrupt move catches me off guard, but I follow suit. Now, we stand maybe five paces apart, staring each other down. For the first time, I get a clear look at her face.

Her features are sharp, and angular in shape; her jaw runs dead straight until it meets her neck, her nose seems to jut out as a perfect right-angle triangle, her pursed lips form a straight line across her mouth. She briefly checks a chunky, obtuse watch before peering beyond me toward the tunnel we just emerged from.

Instinctively looking as well, I hear a faint sound bubble up. A soft whining, accompanied by a low drone. Gradually, they both increase in volume, yet still they remain rather quiet. A small puddle of water near my foot begins to wobble, like jelly on a shaking plate. I can feel it in my feet now, a gentle vibration gradually getting stronger.

These three things are ramping up in intensity, and it feels like a climax is approaching.

And then, it seems like all hell breaks loose.

A jumbled shadow appears on the floor between me and the devil, and a moment later, a booming–

CRASH!

–rings out through the station, and the moment I look up is the moment a shower of fragmented glass comes flying down, amidst of which is a tangle of blades and limbs. The platform is almost shaking now, the puddle of water beside me completely splattered. The low droning seems to groan like some waking beast, and that high whining rises into a shriek that causes a stabbing pain in my temples. A loud thump brings my attention to the two newcomers, both cut to shreds by that glass. I yell out–

And they scramble to their feet, but almost instantly one of the two is flung against the corrugated face of a closed shop, a shock of messy blonde hair disappearing in a cloud of dust upon impact.

The ever rising noises and vibration snap my eyes back to the mouth of the tunnel, just in time to see garish headlights and a flurry of sparks rush out of the tunnel as the sounds become excruciatingly loud. As the screaming blur rushes past, the gun devil and a man with long black hair seem to fling themselves into its path, and they're gone.

With a parting shriek that fades into the distance as it returns to the tunnels, the bullet train vanishes as quickly as it came.

And, the devils went with it.

Which reminds me–

The sound of creaking metal interrupts my thoughts, and I turn to see the other devil's sky-dance partner rise from the cloud of dust. In one hand, he clutches a katana with white knuckles. He looks at the floor, blonde hair spilling down over his forehead. Glass cuts are scattered all across his upper body, and the mask pulled over his face bears a rip, beneath which yet another cut pours blood onto worn skin. He looks up, tugging at the tattered remains of a hood to occupy his free hand.

Blonde hair, katana, blue eyes.

I should've known this would happen sooner or later.

I exhale heavily, and as my breath steams up I realise how cold it is here.

With a sharp tug, the snood slides away from his face.

Yeah.

I knew it.

We stare at each other for some time, neither of us making a move.

Until finally, he speaks in a tone impossible to read.

"I think it's time we had a chat–"

He looks at me pointedly, as if asking me if I've figured it out as well.

And we speak in unison, the same word spoken from two different mouths.

"Brother."

12: A TALK ABOUT FLOWERS AND FLAMES

–IKARI–

Well, there it is.

That cul-de-sac engrained deep into my memory; a patch of struggling grass in the centre, with drab unremarkable houses lining the circle. In silence, we approach the grey door that we both remember all too well. He waits a few paces behind me as I wrestle with the handle, an eventual muffled click rewarding my efforts. On aging hinges, the door swings open, giving way to a host of memories.

Without saying a word, we walk in, heads on a swivel as we pad through the house. I run my hand across the kitchen counter, and it comes back grey with dust. Shaking it off, I move toward the stairs. Each rising step is met with a low creak, and after a moment I find myself facing that white door. Timidly, restricted by a nervousness I can't explain, I reach for the circular handle. My fingers hover a few inches above it, frozen in place.

Just what will I find in there?

Wordlessly, Tengen brushes past me and turns the handle with zero hesitation. I follow after him, and–

"Well done Ikari!"

A warm, smiling face fills my vision, golden sunlight bathing half of it. The woman hands me a small wooden block, and gestures to the board on the floor between us. "Now, which hole does that shape fit in?"

After a bout of uncertainty, I reach out with pudgy hands and drop it confidently into the square-shaped hole. A set of arms lift me skyward, grasping me with gentle hands. Now I'm flying, superhero posters and shelves lined with toy trains and picture books sailing past as the room turns in circles around me. A bubbly laugh fills my ears, and soon I'm laughing too, kicking my feet in joy before my tiny feet once again touch down on the carpet.

Peering through the blinds, a dumb grin spread across my face, my eyes are smitten with the sight of a million stars spilled across the sky. The sound of footsteps passes by my door, and I dive beneath the covers, giggling uncontrollably.

Charging up the stairs on all fours, before flinging the door open and launching myself into the sea of blankets and pillows.

High pitched laughter filling the room, a set of glimmering balloons and streamers floating through the air as joyful hands grasp for them. A deep, comforting voice calling us all downstairs, the enticing promise of cake waiting. We flood out the door, tumbling down the stairs in fits of joyous giggling–

"Ikari?"
A dusty room, toys and shape blocks scattered sadly on the floor, posters peeling away from the walls. Tengen is sitting on the now comically small bed, looking at me with a hint of concern.
"Everything okay?"
Clearing my throat and looking around the room I respond.
"Uh, yeah. I'm– I'm fine."
"Care to sit?"

He gestures to a small chair, positioned so the sitter can look directly out the window. Turning it to face him, I sit. For a small while, neither of us say anything, until finally he breaks the silence.

"So, how've you been?"

"Yeah, I guess I've been doing okay."

The silence returns, but not for long, and this time I speak up first.

"What've you been doing all this time?"

"Hunting. Lots of hunting."

"Oh really? So have I."

He looks at me thoughtfully.

"I know."

I look at him quizzically, waiting for him to continue. He looks away briefly, before coming back with his answer.

"I met a group of people, not long after everything went wrong. They're all like us, young people with a desire to hunt devils, and the strength to do so. After a while, we needed a leader, and they chose me."

He clams up again.

"And what do you call this group of people?"

"We call ourselves survivalists. The survivalist force, to be exact."

I chuckle.

"Survivalist force. Catchy. But that doesn't explain how you knew what *I* was doing."

"Well, the force assigned each of its members to different sections of the city, to cover as much ground as possible. The person assigned to the Nakagyo ward kept on reporting footsteps, burned out fires and dropped items. I figured that since Nakagyo ward is next to the–"

He goes quiet suddenly.

"Next to the what?"

He looks away, before clearing his throat again and continuing.

"Next to the crater, I figured that it was most likely you leaving all those things around the area."

Once again, silence returns. Idly, I clean dirt from beneath my nails, flicking it away. Bleak sunlight files through the blinds, projecting a set of bars against the far wall. A series of loud clicks comes from Tengen, and I look over to see him stretching his arms and fingers. Gearing up the confidence, I run the speech that I've been meaning to make through my head for the final time.

"I think…"

He looks over as my voice involuntarily trails off. I take a breath, and try again.

"I think I owe you an explanation, for… um…"

He looks at me, confused, and I meet his gaze with newfound confidence.

"For what happened, when you fought the representative."

A look that I can't quite read blooms on his face, and he sweeps his hair away from his forehead.

I make the final push, saying what I've been meaning to say. The reason I wanted to talk.

"I think it's time I gave you the full story about Kurayami."

***

"So, what have you got for us?"

A pair of scrutinising eyes peer down at the two figures kneeling before them.

The woman speaks up.

"The group totals 8, with the traitors contractor being the leader."

A satisfied nod grants the two permission to breathe, before the figure standing in front of them speaks again.

"And what of their firepower?"

The male counterpart rubs the plastic protrusion in his neck before speaking.

"Of course, they have the traitor. On top of that, it seems there is a plant devil, an insect devil and the most powerful, a light devil. There may be more, but it is uncertain."

The figure muses over the information for a moment, before speaking.

"Are you certain the insect is not stronger than the light, for humans seem to dislike insects rather strongly?"

"Ordinarily, the insect would be, but it seems the contact they have severely limits the insects power."

"I see. And the others may or may not be contracted?"

"I'm deeply sorry, but I can not be certain about that.."

"Fine. I suppose that can be excused."

The figure gestures for the pair to rise.

"You have done brilliantly, this information is invaluable. With it, we have the grounds that we need to move onto the final phase."

The pair bow excessively, and as they leave, the woman looks back briefly to the figure shrouded in darkness, deciding on a parting thanks.

"Thank you for your hospitality sir."

An unseen look of utter disgust spreads across the figure's face, and they flick their index finger aggressively.

Two dull thuds ring out, and the still smiling face of the woman rolls in a half circle till it faces the figure.

With a tone of deep-rooted loathing for the word, the figure repeats it to themself as they stride away from the scene.

"Sir…"

***

"I guess… the best way to think about it is a field of flowers."

Tengen looks confused but seems to go along with it.

"Imagine that field of flowers is your brain. The red ones are your memories, the yellow ones your emotions, you get the idea…"

He nods.

"Now, imagine a patch of flowers with no colour, separated from the main group. They have no colour, since you don't consciously realise that they're actually there. These flowers, these flowers are your subconscious. Your reflexes, your instinct. When you go into fight or flight, you obey these flowers without actually *thinking* about it."

Tengen nods again.

"Now imagine if the field was predominantly those colourless flowers, and only a few coloured ones."

He wrinkles his eyebrows briefly, before responding.

"So, somebody with more instinct than memories or emotions?"

"Yeah."

I smile dryly, looking around the room.

"That's Kurayami. The second he takes over, all logic, past memories, past emotions, it all goes out the window. He does what he wants in the moment based on what his instincts tell him, and nothing else. Do you get it?"

"I guess so, but still…"

"Still what?"

"What actually *is* he?"

Good question, good question…

"I…, I don't really know how to put it into words. He's like…"

What is he like? Ever since that first time, I've just accepted it without ever actually questioning it.

"I suppose he's just another person. Like your neighbour, except he doesn't live in the house next door, he lives in the corner of your head. And just like your neighbour comes knocking when they need something, he'll jump at the opportunity to take over. When that happens, he's the one deciding it all. For all intents and purposes, another person in the same body."

The room goes quiet as we mull over my words. Stripes of vaguely golden light now cover the wall in front of us, shining particles of dust glimmering as the light passes through the stale air. Tengen exhales deeply, not like an exasperated sigh, but more a sound of acceptance.

"Well, that's clear–"

"But that's not the most important thing when it comes to him. The most important thing is that while yes, he acts upon his own instinct in the moment, he is always bound to my will at the moment of transition."

He looks at me quizzically.

"What do you mean, bound to your will?"

"At the moment we switch, whatever my primary goal is, carries over to him. That first time that we switched by blood, in the boxing ring, my goal was to fight that guy. So we switched, and that's what he did."

I look at the floor, for I don't have the strength to tell him what happened after that.

"So, he does whatever you wish at the moment you… swap?"

"Yeah, in fact, there's this dream, this dream I always have just before something important happens."

"What is it?"

"It's like I'm watching a memory in third person, a memory of this time that we switched, and he… never mind. It's not important right now."

Tengen fidgets, but does not pressure for more. Instead, he simply says;

"Alright then. Kurayami is not a beast within, not a monster in your shadows. He's just another person, connected to you by will and body."

I look over to him, but he avoids my gaze. The moment before I move to get up, he speaks again.

"Guess it's my turn now."

"What do you mean? Your turn?"

He tilts his head slightly and side eyes me.

"You've been meaning to ask about my power. Haven't you?"

He clicks his fingers, and a small flame shimmers to life between them. He moves his fingers apart, and as the flames stretch into a line from fingertip to fingertip.

He looks at the rolling oranges and reds sadly.

"I don't know when it was exactly, but not long after I was born, my father– no, *our* father contracted me to a devil. Not dissimilar to you, my mind was somewhat split. The devil always lurked in the corner, but never speaking to me. For a while, our father simply thought that I needed to get used to having the contract, that soon my powers would show. He wanted a weapon, but one in the form of a son. And so, when it seemed that my power would never show itself, he had no use for me. That's why we never crossed paths. I was kept hidden within our house until I was eight. When it seemed my power would never show, I was dumped."

He turns away, wiping his eyes.

"I failed him, I couldn't live up to what he needed from me. And because of that, he's dead."

For a while, there's no sound except for two sets of breathing, almost perfectly in sync.

"And then, not too long ago, I completed this ritual, this crazy ritual I read about in an old book. I was face to face with *him*, with the devil I've always lived with. And he told me, he told me to fix the weakness that plagues this world. And to do so, he gave me control of this fire."

He slams his other hand into the duvet, and a cloud of dust bursts upward, sparkling as it falls back through the air slowly.

"And now I just don't know *what* I should do? Get rid of the weakness in this world? How? I can't even lead a group of damned children!"

Tengen makes a fist, snuffing out the flame. And when he looks at me, water brims his eyes.

"Ikari?"

"Yeah?"

"Was dad a bad man?"

Was dad a...

"I don't know about the side of him that you saw, but to me..."

Dad.

Father.

A word that brings a whole swirl of emotions into my mind, but there's one predominant one.

"He was a bad man, and an even worse father."

Tengen clenches his fist harder, his knuckles turning white.

"But what if I hadn't failed–"

"Look, you *didn't* fail dad. He wanted you to be a weapon. You might not be the sword he wanted, but you're *human*. And trust me, I've thought a lot about humans."

He goes quiet, and I keep going.

"You didn't fail dad."

I sigh.

"Dad failed *us*."

The sun has reached what we once called golden hour, perfect god rays flooding this dusty old room. Tengen sniffles briefly, before talking in a tone barely held together.

"Yeah, I suppose you're right."

Minutes go by, maybe even an hour. Neither of us say a word, and our breathing is almost silent now. A sad smile rests on my face, and Tengen has long since wiped away his tears. A sombre tone blankets the room, and my gaze flicks from one dusty memory to another. I can't help but wonder, what does Tengen think when he sees this room? What does he remember of this house?

Raised in complete separation, no contact whatsoever. I didn't even know he existed. Then he was thrown out. I don't know when, I don't remember anything. In my childhood, he was non-existent. But I can guess when he was thrown out, because things changed.

Dad forced me to start doing martial arts, training everyday. I suppose when one son failed to be his weapon, he turned to the next. And then of course, his time ran out. My thoughts are interrupted by Tengen, his voice once again steely.

"I've got one last proposal for you."

I think I can guess what's coming.

"The devils are ramping up. The two we chased down were probably spies."

He looks me dead in the eyes.

"A storm is coming, and the survivalists need all the help we can get."

A grim yet hopeful light shines in his eye.

"Can I count on you, brother?"

I sigh, and stand up. Heading to the door, I look back at him.

"So, when do I meet the team?"

13: ZERO PERCENT

Despite the dim lighting, rows and rows of perfectly still figures can be seen within the cavernous space. A certain few tower over the others, and these particular striding silhouettes march between the statue-like figures, scrutinising them from head to toe. At the side of each shadowy form, a chain stretches from their right wrist to an almost comically oversized anchor point. A hundred sets of exasperated breath fill the frigid air, and those that do not breathe in the way we understand release strange, low noises.

Having finished their task, the striding silhouettes return to the foot of a stage that lies before the mass of dark shapes. They turn to face the crowd, hands crossed behind their backs as they too settle into a statue-like form. On a pair of stakes at the back of the stage, two severed heads lie limply on sharpened points; an example.

The soft sound of footfall fills the cavern as a set of four finely dressed men and women stride out from someplace hidden by darkness, spreading out into a sort of flying V, with a young man taking the frontal point. He adjusts his tie with a hint of frustration, and tugs at the bottom of his well-tailored blazer. As he fights with the desire to scuff up his infuriatingly neat hair, he receives his signal.

Stepping up to a rather unremarkable podium, he clears his throat before addressing the crowd in a bored tone.

"We've gathered you here today to give you an idea of how the next forty-eight hours will play out."

He sweeps his arm grandly, before continuing.

"I am the sixth, one of the three remaining devils of the Twelve Fears. At my side are the other two, along with the representative of the ancient one."

He gestures to a middle aged man, excessive bags beneath his eyes and a thin layer of black hair, dressed in a suit so dark it seems to suck in the light around it.

"The second."

He then gestures to an austere looking woman, her hair in a bun so tight it makes one's head itch just looking at it, dressed in a suit so unremarkable one might forget it the moment she leaves your vision.

"The third."

He gestures to a rather old man, a classic cane at his side and an excessively sized cigar between his lips, dressed in a tweed suit that's been out of fashion for some decades.

"The ancient ones representative."

The young man sighs.

"Who I shall now invite up to the podium to speak."

Exchanging curt nods, the two men stroll to their new positions, one atop the podium, the other standing amongst his comrades. After a brief set of coughs, he stands up straight as an arrow and speaks in a booming voice.

"Today marks a great day. Today is the day we rear up from the shadows we lurk in and run amok in the world above. Thanks to the contribution of our late spies, we now hold key information on what we believe to be the most threatening resistance group. A force that refers to themselves as 'survivalists'. A force of children. But, do not underestimate them. And as for our plan–"

He clicks his fingers, and a map appears behind him.

"The remaining Twelve Fears and I will be positioned in defensive positions surrounding this location, with the sixth being the furthest, then the third, then the second, and finally myself. This plan hinges on the ancient one. They have, in an act of utmost generosity, decided that each of you will receive a portion of their soul. In fact, the reason you are chained down is because you *already* have that portion."

A wave of surprise ripples through the crowd, and murmurs begin to arise. The man raises for silence, and continues.

"However, this means the safety of the ancient one is key. This is why the strongest devils will be guarding them. All you must do is wreak havoc. Cause chaos. Crush any resistance, with all the force you want. We expect you to meet the new target, of *zero percent remains*."

A fresh round of murmurs pass through the crowd, but this time the man before them does not raise his hand for silence. For a while, soft, excited conversation is all that can be heard. The man steps down from the podium, and calls the others on the stage closer to him. With the low crowd noise as a background track, they converse in hushed tones.

"Are you sure telling them about the plan's flaw was a good idea?"

"What if they are captured, and reveal it?"

"So what if they reveal it? You think a lowly resistance can beat us? Can they even beat one of us?"

The austere woman tugs on her shirt sleeves.

"I just think it may be a mistake."

The old man snorts.

"Well, I think you worry far too much."

He spreads his arms and injects some quiet bravado into his tone.

"We're *devils*! Second to none! We're born from their fear for crying out loud!"

The woman grumbles, but drops the matter.

"So when are they arriving?"

"Not too long now, a few minutes maximum."

He blows out a long breath. The chatter has not stopped for a moment, the crowd behind them still jabbering away enthusiastically. The man dressed in black rubs his thinning hair, speaking in an almost childlike manner.

"Can we really trust them? I mean what if they tell on us and then we get caught and then we get attacked and then they reach the big boss and then–"

"Please, spare us your mindless and baseless rambling. The hooligans behind us have no reason to betray us, and even if they *do*, as I've stated, a resistance has no chance against *us*."

Lower lip quivering, the balding man looks at the floor and once again is silent. Drumming a beat on the side of his too-tight dress trousers, repeatedly shifting his hair around, kicking the ground with his toes; the young man gives off a restless air, and the others around him begin to feel his discomfort. The next person set to address the crowd, in their eyes, can be rather volatile.

And just as the pot seems ready to boil over, a swath of darkness floods the cavern. In a hushed, angry whisper, a voice can be heard from one of the stage's occupants.

"Second! Is this your doing?!"

"No! I pinkie promise!"

A huffing sound can be heard, and the crowd's excited chatter turns to frenzied screams and shouts. A strong wind bellows through the space, strong enough to force the four figures on the stage to inch backwards, away from the podium into the wings. The screeching and shouting suddenly turns to silence as they realise what's happening, and a sense of nervous tension sets in. Heavy sets of breath can be heard all around, and friends reach for each other in the inky blackness.

Suddenly, unbeknownst to each other, everyone in the crowd looks down simultaneously at the feeling of liquid pooling around their feet. Terrified murmurs begin to pick up again, until a–

Shhhh…

–sounds out, but the harsh undertone it carries sets it more akin to the drawing of a blade than a request for silence. Now, a hundred sets of bated breath wait in both darkness and silence, even those who see themselves as high ranking. At the edges of the stage, the collection of once authoritative figures find themselves under the same pretence of fear as everyone else.

"IT CAN BE QUITE LONELY AT THE TOP, YOU KNOW."

A husky voice seems to ring out from every direction at once, filling the ears of its victims. After the statement, silence once again returns, and hidden panic is felt amongst every last devil.
Once again, darkness and silence.

"ALMOST NOBODY TALKS TO ME UNLESS I FORCE THEM."

A hundred of the most feared, brutal fighters in all of reality, stunned in terror by this almost seductive voice. Somewhere, isolated in the darkness, the devil of blood finds itself sobbing silently.

"IT SEEMS THEY THINK I AM..."

As the voice of fear searches for a suitable word, the devil of sound trembles silently.

"UNSTABLE."

Silence, and darkness.

No sound, no light. The terror of the abyss's inhabitants is almost palpable, as the voice of unrivalled power sounds again in its somewhat provocative tone.

"AND WHEN WE DO SPEAK, THEY SEEM SO..."

The devil of suffocation finds itself hyperventilating.

"SCARED?"

The way the word rings out, in the tone that it almost seems unreasonable for that to be the case. As the devil of needles attempts to still its trembling hands, the voice continues.

"AS IF I'M... SCARY?"

The voice laughs huskily as the devil of dentistry feels itself about to faint.

"ANYWAY, LET'S GET DOWN TO BUSINESS."

Icy gusts of air begin to blow through the cavern, a haunting whistling sound taking the place of that low, husky voice. A sense of finality has overcome the crowd, like soldiers who know they won't be coming home. The wind increases into somewhat of a gale, hair whipped silently around in the dark as feet shift with fearful uncertainty. Despite having composed themselves somewhat, the four suited figures at the side of the stage still can't stop their chattering teeth and flickering eyes.

A returning sense of anticipation fills the cavern, and soon the silent prayers for it to end are met.

Almost akin to a gentle sunrise, reddish light creeps its way through the shadows, creating a gentle hue against the back wall of the stone hall. The whistling of the wind still screams on, but now it's accompanied by the gift of sight. As the crowd turns from dark blobs, to silhouettes, to recognisable figures, the throttling sense of terror begins to subside.

Until footsteps echo from the stage.

The stage itself is still swarmed with shadows, but at the very front a definite figure can be made out. The warm sunrise begins to flicker with orange and vermillion, soon morphing into a heatless inferno flinging light around. Clearing their throat, the half visible figure draws the attention of the crowd.

"AS I WAS SAYING,"

That voice almost causes mass panic, but at this point acceptance has fully run its course amongst the devils. In a fearful quiet, they listen, as the speech that will dictate their actions begins.

"WE MUST NOW GET MOVING, AND GET OUT INTO THE CITY. CAUSE CHAOS, SPREAD *FEAR*. OR RATHER, *YOU* MUST."

Unseen to the crowd, a thin smile plays on their full lips.

"I'LL BE HERE, CHEERING YOU ALL ON WHILE I MAINTAIN THE BOOST OF POWER YOU'LL RECEIVE. MY LOVELY REPRESENTATIVE HAS EXPLAINED MY LITTLE GUARD GROUP, SO YOU KNOW THE DRILL WHEN IT COMES TO THAT. TOGETHER, YOU'LL NUMBER 100, SO SPLIT UP INTO NICE TEAMS. IF YOU ENCOUNTER RESISTANCE, DO SOMETHING THAT EVERYONE WILL BE ABLE TO SEE."

A daring audience member timidly asks *what* they should do, and receives a laugh in response.

"OH, I DON'T KNOW! AN EXPLOSION, OR A HUGE FIRE! YOU'RE DEVILS, SO GO AND DO DEVILTHINGS! KILL, MAIM, TORTURE, DESTROY! THIS IS YOUR BIG DAY, TO GO AND DO WHATEVER YOU WANT!"

In response to the excited uproar, they clap their hands for attention. Once it falls to a sea of murmurs, they continue.

"AS LONG AS, AT THE END OF THE DAY, YOUR WORK MEETS THE QUOTA."

The figure flicks out their fingers and splays their palm, and the following series of dull thuds goes unnoticed by the excited crowd, now a few less in number.

"REMEMBER, *ZERO PERCENT.*"

They click their fingers, and the sound of metal on stone fills the cavern. A raucous cheer erupts as chains hit the floor and devils rubs sore wrists. Moving almost as a singular mob, they barrel toward the exit with newfound gusto and confidence is their freedom. Chants akin to a hyped-up sports crowd fill the ears of the few bystanders, and as the devils flood into the open air they instinctively find their common partners in destruction. Sound and fireworks, hospitals and needles (Needles still feeling rather shaken up).

From the stage, the figure watches with a lazy pleasure as they run their fingers through their hair.

They sigh, turning to walk into the shadow once more.

Just before they fully make their exit, they check to see if anyone is watching. Happy with what they see, they fish a small phone from their pocket.

Quickly checking their surroundings once more, they begin to dial before putting the phone to their ear.

A few short, sharp rings are heard, and then a sound like crumpling paper.

In a bright tone, foreign to the listener, a voice crackles through.

"Hello?"

14: NOW OR NEVER

–IKARI–

What a dump.

A long, meeting style table surrounded by musty chairs, a mess of rust and shadow overhead. The pained choking of a coffee machine, and wallpaper so peeled it could pass for a spiral sculpture.

6 sets of eyes meet mine, each one showing a varying degree of suspicion. Except one pair, warm brown, belonging to an ever-smiling boy called Raito. Surprisingly, nobody looks twice at the light literally emanating from him. The moment Tengen ushered me through that door, he was there with a bouncy handshake

and a flood of personal information. Despite his slight oddness, he seems like the crux of this group.

Looking around at the disgruntled faces of the others tells me that without him this would never work. Tengen gives me a rundown of names that almost instantly vanish from my mind, but I quickly match them to key features.

Long, unwashed hair.

Yasei.

Quiet yet watchful, and young, with such striking red hair.

Kuro.

A bow on his back.

Yuno.

Sinewy yet muscular.

Shoto.

Straightforward, short brown hair.

Kiaran

There's something about them, something that differs from other people. Raito has it too, and Tengen. Only, with Raito and Tengen you wouldn't need to sense it to know. The others however, are clearly more secretive about it. They're contracted.

I wonder, what hell spawn shares their heads.

Coming back to the moment, I realise Tengen is talking once again.

"So, this is Ikari."

With lack of anything better to do, I raise a hand limply in greeting. A few nods in return.

"He can be trusted, and is a highly skilled fighter in close combat."

A hand is raised, belonging to that girl Yasei. When she speaks, it's a kind of distasteful drawl.

"So, what devil's in your head then?"

"None. I don't do contracts."

She scoffs.

"That's bull, and you know it. I can sense that extra presence in your head."

Extra–

Wait, can she sense him? Is that even possible, to sense something like that?

I thought that sense would only work with devils?

Subconsciously, I clench my fist.

"That isn't what you think it is. I can't explain now, but trust me."

Yasei looks at me, smiling slyly. She looks back at her hand, and only now do I notice the plain black glove that covers it. She adjusts it, and for a moment, I can glimpse at a strange pattern that encircles the skin below. Almost like vines wrapped around her hand.

"Sure…"

"I'm telling you–"

Tengen jabs a sharp elbow into my side.

Hmph.

But still, how can that be? Has her perception been increased so much just from her contract?

Tengen clears his throat, and starts again.

"So before, we speculated this may be an attempt at a cull. Since then, devils have stopped appearing on the street, except those two that got away. Knowing that…"

He takes a deep breath.

"We have good reason to believe the devils will make their move *now*."

A young boy, no more than fourteen, speaks up. Kuro.

"Are you sure?"

Shoto responds instantly.

"Yes. It's the only possible reason for them withdrawing all forces."

As that realisation settles in, the room goes quiet. Everyone is looking at everything except each other, and the groaning of that damned coffee machine is the only sound that can be heard. Until, Tengen takes a deep breath and exhales heavily. He speaks.

"So, we can accept that they *will* be making a move within the day. Maybe even within the hour." He shrugs. "Maybe they already have. But all we can do is move in retaliation *now*."

All eyes rest on him, hoping for some kind of plan. And to their surprise, he begins to speak once more.

If you were a bird, and if you were flying above Kyoto at that moment, you might see the chaos that was unfolding. Perhaps if you had swooped amongst the quaint buildings of the Kita ward, your beady eyes might have picked up on the choking black smoke that was spewing from the windows. Or maybe if you perched atop the Kyoto tower, placing your talons carefully for the top was at a great angle, you may be able to see the fires burning across rooftops. Suppose you had sat there a little longer, you may have laid those tiny eyes upon a small group of figures cackling raucously as they swagger down the street, a trail of rubble behind them.

And on the off chance you fluttered those wings and glided to the crater that lies at the edge of Nakagyo, your angular beak may have picked up the scent of gas, and your ears a faint hissing accompanied by a hushed giggle. Maybe you would have heard the click of a lighter, followed by a great rush of heat and wind, as glass shatters from windows all around. Or maybe you had been further east, watching the trees turn to smoke beyond the sprawling city. And perhaps you got bored of the city life, and took to the skies properly. Perhaps you rode the wind west; far, far, west. And if that was the case, perhaps when you found yourself high above Portugal, you may have found yourself battered by the buffeting winds that burst outward from the path of some sleek black jets, almost a blur, heading the way you just came. Maybe you thought nothing off it, and continued on your journey. Or maybe you decided to turn tail, and give chase, riding the eastbound winds. Following those mysterious aircraft, right back to where your journey began.

***

–IKARI–

"–got it?"

As Tengen finishes his speech, a smattering of applause followed by murmurs of understanding award his efforts. I leave my face blank, not letting my thoughts on the plan slip and be revealed to the others.

Because I think it's utterly ridiculous. Stupid even. But looking around, looking at this table surrounded by hard, unsmiling faces, I realise something. This is everything for them. They don't care how outlandish it is, because it's the only thing they have left to do. This is a group of people, young people, who have been backed right into a corner by something they have no control over.

They'll take any chance they can get to fight back, no matter how slim. It's sad how things have led to this. A decision by some superhuman, ancient beings, and in the end all it leads to is a disparate group of borderline children, some of them children entirely. They call themselves survivalists, and that couldn't be closer to the truth. All they want to do is live, to come out on the other side of this mess with a chance at a fresh start.

And man do I hope they get it.

But, none of them have such a free path. Even if they all come out of this mostly unscathed, they'll never really be free.

Kuro.

Yasei.

Raito.

Tengen.

Kiaran.

Shoto.

Yuno.

They'll never be fully separated from this world, from those devils and from this way of life. If we pull this off, if we manage to take them all down, then what?

At the end of the day, they'll still be devils. They'll never have their humanity back, not fully. Because that's the thing with contracts that nobody ever mentions.

There's no way out of them.

And as for myself, I'm not entirely free from that fate either. Of course, I'm human through and through, regardless of whatever the hell happened to my mind. But, even though I will always be human, I won't be…

I won't be…

Whole.

All these thoughts, all these emotions, all these memories. For almost every minute, of every hour, of every day, of every week, of every month, of every year.

Those emotions and memories and thoughts will be *mine*, in *my* body. But then, those times when they're *not*, those times are the ones I remember the most. Ironic, how the times I remember best are the times in which my memory is not mine.

I sigh, and drag myself out of my own head into the conversation. Discussion fills the room, and I watch as heads lean inwards and hands gesticulate calmly yet wildly. Tengen still stands beside me, or rather I stand beside him. Looking over at him, I can see a look of relief in his eyes.

"Happy about something T?"

He looks over, one eyebrow raised.

"Really? T?"

He breaks into a grin.

"I suppose that's not so bad."

Quickly glancing back to the group, he sighs.

"But yeah, I feel pretty good right now. It just feels like..."

He grasps for the right words. "Like I'm finally being a leader, for real. Y'know?"

"Yeah. I get what you mean, after what you told me back home. And by the way, did you figure out how to purge the weakness?"

He scoffs.

"The best thing I can think of is to bring this whole ordeal to an end. I suppose, only those with some strength will have survived."

"A rather inhumane way of looking at it."

"Maybe, but that's all I got."

"I guess so."

As we watch the others talk and plan, a faint smile spreads across my face once more. This room has so much hope. Some would say fool's hope.

But hope nonetheless.

Such difference, from when I first walked in here to those solemn faces and dingy lights. Sure, the lights are still dingy, but the energy in the room gives it a sort of light unseen to the eye. And all it took was a plan, an idea that these people can focus and build on. Something so small and simple, yet something that can make all the difference in the world. It makes me realise, an idea I had long ago needs updating. And all of a sudden, I find myself speaking out loud.

"A while ago, I found myself thinking about what it means to be human."

Tengen looks at me quizzically.

"Back then, the conclusion I came to was that the thing that makes us human is our insignificance, the fact that nothing we do is permanent. I thought that the liberation that gives us makes us human. And I still agree with that, to some degree. But now…"

How should I put it…?

"Now, it feels less like insignificance alone, but more the pairing of insignificance and carefreeness. And I think that carefreeness, the way we can just *keep on going*, no matter the odds, no matter the stakes. Do you get it?"

He laughs, and settles into a surprised smile.

"I never took you for a philosopher."

After a brief shared laugh, he ponders for a moment.

"But I know what you mean. It's strange, how those very ideals are what Azoth considers to be one of the things that weigh us down. He said one thing that day, one thing that stuck with me."

"And what's that?"

"Blinded by hope, all you see is a chance."

We mull over those words for a moment. 'Blinded by hope...'

I guess we are, sometimes.

'All you see is a chance'.

A chance.

That's what we're going on right now, a slim chance.

Hope. Blinding, or liberating? Perhaps both. Or perhaps neither.

"Maybe we should leave the philosophy until after we know we're not dead, ah?"

"Yeah, I can get behind that."

"And brother?"

"Hm?"

"Do you think that there would be a way for us to unify our minds, just for a moment?"

"As in, combine our minds with the others in our heads, to make one conscience?"

"Something like that."

"I don't know. Something tells me if such a thing were to happen, it would be a heat of the moment type thing."

"Yeah, that sounds about right."

With the thought of that possibility heavy on our minds, we watch the others move about with a vigour that can only be found in those ready to act. The once stale air has a fresh tone to it, as if the room itself is feeling the palpable emotions that are running high right now. T looks over them, smiling subtly. He raises his hand, and with a newfound respect for the gesture, the chatter dies down.

"It's clear to me that you are all ready, ready to get out there and take the fight to them. As am I."

His gaze sweeps the room.

"Not too long ago, Raito stood before us as I am doing now, and spoke of heroes. He spoke of how this story will end, of how when the sun rises again, we will be standing there."

He takes a deep breath.

"Things have changed since then. Now, more than ever, we must do this. Last time, we left this room because we *wanted* to fight. Now, it's a *need*. Now, we fight, because if we don't…"

His gaze turns sombre.

"I don't have to tell you what will become of this world if we don't. While we may not know what they want exactly, we think it may be a cull. And if we are wrong, and they are planning something else, it makes no difference. They are devils."

He looks pointedly around the room.

"Those of you who have come into close contact with them will know, that at the end of the day, they are creatures of destruction and fear. Whatever their grand ideal is, we know that life for all except them will be miserable when their mission is complete."

He uncurls his fingers and points his palm to the ceiling, waiting a moment before allowing it to erupt in flame. A column of flowing flame rises, and ten sets of eyes watch it excitedly, while two sets watch it with tiredness and distaste. We watch as the flames morph and stretch, forming vague shapes, reaching out as if alive. As the fire dances, he speaks again.

"A companion of mine, bear in mind I don't like him at all, gave a rather eye opening speech some time ago. All about how humanity is limited, trapped in a cycle. Of how we are blinded by hope."

He grins.

"I think it's stupid what they said. He said, that when blinded by hope, all you see is a chance. I say that when blinded by hope, a chance becomes a guarantee. So we will win this, and we *will* be the ones watching the sun rise after it all."

He grins, and the room erupts in applause. It continues for some time, as we all digest what we just heard. And, without really knowing why, I too raise my hand. It takes longer than for T, but eventually, the room does go quiet.

"I don't know you, and you don't know me."

They watch me intently.

"But, listening to this conversation so far, it's clear to me that we stand for the same thing, and we see things the same way. It's clear to me that with these people, and with this will, we can win. And most of all, it's clear to me that none of you are willing to lie down and be trampled on by those inhuman beasts. You all heard T talk about how it's now or never. About how we must fight, or the world as we know it is over. About hope, and about heroes."

I sigh.

"That's all been said already. So all I want to tell you…"

They wait expectantly.

"Is that when you're on that battlefield, remember what you're fighting for."

I turn, and begin to walk from the room. As I stand in the doorway, I look back at them, and say one final thing.

"So get some rest, because after that, we attack."

They nod, and as I walk down the halfway, I mutter to myself.

"It's now or never, and I choose now."

15: DREAMS, MEMORIES, OR SOMETHING IN BETWEEN

"Kiaran! Dinners ready!"
The boy scrambles down the stairs, grinning from ear to
ear. As he bursts through the living room door, his smiling
eyes search for his dad's wrinkled face. Eventually they
find him, and he runs up to him with open arms. A warm
embrace, and he is released after a few moments. The
chair scrapes as he excitedly pulls it toward him, and he
slides under the table onto a rumpled cushion. A plate

*clatters as his dad brings it over, setting it down with a
weariness. He pulls up a chair opposite him, settling in
tiredly. As the boy rambles on happily about his day, the
dad pushes a plate of microwave chicken toward him.
Taking a break from his speech, the boy munches joyfully,
and downs a cup of water. He looks at his dad, a flash of
concern on his face.*
"Dad? Are you not going to eat anything?"
His dad puts on a smile.
*"No, I'm not very hungry. But don't worry buddy, I'll be
fine."*
"Oh, ok."
*They boy forgets about the exchange after a moment, and
continues to talk aimlessly yet happily. Suddenly, a
memory springs into his mind and he quickly brings it up.*
"Hey dad! Remember what day it is tomorrow?"
His dad wrinkles his face up, pretending not to know.
"What is it Ki?"
*The boy looks sad, his lower lip beginning to quiver. After
a second, his dad erupts into a smile.*
*"Come on Ki, I'm just joking. Don't worry, after school we
can go celebrate."*
"Aww, do I have to go to school?"
"Yeees you do, you have your maths test remember?"
At the prospect of a test, the boy ponders.

*"But those tests are always so easy, when will they get
hard?"*
The dad smiles again.
*"Those tests are meant to be hard, but you're just too
smart!"*
*The chair scrapes again as the boy launches himself from
under the table, before running circles around the cramped
room while laughing.*
"Too smart! I'm too smart!"
Watching with a soft smile, the dad whispers to himself.
*"Yes Kiaran. You're so, so smart. Smart enough to leave
here and live freely."*
*As he watches, a buzz in his pocket draws his hand to his
phone. He wipes away some lint from its small, cracked
screen, and peers at the message. The moment he sees who
it's from, his smile fades. Tapping on it, he unlocks his
phone and looks at what it says.*

'cs money will be late this month'

*He taps away, sending desperate questions, but none of
them deliver. Swiping it closed, he heads to his bank app.
Closing his eyes from fear, he waits for it to open. After a
moment, he opens them, and has to stop himself from
breaking down in front of his boy. A thought suddenly*

*springs into the boy's mind, and he stops his victory
parade to voice it.*
"Dad, is mom coming home?"
Almost choking on his words, the dad replies.
"Mom's away right now, but she'll be back soon."
"But dad, you've been saying that for ages!"
"I know Ki, I know…"
He looks at the clock, ticking sadly on the wall.
"I think you should get to bed now champ."
*The boy ends his parade with a final jump, and heads out
of the room.*
*He bounds back up the stairs, once again forgetting all
about what was said. The man tucks the covers down
around him, and smiles as he wishes the boy sweet dreams.
He smiles all the way to the door, flicking off the light so
only the soft glow of a bedside lamp remains. The door
closes with a soft thud, and the boy looks at the ceiling,
grinning joyfully. He does not hear the man sit at the
bottom of the stairs, sobbing as he looks at his phone. The
man cries, but sources all the money he can. He lies down
on the sofa, hearing his stomach growl. He closes his eyes,
determined not to let life ruin the tenth birthday of his
brilliant son.*
*Upstairs, tucked safely into bed, his son notices something.
In the corner of the room, his piggy bank looks a little
different. It's wobbling, when it was never touched.*

Confused, he tiptoes out of bed toward it. Despite the fact it's always been empty, it rattles as it wobbles back and forth.
And when he gets close, he does a double take.
Because it speaks to him.
And he doesn't know why, but he listens.
And when it asks him a question, he says yes.

***

"Please, clean this dump! Do you have no respect for your surroundings Yuno?"
The boy groans, and makes a rude gesture before slamming the door in the frustrated faces of his parents. He turns and walks to his bed, digging yellow fragments from his nostrils. He stands by his window, sweeping litter from the ledge so he can lean out into the open air. He looks down, gazing at the 10 meters between him and the hard ground. And he sighs, before slamming it shut and cutting off the fresh air.
With another groan, he jumps onto his bed, sending a cloud of dust into the now stale air. He reaches around the cups of stagnant water that clutter his bedside table, and grabs his phone.

*As he is ordering the same meal as every night, there's a
payment error. He angrily texts his parents for more food
money, before swiping onto something else.*

He flicks off the lights.

Downstairs, his parents argue.

*"The boy is a failure! We need to get him to do something
other than rot in that room all day for god's sake!"*

"Yeah, but just forcing him won't work!"

"So what do you suggest?"

They go quiet, before one comes back with a suggestion.

*"He's always playing those funny fantasy games, how
about something to do with those?"*

*"Oh great, we can sign him up for the dragon raising club!
What the hell do you mean, those stupid games are called
fantasy for a reason!"*

"Just give me five, I have an idea."

"Fine."

*Upstairs, the lights flick back on as Yuno drags himself
from his bed to the bathroom. He tosses a bundle of tissue
into the toilet, before heading back to his room and sitting
at his desk. An email pops up relating to schoolwork,
which he instantly closes before blocking the sender. Lazily
double clicking the all too familiar logo, he watches with a
tired excitement as a golden L surrounded by blue swirls
fills the screen. As it loads, he checks his phone, awaiting
the money he wanted.*

Instead, he finds a message from his parents.
He curses aloud, but opens it.
'Yuno, we've signed you up for a trial at the local archery
club later. Come down at 2:30, the trial is at 3:00.'
The boy slams his desk, and checks the time.
2:00.
His first reaction is to go downstairs and yell at them, but
he decides to think for a moment. He closes his eyes, and
when he opens them, the game's loaded. Before him,
bobbing up and down faintly, is his most used character.
An archer, tall and slender, with long blonde hair and
unrealistic proportions.
In her hand is a bow almost as tall as her, adorned with
spikes and flowers. As he looks at her, he comes to a
realisation.
Maybe it was worth a try.
And so, for the first time ever, he replies to his mom in
agreement. Heading back into the bathroom, he flips the
shower on and dredges the grime from his body. The water
running down his skin is an unfamiliar feeling, but he finds
it pleasant.
Coming out of the shower, he is forced to raid his dad's
room for any clothes that aren't stained to hell and don't
stink of that unwashed odour.
He checks the clock, and heads down to the living room.

When he opens the door, his parents stare at him as if he was an alien. Their gaze lingers on his clean hair, his clean clothes, and most of all, the fact he's there.

They both erupt into smiles, and indicate for him to come with them.

"So, you like the sound of archery?"

The boy huffs.

"More like–"

He stops himself.

"–Yeah, I do."

They smile at him.

"That's good to hear."

After some time, the car pulls up to the range. Stepping out, the three of them head to a small crowd of boys standing by the door. After saying goodbye, Yuno quietly joins them. An instructor leads the crowd to the end of the range, and gives a brief talk. Yuno doesn't hear a word, for his gaze is fixed upon the bows hung up on the wall. The moment the instructor allows them, he goes straight for the largest one he sees, almost half as tall as him.

"Oh no, that one is far too tall for a kid. How about this–"

"Please, can I just try this one?"

"I really don't think…"

The instructor sees the look on his face, and decides to allow it. After a brief demonstration of technique, the first round of boys take aim. Arrows fly all over, and not one

meets the target. The second round fires, and again, not a
single hit. Yuno's group steps up, and takes aim.
His arms shake as he draws back the enormous bowstring,
but his feet are dead still. The bow reaches across his
body, shoulder to shoulder, and he closes one eye.
The command to fire is given, and he releases the arrow.
It flies straight, and buries itself into the centre of the
target. A wave of stunned faces turn to him, and he has but
one thing to say.
"I like this."
He goes to knock another arrow, but the one he grabs
seems different from the others. He moves to put it back,
for the strange patterns on it disconcert him, but something
rather odd happens.
The arrow speaks to him.
And although he doesn't really know why, he listens.
And when it asks him a question, he says yes.

***

"Are you excited Yasei?"
The little girl gives an emphatic yes, giggling as the
buildings go by beyond the windows of the car. She
watches with wide eyes as small townhouses turn to low

apartments, and then to towering high-rises. The roads are quiet at this time, since she got to skip school just for this. Her parents are singing along to a tune in the front seat, smiling happily. The car comes to a stop across the road from a huge pair of scissors, which she looks at in wonder. They cross and walk in, before finding themselves surrounded by spangly looking chairs and mirrors.

A friendly man welcomes them, and finds their booking on a fancy looking computer. He gestures to a seat, where a smiling woman waits.

She indicates for the girl to get into the chair, and goes to get a wheeled tray loaded with a variety of scissors, spray bottles, and dryer attachments. The woman gathers up the girl's hair, handful by handful. She takes a few steps back, and the girl's hair stretches out all the way with her.

"Such incredibly long hair young lady, have you ever cut it?"

With a joyful vigour, the girl shakes her head.

"So, how short are we going then?"

The girl places her hand just below her shoulder. The stylist smiles and nods.

"Sounds good."

She picks up a few tools, and begins to work.

Both the parents and the girl watch excitedly as huge lengths of hair fall to the floor, and the base of it gradually climbs toward her shoulders. After some time, the hairdresser steps back, and grabs a mirror. The girl and her parents laugh and smile, and the girl pushes her remaining hair around happily.

As she gets out of the chair, her parents and the dresser go over to a desk. Her mom swipes a card, and gets a smile and a thanks in return. Her parents come over to her, and the three of them say thanks together.

As they walk out of the building, her parents complement the new look.

They approach the road, and as always, she takes her mothers hand on one side, and her fathers on the other.

They reach the island, and the man flashes green for them to cross all the way.

At that moment, the girl finds herself enthralled by an unusually colourful plant sprouting from the curb next to her.

In a brief lapse of judgement, her parents walk on without her as her hands slip from theirs.

And they realise, perhaps halfway into the road.

They call her name, and turn to go get her.

And a horn blares, tires screech.

And her parents are gone.

And at that moment, she cannot explain why she does it, but she looks back at that plant. And the plant reaches out, and begins to speak to her. It begins to wrap around her hand, and it keeps speaking.

And she listens.
And when it asks her a question, she says yes.

***

"Come on Shoto, just try it. Please."
He picks up his fork limply, and pushes the food around the
plate distastefully. Gathering a small portion on the tip of
his fork, he begins to raise it to his mouth. Halfway there,
he turns the fork and it falls to the plate. Placing the fork
down, he declares something.
"I don't want it. I can't eat at this time."
With an exasperated sigh, his mom responds.
"So when can you eat then?"
The boy raises a narrow finger, and the look on his face
shows that this isn't the first time he's explained this.
"Once a day, at one o'clock. No more than eight-hundred
calories."
"Come on, that isn't healthy! Growing boy like you, you
need food for Pete's sake!"
"I can't, or I'll lose my definition and become fat and
ugly."
He splays his fingers, and watches as the tendons ripple
and change. His skin appears almost shrink wrapped to his

bone, but despite that, he maintains some portion of sinewy muscle around his shoulders and arms. He checks his phone briefly, and sees a message about going out to eat with friends. Swiping it away, he opens a calorie tracker. As he meticulously inputs every possible piece of data, his mother watches with a face full of concern. She can't help but pray for this to be over, for her son to just eat again. She recalls the moment this started, when they had been walking down the road.

Shoto had seen a billboard, advertising some strange supplement. But what really drew his eye were the figures advertising it, men so incredibly lean they appear more like anatomy models. Since that moment, he had been utterly obsessed. He did nothing but exercise, not eating a gram except for a salad or something small just after midday. He limited how much water he drank, causing headaches and grouchiness.

All this was tearing his household apart, but all he cared about was when he looked in the mirror for the first time and saw something akin to a science classroom plastic model.

He had smiled, and decided that this is the shape he wants to live in. After that, he began to feel that if he wasn't like that, he would have failed his old aspiration. And so he eats as little as he can, drinks as little as he can, all for the sake of that shape.

*That was many years ago now, he was just a young child
when it started. Now, as he approaches the elder years of
teenage life, his parents have finally had enough for good.
"That's ridiculous, you need to eat more! You're bloody
starving yourself!"*

"Me? Starving myself?"

*A shocked expression blooms on his taught, gaunt face.
"I'm just dieting!"*

"That's not true, and you know it!"

Was it true? He thinks it's true.

*His mom brings over a new plate, this time laden with piles
of food, steam curling away from it as she hurries it to be
in front of the boy. Meat, fish, carbs, veg, sugar.
Everything was there, in the hope he would take a liking to
something. But alas, he pushes the plate away. However,
for the first time, he spies something at its edge that
interests him. Some fried meat of some kind, he can't tell
them apart anymore. But what catches his eye is the
seasoning, like a white powder sprinkled softly over the
top.*

"What's on that meat?"

*Shocked at the slight signs of any engagement with the
food, his mom scrambles to answer.*

*"Oh, it's err, white lemon pepper. And the meat is fried
chicken."*

"White lemon pepper…"

He pulls the plate back to him, and his mom can barely hide her excitement and shock. The boy looks at the clock. 3 PM.

He grinds his jaw for a moment, and looks back at the food. He can't help but think that powder looks exactly like the supplement on that billboard that started this. He looks at it some more.

"I don't want it."

Crestfallen, his mom goes to pick up the plate, sighing. But he places his hand on the edge, and says something she finds rather confusing.

"The plate can stay."

Confused, she thinks about questioning why, but decides against it. She mutters something about work, and heads toward the door. Behind her back, the boy stares intently at the 'fried chicken with white lemon pepper'. Those words mean nothing to him, but all he can think of is that billboard.

The door closes with a thud, and his mom pauses for a moment. And she hears it.

Crunch.

And then again.

Crunch.

And again.

Crunch.

A muffled scraping as something moves on ceramic.

Crunch.

Crunch.

And his mom, unbeknownst to him, slides down the door, sitting with her back against it.

And she cries.

She cries tears of joy.

Back in the room, as he munches on food he doesn't quite understand, he sees something in the corner of the room. He stops eating for a moment, and spots a tick. Usually, ticks are rather small, but this one is different. In fact, it was so fat it could no longer crawl, as its legs were now pushed too far apart to touch the ground.

He crouches down, and the strangest thing happens.

It speaks, the tick speaks to him.

Though he doesn't really know why, he doesn't kill it. He listens.

And when it asks him a question, he says yes.

***

"Let's go everyone, let's go! Kuro, can you grab that for me?"

Obliging, the boy hands his father his phone. All around him, the chaos of holiday preparation is almost deafening.

He doesn't like the noise, he finds it makes him very sad.
He's young, not yet a teenager. And already, he has seen
more of the world than most people on their deathbeds.
India, China, England, Indonesia, Holland, Norway,
California, Oregon, Canada, Alaska.
Sometimes, he forgets where he has been. Those countries
and states are what he remembers, though his family
always talks of memories made in places he cannot for the
life of him recall being to. His siblings, for they are all far
older than him, tease him relentlessly for it. And so, most
of the time, even when surrounded by the most wonder this
world has to offer, he finds himself shut in a room, or
curled up in the corner. He likes to play, to move around
his insect action figures and get lost in the world of
imagination. His siblings find his plastic bugs creepy, and
again, tease him for it. But he's always loved bugs.
Wherever they go, that's the highlight for him.
Big shelled beetles, little furry critters that scurry under
logs, minute caterpillars that inch along leaves. All of them
need to be inspected, to be picked up, to be shown to the
others.
Only to be slapped out of his hand, followed by a shriek or
a disgusted look.
They just don't see them the way he does.

He snaps out of his memories as his father places a hand on his shoulder, and steers him into a side room where his mother is waiting, a mask of sadness on her face.

And they deliver the news, with a tinge of sadness, but a primarily blunt tone.

"You can't come with us on this trip. Your siblings say they aren't comfortable with you there, they say your obsession with bugs makes it impossible to relax with you around. So you'll be staying with aunt Georgia. Come, I'll drop you there now."

And without a chance to say a word, his father steers him out the door, down the drive, and to the car.

He opens the door wordlessly, and indicates for the boy to climb in. The boy does, and the father gets in the driver's seat. Still not saying a word, the mother climbs in too, and the car pulls away from the house.

The boy listens to the soft sound of the engine purr beneath him, and all he thinks is how he wished he had the chance to grab his action figures. The car takes many turns, and if the boy had been paying attention, he may have noticed that they are not the usual ones.

They turn onto a highway, and the sound of the engine ramps up. The boy watches lights flash past, and he then notices a fly trapped by a spider's web in the corner of the window. He watches sadly as the fly is repeatedly battered against the car by the window. Deciding that it can't

continue, he rolls down the window. Ignoring the annoyed
sounds coming from the front seats, he reaches out the
window. Struggling to stop his hands from being pushed
around by the wind, he cups them gently around the
helpless bug. Closing his hands fully, he pulls them back
into the car. He quickly rolls up the window with an
extended pinkie, then he opens his hands. A few wisps of
spider web fall out onto his thigh, and with them is a black
dot. Pulling the web away, he brings the dot closer to his
face.
The fly scuttles about on his hand, and after a moment, it
turns and crawls to the edge of his hand, right in front of
his left eye. He closes his right eye, and brings the fly
closer still.
One eye looks into two, bulbous ones, each with thousands
upon thousands of dots.
So really, one eye looks into ten thousand eyes.
And ten thousand look into one.
The boy and his fly sit peacefully, listening to the car.
Their peace is interrupted by his father saying they've
arrived, despite the windows showing nothing but trees.
His mother speaks.
"Okay Kuro, me and your dad are really busy so we don't
have time to walk you to the front door."
She points to a small path.

"Head down there, and take the first left. Aunt Georgia's is right there."

The boy knows that this is not where aunt Georgia lives, but he obliges anyway. Tucking his fly into his pocket, he closes the door softly behind him. He walks around the car, and into the trees.

He walks down the path for a few minutes, and he sees a left turn.

He turns left, and of course.

There's no house, only trees.

It isn't even a path, just a patch of trees further back than the others. And, as if confirming his theory, the sound of screeching tires and a revving engine fill his ears, before settling into the growl of a pedal pressed to the floor, and finally fading into the distance.

The boy sighs, and slumps down against the nearest tree. Sitting there, amongst all the weird and wonderful wildlife, he smiles. Finally, he is alone with his friends.

And as he thinks that, he notices something. Bugs, swarms of them, are crawling through the grass toward him. Spiders and beetles and caterpillars and centipedes and cicadas.

And the air begins to fill with wings, buzzing flies and hornets and bees. In only a few moments, he finds himself before hundreds, probably thousands of bugs. They've stopped about a foot away from him, making him feel like a leader about to address his subjects. He feels something move in his pocket, and he fishes out his fly. He holds it in his fist, before opening his palm. The fly buzzes its wings, and takes flight.

But instead of flying away, it does something rather strange.

It hovers in the air between him and the bug cloud, and turns to face him.

And then, something even stranger happens.

It speaks to him.

Or rather, they speak to him, the thousands of insects before him. Their voices come together into one, a single voice with uncountable layers. And he feels them on his skin, despite the fact they have not touched him. He feels them crawling, crawling all over his arms and legs and face.

But they do not touch him.

And so, he feels them crawl, and listens to them speak. He listens, although he doesn't really know why.

And when they ask him a question, he says yes.

***

"So what kind of hero do you want to be Raito?"
The boy's face lights up at the mention of that word, and he instantly begins to give an answer.

"I want to be the kind that saves people!"
His friend laughs, and then puts on a sinister voice.
*"Look, I'm a villain about to attack those innocent
people..."*
*Raito puts on a deep, booming voice (or as deep and
booming as his eight year old vocal cords can handle) and
says his favourite line.*
"No you won't, because I will stop you!"
"And who might you be?"
*He strikes a pose, one hand reaching for the sky, the other
pointed directly at the villain.*
"The hero this world needs!"
*They both burst into laughter, doubling over. His friend
ends up rolling on the floor, crying from laughing so hard.
The wind whistles around them, and the striking of a bell
reminds them what time it is. Quickly grabbing their bags
from the bench at the end of the park, they break into a jog,
still giggling breathlessly. They round a final corner, and
the sight of that square-ish concrete building puts a sense
of dread over them. With a heavy sigh, they walk through
the gates. To their left, a small group is arguing over four-
square, one of them so heated he's gone completely red in
the face. Beyond that, a boy with short curly hair is getting
interrogated about his new braces by that girl that always
follows him around, and it seems that she just doesn't
understand why he got them blue, or why he didn't respond*

to the message she wrote rather creepily in his science book. He mutters something about her not even knowing, and walks away. Having just seen the same thing, Raito's friend whispers in his ear.

"So cool!"

Raito snorts, and keeps walking. They approach the entrance, and say their goodbyes as they go their separate ways. As a fresh year seven, the boy finds it rather overwhelming as he says goodbye to his only friend and squeezes past all the older years to make it to his class. He notices a boy with a middle part talking about bins on the school TV's, and a gray haired teacher with a rather thick accent telling another science teacher about how good her class was. He squeezes past the football team, overhearing their excited chatter about some cup final after the holidays.

Finally, he reaches his classroom, and the day begins. Some seven hours later, he walks back out through that concrete ground, searching for his friend. He finds him at the main gate, after accidentally running into a group of boys with excessively fluffed up hair talking excitedly about their plans to 'chong'. Whatever that means.

They begin to walk together, taking their usual route through the woods down a hill. They reach the bottom, and begin to walk back up the other hill, when they hear some muffled shouts. Maybe ten metres away, a group of rowdy

*looking boys with half covered faces speaking a language
barely recognisable as English are marching down the
road, and as they approach the boy tugs on his friend's
arm to pull him out of their path. To Raito's horror, his
friend speaks up, looking directly at them.*

"You look stupid with your pants that low."

*They stop walking for a moment, and look at each other, as
if to confirm they heard what they thought they did.*

"You 'alking 'o 'ss?"

"Yeah, I'm talking to you."

*And without warning, the lead boy lashes out. His fist
connects directly with his friend's nose, and blood sprays
as his friend staggers back.*

*Raito watches in shock, feet frozen in fear. But as he
watches his only friend stagger back, blood dripping down
his lips and clothes, the boy realises that now is the time to
fulfil his dream.*

"GET BACK! STAY AWAY FROM HIM!"

*Raito's voice comes out shrill, wobbly with fear. His legs,
still shaking, obey him now, and he plants himself firmly
between the group and his friend. A round of raucous
laughs fill Raito's little ears as the bunch of boys double
over with laughter.*

"And w't' 'r 'oo gonna 'o?"

*The boy's voice shakes more and more with each word, but
he stands his ground.*

"I'll stop you, because I'm… because I'm a…"

"A 'w't?

"BECAUSE I'M A HERO!"

The lead boy snorts, then snorts again. The corners of his mouth begin to wobble, then he starts to turn red.

And after a moment, he bursts into the hardest laughter anyone there has ever heard. In fact, he's laughing so hard he seems to be struggling to breathe. He drops to one knee, and Raito notices all the boys behind him have had the exact same reaction. One of them, slightly more functional than the others, walks up. He smiles, and draws his arm back.

"Then stop this, Superman."

Ratio can do nothing but watch, petrified, as the back of the boy's hand smashes into the side of his face. He staggers and falls to the concrete. His friend crouches down and is pushed onto the floor. The group walk over them, laughing as they turn the corner.

His friend, having recovered somewhat, scrambles to his feet, and looks down at Raito.

"Why would you do that, that was so stupid!"

Raito feels his vision fading, but he smiles.

"Because… because it was what a hero would do."

And as his light-headedness takes over, he hears his friend calling for help from anyone passing by.

Blackness creeps into his vision, but he sees something just before it closes completely.

A ray of light, cast through the bank of clouds onto the ground beside him. Dust and dirt shimmer within it, mundane things turned to beautiful sparkles.

And then, as he fades out of consciousness, the strangest thing happens.

It speaks to him.

The light speaks to him.

And although he doesn't know why, he listens.

And when it asks him a question, he says yes.

***

The boy realises that it's that same dream.
He watches from afar, seeing himself.

The boy reaches out to help his mom, handing her a bunch of flowers.

"Thanks Ikari, you're such a good helper."

The boy grins from ear to ear, and reaches for the next bunch. The two of them, kneeling in the dirt, happy to be there. Gardening.

*It goes on like that for a while, nothing but smiles and
gardening.*

*His mom asks him to open a bag of dirt for her, and he
grabs the trowel. He holds the bag up, and impales it with
the sharp end of the trowel. Instantly, he drops both items
and clutches his hand. A small patch of blood spreads on
the end of the trowel, and he peers in pain at the cut on the
end of his finger. His mom rushes over, asking to see it.
The boy still wants to help his mom, more than ever.
Even when hurt, all he thinks is;
I should help mom.*

*As she approaches, the boy instinctively puts his wounded
finger in his mouth. His mom shrieks for him not to do that,
but it's too late. The blood slides down his tongue, and he
collapses.*

After a moment, he picks himself back up.

His mom scrambles away in fear.

*The boy gets up, looking around with a confused manner.
He sees his mom, white faced, backing away. He looks
down at his finger, curious at the blood trickling down. He
looks back at his mom, and says something in her son's
voice.*

"I should help mom."

His mom's voice shakes.

"What was that?"

"I should help mom. Are you mom?"

*She looks at him, fear in her eyes. But alongside that, some
inkling of confusion. The boy speaks again.*

"Are you mom?"

"Y-yes, I am."

The boy smiles.

*"I should help you then. What do you need help with?
What was the other one doing before?"*

*The fear has further faded from her eyes, and she begins to
come closer to the boy.*

*"Me and Ikari were just gardening. Would– would you like
to do some too?"*

His face lights up.

"Yeah, sure!"

*And so, despite the slight tremble in her hands or her
instinctive flinch every time the boy moved, the two of them
did some ordinary gardening. They didn't talk much, but
they exchanged flowers and dirt and trowels on a regular
basis. After some time, it looked as if a mother and her son
were just spending some time together.*

"I want a name."

The mom looks up from her latest excavation quizzically.

"A name? You have one–"

*She realises just in time. She's not gardening with Ikari,
but with the other one.*

*"Well, the men in the hospital called you Kurayami. Do
you like that?"*

"Kurayami?"

The boy ponders for a moment, examining his hands as if he never gets to use them.

"I like that. From now on, call me Kurayami."

The boy's smile grows even wider.

The mom stands up, and turns to head toward the house for a drink. As she leaves the flowerbed, she catches her foot on the raised ledge and starts to tip. Right as she begins to fall toward the floor, she feels a hand grabbing the back of her shirt. She feels herself slowly rising, the ground getting further and further away. Until, she's standing up straight again.

She turns, and sees the boy smiling happily.

"I should help mom. So I did."

She tries to hide her shock and thanks him, but in her mind questions swirl.

How did he react so fast?

How did he get here so fast?

How did a ten year old pick her up by one arm?

But most of all, why was the other one so friendly?

She turns to her boy, to ask him.

But she finds him collapsed, face first in the dirt. She rushes to take a look at him, but a sharp pain wracks her body with no warning. She's forced to drop to one knee, clutching her chest as she struggles for breath. She pulls

an inhaler from her belt and takes desperate puffs, hoping
to escape this suffocating sensation.
And the boy rises from the dirt, Ikari once again. Despite
his confusion of how he was in a different place to a
moment ago, and how the sun was far further in its cycle,
he can see one thing clearly.
Mom needed help.
And so he runs inside, calling urgently for his father.

***

And the final boy does not dream of his past, but instead
his mind shows him ideas of the future.

The streets are strewn with broken glass, the few buildings
that are still standing are coated in graffiti. Gangs of
devils roam the streets, laughing raucously and destroying
their surroundings for fun. Overhead, the sun no longer
shines, for the veil placed by darkness envelops the sky. In
the darkness, a few lone humans dash from shadow to
shadow, nervously looking around. Burlap sacks are
thrown over them, hiding them completely. They must be in
their mid-twenties, and there are perhaps four of them.
One takes the risk to lower his tattered hood, and blonde

hair spills out. He scans the area with sharp blue eyes, and indicates for the others to follow. He leads them into the lobby of what was once a hotel, and signals them to hide behind what was once a check in desk. The blonde one peeks up from behind the desk, checking if they were tailed. He shakes his head.

A woman with long, matted hair crawls from behind the desk, and leaps to her feet at the bottom of the stairs. They run to follow her, and begin to climb. The woman makes a hand gesture, and thick vines begin to close off the entrance. They reach the floor they were told about, and on the count of three, burst the door open.

Expecting to find a group of human refugees, it would be hard to put into words the shock and horror they feel when they see a group of devils with blood splattered mouths. Simultaneously, they realise it was a trap, and start to back away. The devils begin to enclose on them, and the blonde one draws his sword. His demeanour changes, and he flips the sword so he's holding it in reverse. Another one next to him makes a hand sign and mutters something, and balls of flame appear around him in the air. The woman clenches her fists and vines wrap around them, thick thorns protruding from her knuckles. The final member at the back, a mess of wildly red hair tussling as he moves, makes a strange clicking sound, and bugs begin to pour from every crack and crevice in the building. They surround

*him, and form themselves into large figures. He gives a
command, and they shriek a war cry from saw-like mouths.
The four of them face the devils, and smile.
It's been a while since they fought head on like this, been a
while since they could fight together in one place.
So they attack, moving with the practiced ease and
communication of a group that has fought side by side for
years.*

*Light shimmers in every corner, refracting through the
floor to ceiling windows before the four figures. An
assistant approaches from behind, and hands the red-
haired one a small cup of coffee. He sighs as he drinks it,
watching the traffic go by some eighty stories below. He
glances at the three beside him, and smiles. The man with
short, black hair and one rather uncanny eye notices and
smiles back with a warmth akin to a soft flame. The blonde
one flicks his blade-like blue eyes toward him, and softens
his expression to grin, each side of his face scrunched to
slightly different heights. The long haired one laughs at the
three of them, and soon all four are laughing together.
A round, red faced man bursts through the door blabbering
about something he claims to be urgent. An ANGEL attack
somewhere. The red haired man rolls his eyes, and
whistles a sharp tone.*

A strong buzzling rumbles from beyond the windows, and a most terrifying creature rises up into view. Wings that span as wide as a small plane, scales rippling along its body, an insectoid face with mandibles the length of a forearm. Four beady eyes meet with its master, and it awaits commands. The red haired man makes a series of shrieking clicks and whistles, and the beast flies away.

The red faced man bows, and leaves.

Another set of laughter fills the room, and the four of them take their seats. They discuss matters ranging from the fate of the world to what the best chocolate bar is, and they talk until the sun fades to a deep red. A meal is brought to them, and they keep on talking. Eventually, the red haired man says he needs to go home and see his kids, and the others wish him goodbyes and see you soon's. After a little longer, the woman says that she should get to sleep, because her son's graduation ceremony is early tomorrow. She receives the same warm goodbye.

And then, it's just the two of them.

They smile, and stare at the fading sun.

And for the first time since it happened, they talk about the girl whose death sent them down this path all those years ago.

The boy, conscious of these dreams being dreams, wonders how true those ideas are, or if they are even true at all. He can't help but notice one common element however, and that is the same four people depicted in each dream. The gears turn in his mind, and with a start, he wakes up.

He jolts awake in a cold sweat, and checks the time.
3 in the morning.
He shrugs off the covers, and sounds the building alarm.
It's time.

16: TARTARUS

−TENGEN−

We stalk slowly amongst the rubble, communicating in hand signals only. Burlap sacks are thrown over our heads and shoulders, masks covering our faces. Every single one of us are on edge, every minute sound causing a frantic grab toward a weapon. Deep in the inner city, devils roam the streets with a destructive abandon, and they are all on the lookout for humans.

Especially us.

According to the plan, we find ourselves tailing behind a small gang of devils, keeping to the shadows. Their lack of distraction and the serious looks on their distorted faces tells us they're either on a mission, or returning home. Either way, we need to figure out where they're going. So we follow, making no sound bar the soft taps of our footfall, slinking from shadow to shadow. It continues like this for a while, until we come to an open junction, with no places to hide. In all directions, devils are converging upon this spot, as if it was a giant meetup. Quickly, Ikari leads us into a building on the side of the road, and we scramble up the stairs. Nervously, Kuro sends a small bug to check if the floor is clear. It returns, and we sneak through the door, tiptoeing to the nearest window. Looking out onto the crossroads, it's a sea of creatures. Every square inch of concrete is covered by a devil, and the few that can fly hover about with a worried uncertainty. It seems as if they are all waiting for something, akin to fans at a concert waiting for the artist to make an appearance. They mill about, confused. Some of them begin to get frustrated, taking their anger out on the weaker devils around them. Suddenly, a sound like a low whoosh splitting into jagged rumbling fills the air, only for a moment. A high pitched whistle is heard, and it turns to a haunting scream as something barrels through the air. At once, all of us, and all of them, look up. Kuro suddenly screams at us to get back, and despite our shock at hearing him shout, we listen. The moment we back away from the window, a deafening boom followed by a rush of air shatters the glass, and outside everything turns red and fiery. The wails of devils pierce through the roaring of flames and the pitter patter of falling rubble, and Kiaran clamps his hands over his ears. As visibility returns outside, we all see the same thing instantly. A devilish bird, with great flapping wings and razor-like claws is gunning straight for the window, unfazed by the explosion.

Yuno scrambles to nock an arrow, but it's too late. The empty window frames are filled by its almost dinosaur like appearance, and Ikari reaches for his sword in preparation. Involuntarily, I cry out and feel the flames flare up within my palms, ready to try a desperate head on attack.

But then, without warning, that same whoosh turning into a rumbling sound, this time followed by a great roar as if a thousand tiny explosions were sounding one after the other.

The bird is torn from the sky by some invisible force, green blood splattering the inside of the room. Still jacked up by the adrenaline, I dash to the window to catch a glimpse of our saviours. I see it just before it disappears into the clouds, a black blur flashing through the air. Across the road, another black blur passes in front of a building, and a moment later that same woosh-rumble.

Kuro taps my shoulder, and I glance over at him.

"Fighter jets."

"Are you sure?"

He nods with confidence, and I have no reason not to believe him. But if they are fighter jets, who's piloting them? Are they even Japanese, or were they sent by some other country? If that's the case, who called them here? And most of all, how can they kill devils with bullets? So many questions, not a single answer.

"Tengen?"

I turn, and see Yasei looking at me.

"Yeah?"

"How exactly are we going to find their base," She gestures to the sight beyond the window frame, "When we can't follow dead creatures?"

She makes a good point, how can we?

Unless… But how could we–

"I've got an idea."

Ikari steps forward, a worrying smile on his face.

"Where would devils reside? How about the place where every devil that has been caught is held?"

Kuro looks at him, worried. Shoto clenches his fist, and speaks for the first time.

"What are you suggesting?"

That smile on Ikari's face, it reminds me eerily of Kurayami's look in the battle.

"The devils will be beneath the primary JSDF prison."

Shoto looks confused.

"Beneath?"

"Oh, at least some of you must know what I'm talking about. The secret NEA prison, in a cavern deep under the surface of Japan. The absolute maximum-security prison." He pauses for effect, still smiling. I can see the gears turning in the heads of the others, and after a moment I too catch his drift.

"Tartarus."

***

Shrouded by darkness, tucked away in the valleys just beyond the Biwa lake, south of Mount Haku, a compound of shadows and blinking lights lies in wait.

Signs of the JSDF's presence can be seen in small informative signs, or on the lapels of the guard uniforms, but it would seem that they don't want their association with this place to be obvious.

After a long, long walk across the foothills and around the banks of the lake, we find ourselves tucked behind a ledge, looking down on the compound. Long ago, we ditched the burlap sacks, and now all of us feel the wind rustle our hair. As we watch soldiers mill about, nothing more than ants from this distance, the sun begins to set behind the hills again. Walking for a whole day has left us tired as ever, but we've no choice except to continue. Quietly, Tengen signals all of us to gather together, and he begins to speak softly.

"Let's think for a moment. Are you all aware of the twelve Fears?"

We nod.

"So, we can cross off 9 of them. Either we've killed them, or they have been hunted, or they've defected. Either way, nine are gone. That leaves three. Logic says we'll need to fight them all to reach the final two devils. Now, do any of you have any idea which devils we may face?"

"Yeah. I do."

"What are they, Ikari?"

"Chances are, one of them will be darkness."

He doesn't notice since he's busy watching the prison, but we all subtly look at Raito. All this time, he's been smiling, encouraging, sharing optimism. It seems that no matter how down things are, how narrow the odds are of success, he never stops smiling.

Like a hero would.

We turn back to Tengen.

"Ok. Anything else?"

His question is met with silence. The soft breeze rustles the leaves of trees around us, and the moon is slowly beginning its ascent into the sky. He nods his realisation, and continues.

"I realise that Ikari does not know the devils that you all contract with. I know that you don't like to share them, but he needs to know, to be able to fight alongside you."

A series of huffing and puffing, and several distasteful glances in T's direction, but they too realise that I need to know.

Kiaran steps forward.

"Devil of poverty."

Strong, but not incredibly so. A lot of people fear that, but the nature in which they fear it limits its effectiveness.

Reluctantly, Shoto comes next.

"Devil of obesity."

Again, very strong, but the fact that it's the fear of a situation limits its ability.

Yasei steps up.

"Devil of plants. I know that you may not think people fear plants, but enough do."

Strong, and the nature of that fear will give it brilliant combat ability.

Yuno scratches at his filthy beard, and gives his answer.

"Devil of archery."

Perfect, perfect. The fear of something like that is the perfect combat devil.

Finally, the young boy Kuro speaks timidly.

"My friend is the devil of insects."

"What? Insects? Are you sure?"

"Yeah…"

I can barely believe what I'm hearing. Insects? Something that ancient, that instinctive… it has to be on par with the twelve fears in terms of strength. Maybe even greater.

Tengen takes a step toward me, and whispers in my ear.

"I know how strong it sounds, but it's not at full ability. The nature of their contract limits it heavily. I can't explain further, not now."

With that, he steps away and goes back to addressing the group.

"Ok, now that we're all acquainted–"

"Hey guys? You might wanna come look at this…"

Raito's tone makes us all scramble to see what he sees, and we head up to look over the ledge. Yasei puts what we all see into words, her voice just above a whisper.

"Tartarus has gone dark."

***

Deep in the dark underbelly of the prison, the figure hangs up the phone, smiling. They stride from the seat overlooking the CCTV footage, and head into what was once the head marshals office. They settle into the chair, kicking their feet up, and giggling at the thought of all the unknowing officers hundreds of metres above them. Their phone buzzes again, and they fish it from their pocket with eloquent fingers.

"Yes?"

The frantic, non-human voice on the other end rambles on about a whole load of things, but emphasises two.

Almost all the devils they sent to the city have been killed. And the group of survivalists are on their way.

The figure hangs up the phone the moment they hear the second thing, and they dash back to the CCTV, their face lit up with a grin. And low and behold, up on the mountain, there they are. They think they're hidden, sneaking behind that ledge, having a little group discussion. As for the defeat of the devils, they addressed the aftermath of that earlier. They exhale heavily, and settle into the chair. They miss their mansion, their daily entertainment, that little girl with one of the greatest powers on the face of the earth. But now, they force themselves to look ahead, at what the future may become. They can think of two outcomes, depending on who emerges victorious from the approaching clash. They reminisce about the other ancients, about how much fun they had with that church in the medieval times. What was he called, the man that almost took them down? Ah, yes. Arthur. That was it, Arthur.

What a man he was. Came so close, and he fought so well with that comparison of his. A woman, he fought alongside a woman. Perhaps his wife?

Brilliant fighters, both of them. What was it they used? Was it the devil of blood, or the devil of sound? The figure smiles, and makes a mental note to ask blood and sound about it. They were so unique, one of the only cases of sharing a contract with multiple people.

But they fell at the last hurdle, for their greed betrayed them.

Ah well.

Maybe this time the best Japan has to offer will succeed. They lean down, and speak into a microphone, broadcasting to all of Tartarus.

"Cut power to the JSDF section. Storm boy, you're up."

On the other side of the prison, the sixth fear steps into an elevator excitedly. He's well aware that he might die today, but the prospect of it only excites him more. He cannot remember the last time he was given the command to use maximum force, until today. Tussling his black and blonde hair affectionately, he silently hopes he can keep it in the afterlife if he dies.

The elevator climbs further toward the surface, and when he steps out, he finds himself in a dark hallway, shouting and screaming somewhere far off. Of course, the JSDF staff will be panicking, having lost power in their maximum security prison. But, the only people locked away on the surface level are just that. People. All the real dangers, the devils, have already escaped after the ancient one broke them out, and then took control of Tartarus. The place he is in now, JSDF maximum security, matters about as much as a fly on the outside of the empire state building. All it is is the entrance to Tartarus.

And so, he concentrates for a moment, and lightning begins to arc off of him. The sky above begins to rumble, and flashes of light are seen through the tiny windows. He bursts through the ceiling, and locks eyes with his targets.

Down below, the figure playfully tosses a small white pill bottle away, the label long faded, having emptied the contents out onto the floor.

They get all of the small white contents in a pile, and crush it beneath their heel. With a wave of their hand, the white dust is flung into the air, and dispersed, gone forever.

***

–IKARI–

A terrible thunderstorm is raging in the sky above, lighting flashes illuminating the otherwise dark complex below them. The sound of panicking staff is lost to the great booming from the sky, and not a single light is on in the complex below.

A small explosion draws our attention to a building at the closest edge of the compound, a cloud of smoke visible intermittently as it turns white from the flashing sky.

Nothing but an ant against the backdrop of the compound, a figure rises from the flashing smoke. Blue energy arcs off them in waves, and they float some twenty metres above the roofs of Tartarus.

I look at them, and despite the distance, I could swear that I see it grin.

It places its hand on what appears to be the hilt of a sword, and with a flash and a thunderclap, it disappears.

Here we are.

Atop a mountain.

Amidst a raging storm.

Against a devil too fast to see.

Well, it was now or never.

And I chose now.

Time to prove that wasn't a mistake.

PART FOUR;
SUNRISE

17: THE SIXTH

"I can't help but wonder, just what were they thinking?"

"It's strange, isn't it…"

The two men lounge about, sipping idly at lukewarm cups of tea. Outside, traffic barrels down all seventeen lanes of the M61, hundreds of people heading into the nearby city. The men watch with a tired disinterest, this view all too familiar to them.

"But I suppose it isn't our place to ask questions, we're not even real members."

"True that, but it just seems odd y'know? I mean, why would you possibly want to call a strike on your own forces?"

"Couldn't tell you mate."

They turn their attention to a plane passing overhead, a white speck on the ever-grey sky.

"Tell you what, I sure would love a holiday soon. The missus has been hoping to head Ibiza, but I just dunno if it's right for me, y'know?"

"Yeah, I can see where you're coming from with that, it's a tough one. But you know what they say…"

The two men look at each other, not even needing to put the classic phrase about a happy life into words.

Far above their heads, in the clouds many miles up, the white plane which they saw changes course, heading dead south. On board, the interior of the commercial liner has been ripped out to make room for a series of luxurious and eccentric furnishings. A large sofa, complete with a stupidly large TV, an entire bar, a full dining setup, and a pool table. Down the end of the tube-shaped cabin, a wall and a sliding door blocks off a large, posted bed, in which a man lays restlessly. He tosses and turns, and stares with bloodshot eyes at the screen embedded in the ceiling above him. He can't sleep, he can never sleep. His mind buzzes with ideas, ideas for innovation that in his head would be world changing. But every time one of those ideas springs up, he forces himself to concentrate on the very real project that is so close to completion. Up here, in this plane, so close to heaven, he feels all the more connected to his plan, to the ANGEL's that he wishes for. All around the world, people under *his* command are tirelessly working for the better future he promises them. But to do that, he needs control. Total control.

And, if everything goes right, his ANGELs will grant him that.

***

–IKARI–

The rain hammers down, unrelenting in its barrage. Lighting flashes in the sky above, each time illuminating the lightless compound and the steep walls of the valley in a haunting white glow. We all look around nervously, muscles tense, hands on weapons. That devil is in the air, and we all know he can strike whenever he wants. A twig breaks behind me, and I spin around to see a flash of blue and silver. On pure instinct, I throw myself to the side, and as the blur passes a strong stormy scent assaults my nostrils. Gathering my breath, the eight of us form a circle back to back. Only now, now that I feel some tiny sense of security, do I notice the warm blood trickling down my neck and soaking the hem of my shirt. A second later, and my head would be rolling on the floor. I feel a searing heat as T aims for something I can't see, and a second later a childish laugh rings out from above us. At once, we strain our necks to look directly up, and there he is. A youngish man, with a white shirt that remains perfectly dry, baggy grey trousers, and black and blonde hair. Black and blonde? What a strange choice–

My train of thought is derailed as he disappears again, but this time is different. I can almost feel his presence, feel my hairs standing on end. Suddenly, I can taste the strong flavour of iron, and I yell out in warning.

"He's coming!"

The instant I finish my words, I hear somebody cry out. Whipping around to see what happened, my eyes fall on Shoto. A deep gash in his lean bicep, blood pouring from it only to be washed away by the rain. He clutches at it and doubles over, but the grimace on his face tells me he's not done yet. With a single movement, he rips off his shirt, and ties it tightly around the wound. Still clenching his jaw, he stands up fully again, a strange light in his eyes. The blur passes around our group, circling us, like a hunter stalking prey.

I still hear his laugh echoing through the wind and rain, despite the thunder booming viciously overhead.

He passes by again, but this time, out of the corner of my eye, I see Shoto make a move. Raising his non-injured arm, he holds an open palm directly in front of him. The blur reaches him, and although it was only in front of him for a fraction of a moment, he clenches his fist at exactly the right time.

Instantly, the blur becomes a person again, slowed down by whatever Shoto did.

The devil of obesity contract. I wonder–

Raito launches himself at the now still figure, and wraps his arms around him. Light flares up at his feet, and they launch into the open air.

After a moment, the devil breaks free of Raito's grasp. Moving too fast to have visible form, the two of them become white and blue lines in the sky, the white one moving in sweeping bends and curves, the blue one in jagged, erratic dashes. Every second or so, the two lines meet, and the clash of steel on steel rings out.

Reduced to bystanders, we watch in fearful awe.

"What's Raito fighting with? He wasn't carrying a weapon…"

Kuro's voice is nervous as his eyes flicker back and forth, attempting to keep up with those flashing lines that his friend's life depends upon.

"I just want to know when he got so much faster… how can he keep up with that guy?"

"He has his tricks. And he's been training. He might act like a hopeful child, but he's quite the fighter…"

Despite his confident words, a slight tremble in his voice betrays Tengen's true feelings about this fight.

"Can we not do anything?"

"I wish we could, but we have no ranged attackers–"

"Really? Forgot about me so soon?"

Yuno steps forward, eyeing up that frantic blue line against the dark backdrop. He scratches his mess of a beard, and rubs his eyes. Wordlessly, he reaches for an arrow. Nocking it, he closes one tired eye, and draws back the string. His body goes still, and he takes a deep breath, watching the blue line as it clashes and separates from the white one.

Left.

Right.

Clash.

Right.

Up.

Down.

Clash.

Right.

Left–

Now.

He releases the arrow, and it flies dead straight. It disappears in the darkness of the stormy sky, but I can see in Yuno's eyes, he knows it's bound for the target.

The blue line jerks to the left, and I see the moment it hits. The line disappears, and the silhouette of a man doubles over as lightning flashes once again. Raito sees this, and the white line curves into him, connecting with a flash. Entwined, they barrel towards us, like a star falling from the sky. We disperse frantically, taking what little cover we can.

They meet the floor, and deafening-

CRASH!

-pierces the sounds of the storm.

Dust billows up, obscuring the impact site completely.

With bated breath, too cautious to charge in, we wait as it slowly settles. The sounds of a struggle and clashing blades only adds to the tension–

With a final gust of wind, the dust is cleared, and the scene is revealed. Raito lays on his back, struggling against the devil as it presses a blade toward his throat. A bar of light holds it back, but ever so slowly, it inches lower and lower. Looking down at him the devil grins. The arrow lodged in his flank appears to be nothing but a minor inconvenience, not the kill shot we were praying for. The devil speaks in a young, confident tone.

"Your strength is fading, glow stick, I can feel it!"

He presses with all his force, and bar of light inches closer and closer to Raito's throat–

A rush of arrows whistles through the air, and at the last moment, the devil sees them. He disappears, but he's slower now, and he wasn't fast enough to evade them all.

A few metres away, the blur snaps back into a humanoid, staggering from the arrow stuck fast in their thigh. They stare at it with discontent, and the storm above us begins to churn, threatening to become something truly overbearing. The devil spits blood, and advances.

Yasei yells something, and thick, gnarled roots curl out of the dirt, wrapping around his ankles. He looks at them the way a car looks at a twig, and he takes another step. The roots are torn from the ground, and disconnected from their source, fall away limply. Behind me, I can hear Yasei's frustration.

Waves and waves of roots rise up, each time ripped away with a single step.

The devil nears, and I grip my sword handle. Without thinking, my feet settled into a stance, my body turned at an angle, my sword primed.

A quick draw.

And, to my shock, he does the same. Feet apart, knees slightly bent, sword primed. But his angle is wrong. He should be facing me at thirty degrees, but instead he's almost side on.

We go still, muscles twitching with the urge to draw. But it's about patience, about seeing a moment of weakness. And we both see one.

There's a clap of thunder, and he's gone–

My sword flashes out of the saya, slicing straight through–

Air?

Too late, I realise what's happening.

Time seems to slow as I realise, he wasn't aiming for me.

And I whip around as fast as I can, just in time to see a red cascade spilling from the side of Kiaran's throat.

***

Emphatic applause fills the almost empty room, the noise emanating from one person only. The figure clutches at a bucket of popcorn, watching with great interest. A battle plays out on the crackly screen; nothing more than a TV series to them. They watch as the white and blue lines clash, they watch as the vines make a futile attempt to hold back the sixth, they watch as the two boys settle into quick draw stances. Secretly, they cheer the survivalists on, for they see the sixth as disposable, and as nothing but a first test for their new guests.

As the next few moments play out they laugh with surprised joy, for what happened next surprised even them.

***

The body hits the floor with a damp thud, and lighting fizzles out as he sheathes his sword.

The devil grumbles in a low tone dismissively at the unmoving body on the floor next to him.

"Don't come to a devil fight if you don't know how to use your contract."

The rain has eased off, only a gentle drizzle now, but the wind is still roaring in our ears. The devil looks around, grinning at each of us.

And one of us snaps.

Kuro screams, screams so loud the whole mountain range could probably hear it. His scream turns to a shout, then a roar of anger and sadness, echoing amongst the booming thunder and whistling wind between the green slopes of the valleys. He screams and screams, unrelenting in his outburst.

Too shocked to move or speak, we can only watch as he steps slowly forward, his scream finally coming to an end. He walks toward the slightly stunned devil, his face twisted with sad anger.

He hisses, akin to a wounded cat, and it seems the grass itself answers his call. The blades ruffle and fall, as if millions of tiny things are walking through them. A strong buzzing fills the air, drowning out the wind and thunder. A cloud of darkness crests the hill, some moving mass of dark spots hovering in the open air.

The devil sees all of this, and smiles.

"I was told you had a rather limiting contract. It would appear I was misinformed."

In response, Kuro raises his arm, simply pointing at the devil. The creatures, the insects, obey his command, and swarm toward him. At first, each one is shrugged off with nothing but a twitch, but slowly, they begin to pile up. The latch onto his skin, burrow into his hair, bury stingers into his flesh. After a moment, a realisation seems to come over the devil as he notices the ever-piling bugs. He begins to struggle, soon turning to a desperate scramble–

He fights and fights, but soon he becomes weighed down. The insects are endless, constantly piling up on each other. Yasei grins, and plants too begin to reach up, wrapping over the insects and binding them all together. The two of them work in wordless communication, like architects that can read each other's minds. And after a moment, it's clear what kind of architects they are.

The devil strains against his prison of hardened plants and seething bugs, but to no avail.

His arms are trapped to his sides, his legs attached to the earth by tree roots and countless bugs. He snarls, and the storm above us spins into a great swirling mass of lightning and wind, forming some kind of whirling cyclone. A great column of spiralling air touches down on the edge of the dark compound and starts to climb the walls of the valley.

Do it.

Huh? What was that? I look around to see if anybody spoke, but nothing.

Finish this off.

What's going on? Who is that? How are they in my head– Wait.

That's your strongest will right now, to kill the devil in front of you.

But he shouldn't be able to speak while I'm in control, that's not possible... unless–

"You fight well, for humans and half-bloods; colour me impressed. Especially you, insect boy. But hear this and hear it well."

His tone turns grave, and all our eyes rest upon the imprisoned devil before us.

"I am the least of the remaining forces, the weakest of the bunch. The next one you meet is not a fighter, and force will not work. So heed this: To beat her, rely on bonds."

With that, he goes quiet. Suddenly, he begins to thrash and thrash, and the storm approaches–

Yuno lowers his bow as he admires the arrow he just buried in the devil's forehead, before yawning.

Lightning flashes again, and it illuminates the body of the boy, slumped in the grass. Raito rushes to help, but T grabs his arm.

"We knew what we signed up for when we came here."

Above us, the storm simply dissipates silently, a befitting end after the almost anticlimactic death of its creator, and the quiet loss of a child's life.

The moon hangs high in the sky, casting just enough silver light to illuminate a path down the valleyside, and into Tartarus.

Raito, wiping his eyes, comes to the front of the group, and looks back at us. He begins to descend, and we follow.

Halfway down, he looks back at us.

"The devil of storms is dead. One down, four to go."

18: THE THIRD

The darkness of the compound is like black hole, drawing us closer and closer. We reach the bottom of the valley-side, and approach a towering chain link fence topped with lethal-looking wire. Beyond the fence, the vague shape of buildings can be seen, and now that the screaming of the storm has faded, the faint panicked yelling of staff can be heard.

"Shall we?"

Raito gestures to the fence. Instinctively, flames begin to well in my palms, and I walk up the base of it.

"I think we shall."

Flames rush forth, coating the metal in a bath of swirling red and orange. Slowly, the grey colour fades to a dull maroon, and as my fingers strain from calling upon so much power, the metal whitens and whitens. The defined shape of the fence begins to weaken, and the rigid mesh starts to deform. The first drop of liquid metal falls to the floor, sizzling as it hits the damp grass. Then another, and another.

Without warning, the whole section collapses into a paste, blackening as it touches the wet earth.

I hear a low whistle, and turn to find the source of the sound. Ikari looks at the sight, and laughs.

"A bit overkill, wouldn't you say?"

Laughing, I respond.

"I thought it was perfectly reasonable."

The group chuckles, and we carefully step over the smoking pile as we enter the compound. Those dark silhouettes of buildings seem much more imposing up close, towering above us. Yasei speaks in her usual dry tone.

"I suppose this is the first level of Tartarus."

"I would say it's more like the entrance."

Kuro says, and smiles at her.

"But same difference."

She smiles back.

"Yeah, I guess."

The rest of us look back and forth between them, surprised at Kuro's talkativeness and Yasei's friendliness. Ikari looks at me and smirks, and I can't help but smirk back. But I know that all this banter and happiness is only on the surface, because in reality...

Our moment of peace is interrupted by the sound of a door swinging open on rusty hinges, but nobody steps out. Raito looks at it and frowns.

"I suppose they're inviting us in."

"Shall we accept?"

In response to Yuno's question, we walk toward the door, treading softly on the wet concrete. As we enter, shadow absorbs us. It reminds me eerily of that time in the railway tunnel, chasing the devil of guns. A soft light emanates from Raito, but not enough to disperse the shadows. Immediately, we find ourselves met with a steep staircase, leading even further into the darkness. Each step we take down it creaks, shattering the silence. We descend further and further into the eerie dark, and soon the small splinter of moonlight from the entrance is gone.

After a few minutes, the stairs come to an abrupt end, and light returns in the form of a few humming electric lamps, flies zipping around them. The moment Kuro steps down from the stairs, they stop their aimless buzzing around the lights, and sit quietly on the walls.

"The first level of Tartarus."

None of us argue with Ikari's statement, but our eyes strain into the dark beyond the glow of these few lights.

"Correct."

The voice that replies is dry, emotionless, and definitely not one of us

"Who's there!?"

For a moment, my challenge goes unanswered, until a person emerges from the darkness, entering the light. A woman, dressed in a well tailored suit, brunette hair pulled into a tight bun. She's pretty, in an austere way. But, the way she moves, the way she does things. I've only seen her for thirty seconds, but I already get the sense that she's acting. As if this suited, stern person is not actually her.

Or maybe, I'm just imagining things.

Either way, she is one thing for certain.

"Third devil of the twelve. Will you surrender, or will you fight?"

She laughs; a basic, forgettable laugh.

"I think I'll fight, host of Azoth."

She opens her mouth to speak again, but an arrow whistles past her head. Yuno nocks another one, and draws back the string. She draws a small dagger, and stalks toward him. He fires again, clipping a loose strand of hair as she ducks just in time. Out of the corner of my eye, I see Ikari rush toward her, sword sliding out of the sheath–

With an open palm, she strikes his chest, and as if a light switch was flicked off in his body, he collapses.

His body hits the floor with a dry thump, and she smiles.

***

–IKARI–

What is this?

Where am I?

Looking around, I see a playground. I'm sitting on a bench at the edge of a sandpit, atop a small mound of grass. Behind me, a climbing frame towers up, seeming impossibly tall. In front of me, a large purple dinosaur– I know this place. When I was little, we called it the park with the different things. Me and my grandma used to come here, sometimes my parents too.

But why am I here?

How am I here?

The sound of soft footsteps makes me turn around, and I see the strangest thing.

It's me, walking toward me. Same messy blonde hair, same blue eyes. But a few things are different. He walks differently, and he has his left hand in his pocket.

"Hullo, Ikari."

"Hello, Kurayami."

Wordlessly, he takes a seat next to me. We look out over the same view, and I can't help but wonder what comes to mind for him when he sees this.

"What's going on? How am I here, talking to you?"

Kurayami smiles.

"The devil of self put you in touch with me. Right now, your friends are fighting while your body is slumped on the floor."

"How long am I stuck here?"

He smiles again.

"Until we reach an agreement, me and you."

"Agreement? What do you mean?"

He sighs wistfully, and looks out over the playground.

"It gets rather boring in your subconscious, you know? Nothing to do except wait for the next moment you slip up so I can have a go."

He smiles.

"An agreement is a way for both of us to feed off each other, and become something better."

He picks dirt from beneath his fingernails.

"Have you ever thought about the differences between us?"

"Not really…"

He laughs.

"I don't suppose you would have. But think. A person with lots of thoughts and little impulse. A person with lots of

impulse and little thoughts. We fit together like a puzzle
piece. Ever wondered why that is?"
Slowly, the gears in my head turn, and I realise.
But can that be right? We're so different in so many ways,
and yet it all makes sense for us to be...
I respond slowly.
"We're the same person."

***

–TENGEN–

The knife flashes toward me, and I barely slip out of its range. One of Yuno's arrows whistles between us, forcing her to back up. Since Ikari fell, she did the same thing to Kuro and Yasei. Me, Shoto, Raito and Yuno have been holding our own, but for somebody with nothing but a knife, she's proving to be formidable. On top of that, Shoto's shoulder means his abilities are pretty limited, and Yuno's running out of arrows.

As for myself, I'm hanging in there. I can feel my skin heating up, a sign that I'm overusing my flames. Stepping back as Raito dashes in, I let myself cool off for a moment. Too late, I realise my guard is down.

She sidesteps Raito, gets behind me, and I feel the cool touch of a palm on my back.

***

–IKARI–

He claps slowly.
"Very good. There's a slight difference though. Right now, we are not the
same person. No, we originated from the same person. Like a steak cut in
half, and fried in different pans with different seasoning.
It's the same meat, but it'll taste completely different."
We sit in silence for a moment.
"So what I'm getting, is that this 'agreement' will be going
back to how it was. Like fusing the cooked steaks back into
one cooked steak."
He chuckles.
"Spot on."
"And you're saying that's my only way out?"
He nods.
"In that case, what choice do I have?"
He looks at me solemnly.
"That's for you to decide."

For me to decide. Either I... join with him, and he joins with me, or I stay here. And let the others fight alone. And die alone.

What choice do I have?

No choice.

"I'll do it."

He looks at me, showing no emotion, not letting his feelings on the matter slip. But he says a few things.

"I'll warn you here and now. There will be side effects."

"Like what? What will happen to the current me?"

"For the first few hours, maybe a day, we will coexist simultaneously in your head. We will be able to communicate by thinking alone. Gradually, my memories will seep into yours. You may forget things, as my memories cloud some of yours. I will forget things, as yours cloud mine. My mannerisms will begin to influence yours, like the way you hold your sword. As for the current you, it will..."

He seems to fumble for the right words.

"I don't know. You will still be Ikari, but... so will I. And Kurayami will cease to exist. Or he may become us both."

His solemness takes a back seat, and he grins.

"And before you make your decision, you should know one thing. That brilliant strength and speed of yours... those abilities that have saved you time and time again."

He jabs a thumb toward his chest.

"Those are my physical attributes that you call upon. When we split, you subconsciously swore away your physical ability, for in your childish mind you thought they were to blame for your mothers diagnosis. So, when we combine, they will return to you. Fully."

I swore away my strength? And if I form this agreement, it will...

With the approaching fight, I need that strength.

"You made it seem like there was, but there was never a choice, was there? And also, this was a test."

He smiles wordlessly, and extends a hand.

"This was a test to see if I'm afraid of myself."

This is it, I suppose.

I reach out, and take it.

***

–TENGEN–

What is this?

Where am I?

What happened?

I'm floating in darkness, not a single sense is working.

I hear nothing, see nothing, feel nothing, touch nothing, smell nothing.

That devil touched me with an open palm, just like she did Ikari and Kuro and Yasei–

What has become of the others? If four of us are… like this, what will happen to the last three. To Raito, to Yuno, to Shoto! I thrash in the dark, hoping, praying, for anything to happen, any clue of what this may be. I need to get back the others, I need to help them–

"Hello, Tengen."

That voice– where did it come from? And why does it seem so familiar–

The realisation hits me like a truck, and my throat manages to form the name that rattles through my head.

"Azoth."

A cold, grating laugh. Suddenly, the darkness in front of me begins to compile, to take shape. It forms a figure, and slowly, detail is added. A flowing cape, swirling hair, sharp features. It all forms out of shadow, black on black. Until a small spark appears at the tip of its toe. Slowly, like paper touched to a flame, the blackness burns away, and in its place, colour.

The cape is flowing vermillion, the eyes are pools of crimson and terracotta. The hair billows in untraceable wind, a swirl of reds and oranges.

"Indeed. Good to see you haven't forgotten me."

"How could I?"

He laughs again, a chilling sound.

"I suppose so. Now, have you been completing the task I gave you?"

I scoff.

"Shining the light of the strong into the eyes of humanity? Tch. But, you also wanted the weak dead. And even if it wasn't my doing, they are. The pillaging and rioting of the devils has wiped out only but the best fighters we have. So yeah, your little task has been completed."

His lips pull away from his teeth in a grin.

"Good. Very, very good. The time for you to move onto the next stage is fast approaching."

"Next stage? What do you mean?"

"The role you will take on if you win this upcoming fight."

"Role? What are you on about?"

"I can't spoil that for you. It is a role as old as devils, the name given to the greatest hunters. The hunters who bring down an ancient devil."

He spreads his arms.

"So, I have a proposal for you."

"A proposal?"

That grin sends a chill down my spine.

"Assimilation."

"Assimilation? What do you mean?"

"The entity known as Azoth will combine fully with the entity known as Tengen."

"Combine?"

"I will cease to exist, you will cease to exist. We will join into one, under your name. Your memories will remain intact, mine will as well. We will share memories, share mannerisms."

In his palm, flames flare up in a great spiral, and the darkness makes it impossible to tell how high.

"And most importantly, share power. You will fight like me though, so some other devils may notice."

Power.

And his fighting style.

In this battle... but is it worth it? To combine with somebody like Azoth? Will I become cold, will I become murderous?

No. My spirit is stronger than his, I know it is.

I will stay myself, and use that power to win.

I must win.

"Tell me, how do you fight?"

"That is something you will figure out the moment you attack anything."

Of course, he won't tell me. But, it doesn't matter how I fight, as long as I win.

"Fine then. Let's combine, devil."

"Good, very good. You will wake up now, and you will not feel anything different. Your companions may notice something, or they may not."

A smile gleams in his eyes.

"But that is the risk you've accepted, is it not?"

"It is. Now hurry up."

He winks, and a moment later, his body crumbles. Where his heart was, a bright ball of flame. It floats in the darkness, almost calling to me.

I extend a hand, and it floats ever closer. It rests on my palm, pleasantly warm to the touch. I hear a whisper–

"You pass the test."

And a searing heat slams into my body, the flesh beneath my skin burning. I spasm in the dark, convulsing from the searing burns that seem to ignite within me. I open my mouth to scream, and–

–a knife rushes toward my throat.

Without thinking, I roll to the side. The devil huffs as she pulls the knife from the concrete where my head was, and lines it up again. She raises the blade above her head–

An arrow knocks it from her hand, and a wall of light slams her away. I scramble to my feet, and look around. Yuno limps with each step, but still he raises his bow. Raito appears unchanged, still fighting as he was when I was hit.

And Shoto.

His body lies slumped against the wall, his chin against his chest. A red smear decorates the cracked wall behind him, and streaks of crimson run down his chest from a rip in his shirt. Kuro and Yasei are still slumped on the floor, and Ikari–

The second my gaze finds him, he regains consciousness, fist clenching and eyes snapping open.

He jumps to his feet, rushing the devil. He moves erratically, dashing left and right as he closes in on her. His sword is gripped in his left hand, facing the ceiling.

He slashes up.

Down.

Across.

Up.

He turns his sword, and drives it straight at her.

The devil nimbly evades his cross of cuts, and steps just far enough back to render his attempt at a stab ineffective.

So that must be Kurayami... but then, the way he twists his body to avoid each slash... that's Ikari's movement.

No time to think about it, either way they need support–

Instinctively, I begin to harden my forearms, but something stops me. And, without really knowing why, I try something different. I hold my hands out in front of me.

They form a circle, as if wrapping around a sphere. Flame forms around the devil, matching the shape of my hands. Without thinking, I clamp my hands together.

The flames form chains, and enclose upon her like a straightjacket. They lock the devil in place, and they steam as they contact her skin.

Seeing an opportunity, Ikari makes his move.

His sword flashes like a wild snake, and two diagonal slashes of red spray into the air.

Two gashes, one from left to right, the other from right to left, forming an X on her torso.

The chains dissipate, and her body crumples to the floor.

19: THE SECOND, AND A HERO

The sound of the body crumpling echoes through the dimly lit room, accompanied by several sets of heavy breath. I hear a groan, and turn around to see Kuro slowly picking himself up from the floor. Moments later, Yasei does the same. They look at each other, then at us, then at the devil. And finally, at the sight of Shoto, his lean form resting lifeless against the wall. The sound of breathing subsides, giving way to the gentle whine of the lamps. Ahead of us, shadows fill the air, an inky soup that absorbs all light.

"Let's get going."

Ikari's voice breaks the silence, as a slightly dazed Kuro responds.

"Yeah."

That's odd, he's never usually the first to respond.

Regardless, the remaining six of us turn to the darkness. Raito takes the first step, the soft light that bleeds off his skin instantly swallowed up. He takes a deep breath, and looks back at us.

"Two down, three to go. You coming?"

I smile, and the rest of us follow on behind him. We all try to clutch at any hope and joy we can, doing everything possible to not think about the body of our friends behind us. The darkness reaches around us, wrapping cold arms over our bodies, holding us away from the light. Further and further we travel into this inky world, until even vague silhouettes cannot be made out. It seems palpable, like pushing through a thick syrup, but it doesn't slow us down. Further and further we stray from the light, into the depths of Tartarus. Soon, the distant yelling and humming of electric lamps fade, leaving us with nothing but footfall.

"Link hands."

I can't tell who said it, but we oblige. I feel a rough hand brush my shoulder, and I grab it. A warm, smallish hand grasps mine on the other side.

And so, we walk through the darkness.

"Everyone linked?"

A chorus of yes's reassures me, and soon a new sound can be heard. A faint whispering, impossible to make out the words being said. I grasp the hand in mine harder, and the person holding mine does the same. I feel us pull each other in, until on both sides my shoulders brush against somebody else's. The whispers become slightly clearer, occasional words becoming audible.

"Scared...monsters... hands... under... bed..."

The whispers of children. Children scared of something.

"Children scared of the dark."

I think that was Yuno, but it's hard to tell amongst the voices clouding my ears. Either way, they're right. So that means this is the second's doing. Suddenly, something whistles through the air, and I hear somebody cry out. In a panic, the hands slip from away from mine, and after only a moment, I'm alone.

Raito calls out frantically, somewhere not too far off.

"Hello? Where are you!?"

My voice is steady, and for once there is not a hint of tremoring.

"Stay calm, the devil has split us up. Raito, can you form light?"

"Trying…"

I open my palm, and attempt to gather flames. A small spark appears, but the moment I try anything more, it gets smothered into nothing. Damn, are my flames really rendered useless again?

It's just like that time in the hospital–

My voice pierces the silence once again.

"Is everyone OK?"

Yasei sounds unharmed, and mostly calm.

"Yeah."

Ikari too speaks up, sounding shocked but fine.

"Yeah, not too bad."

Then Kuro. Then Raito.

I realise something, somebody hasn't replied yet.

"Yuno?! Yunooo? Yu–"

That cry, when we first split. Don't tell me…

"He's gone."

Ikari's words affirm my thoughts, as we all fall silent once again. fOn this damn mission, will any of us even survive?

First Kiaran.

Then Shoto.

And now Yuno.

The fights, three dead.

If this rate continues, one of us will die in the coming battle. And after that, there will be four. And then...

No. We can't lose any more people. Any more fighters. We won't.

My ears once again fill with whispers, this time more forceful.

"Monster... dark... under... hands... bed."

They interrupt my thoughts, throwing me off guard. All these children, all these children terrified of being alone in the dark. And now that's us. Alone, wrapped in shadow.

Ikari can't fight if he can't see.

My flames won't ignite.

Kuro's insects might work, but there won't be any down here to call upon.

And Yasei's plants have no earth to grow from, the ground underfoot is solid concrete.

The only one of us with any chance to counter this is Raito. It's befitting, isn't it.

Trapped in darkness, blind, and alone, the only hope you have is for light to return. And now, I beg that chance falls our way, and Raito becomes the hero he always wanted to be. I hear a grunt of strain over the whispers, and a light appears to my side.

As if I had willed it to happen, Raito managed to make light. Not much, just a small pinprick cupped in his hand, but it casts a sphere of dull golden glow around him. He smiles, and takes a deep breath.

Something hisses, and the darkness seems to press in on him, but he resists.

A bead of sweat trickles down his brow, and he redoubles his efforts.

As I watch, the whispers in my ear become a drumming beat of wailing.

"MONSTER... DARK... SCARED... HANDS, CLAWS... UNDER... IN..."

My head feels like it's splitting open as the terrible beat drums at my ears, blocking me from thinking. But despite that, I can still see Raito struggling against the darkness, that dot of light shrinking and growing as the tide of the battle flows back and forth.

He clenches his jaw, and his lips peel back from his teeth in a strained grimace, but he keeps fighting. And then, from seemingly nowhere, a shaft of light shines from above.

How–?

It skewers the shadow, and something hisses again, this time in pain.

The light settles on Raito's face, bathing it in a golden glow, giving it radiance and lustre.

He looks into it, his eyes filling with luminescence.

And for a split second, they roll back in his head, leaving nothing but the whites of his eyes bathed in shining gold–

***

Raito floats in darkness, no light, no sound. He looks around, a mix of confusion and panic clear to see in his expression. Gradually, his moves become less frantic as he realises that there's nothing he can do except figure out what happened.

He opens his palm, and strains, but his hand stays dark. He curses, and looks around again. It's impossible to know what is up and down, what is left and right, and so he simply turns in circles. The darkness is not oppressive, nor is it thick and malicious like the one he walked through earlier. Instead, it seems like a veil, as if something is hidden just beyond it. He stops twisting and turning, and settles still.

The sound of his deep breathing is heard by nobody except himself, and after a moment he begins to feel a strong sense of isolation. Alone, separated from not just his friends, but from the world. He thinks of the survivalists, his only real companions, fighting those hissing, malicious shadows far away from him. He worries for them.

*To him, it seems almost an hour has passed. Out of
curiosity, he tries speaking into the void.*

"Hello?"

Hello, hello, hello…

*His voice echoes through the emptiness, and he realises
that this can't be some infinite plane, if his voice can echo.
So he speaks again.*

"What is this?"

This, this, this…

*He receives no answer, only the sound of his own words.
He sighs, and tries to think. He was fighting with the
darkness, giving everything he had to hold it back. He was
almost succeeding, until…*

*When he had looked into that unexplainable stream of
light, in an instant, he was here. The scene had switched,
from that gritty battle to this nothingness.*

*Out of frustration, he opens his palm again, and tries with
all his might. In response to his effort, a single pinprick of
light burns to life. It only casts enough of a glow to turn his
wrist and fingers a soft gold, but for him it's enough.*

He likes light.

It brings him comfort, warmth.

He remembers the first time he felt that warmth.

*Slumped on the floor, a trickle of red from his nose
straining the hem of his white button up shirt. Despite him
still reeling from the blow he just took, his eyes settle on a*

gap in the clouds far above. He feels that warmth, like a gentle hug.

He liked that.

And now, in this darkness that hides something from him, he hopes for nothing more than for that light to once again return. His skin aches for the apricity he used to feel, aches for the bath of golden light when the grey clouds far above him split open. In this dark, that seems a million miles away. Perhaps it really is a million miles away, or perhaps it is only a few metres away.

When you don't have an inkling of where you are, everything becomes a question, nothing can be absolute.

He begins to feel tears well in the corners of his eyes, realising that whatever this is has ripped his dream right from his hands. How can he be a hero, trapped in this place?

He wonders, does he even want to be a hero?

Or is that nothing but a childish dream he hung onto because he was scared to have no aspirations, scared to have no end goal?

No.

That look on his friends face, that shocked gratitude.

That look, that's the look he wants to see on the faces of the people he's been fighting alongside.

When they needed him most, he had failed them.

Kiaran.

Shoto.

Yuno.

But no more. He will save the rest of them.

*He knows what he wants to do now, what he's always
wanted to do. He doesn't want to be some comic book
hero, some man in a tight bodysuit with a catchphrase. He
wants to be a real hero, one he who lives for nothing more
than to give without the expectation to receive.*

And now, he'll give his friends a real gift.

He'll give them the chance to win this battle.

Whether it costs him his life or not.

*At that moment, something begins to happen. The light in
his hand dissipates, dissolving into nothingness. Far above
him, or maybe right in front of him, the darkness begins to
lighten.*

*Like a snake shedding its skin, the layers of shadow fall
away.*

*God rays begin to shine through the cracks in that inky
ceiling, and whole chunks of black give way to patches of
ethereal blue.*

*The sun's light shreds through any remaining darkness,
and the boy looks around in a completely different world.
His eyes widen in amazement, and a memory springs into
the back of his mind. Standing with his friend that day back
in school, the morning before that fateful event had taken*

place. Looking up, and smiling alongside the one person
that in that moment, he knew he could trust entirely.
Somebody he could tell anything to.
Somebody who was always there.
Somebody who did the most, no matter what was
happening, to help others.
Right now…
As he stares at the view above him, that's who he wants to
be.
Above, a stunningly blue sky that remains uninterrupted by
clouds. Directly above him, the sun looks down. He stands
in a field of snow, and he takes a step, listening to the
crunch underfoot. A cold wind chills his face, and he looks
up.
And there it is, that warm hug.
That apricity that he missed so much, soothing his skin.
And as he smiles into the light, he realises something.
All he has to do is outrun the shadow, all he has to do is
move fast enough that more shadow can't form. As he
makes that realisation, he looks straight ahead, out over
the horizon—

***

–TENGEN–

–his head snaps forward again, and the shaft of light
disappears. The glow in his eyes never fades, and it's clear
that in that split second something changed.

The seemingly conscious shadow has sensed it too, and shrinks away from him with another hiss. The shadow condenses, taking on a humanoid form.

A figure, lacking all facial features except a mouth, and large bat wings sprouting from the back of its shoulder blades.

The room seems to split in half; Raito's side, and the devil's side.

Down the middle is a grey blur where the light that spills from Raito's literally radiant skin mixes with the palpable, dark murkiness that the devil is formed from. It's only visible as a silhouette, except for one part.

Its singular facial feature, that uncanny human mouth, bends into a grin. Its blinding teeth create a patch of white amongst the shadow, a taunt.

Raito grins back, and re-aborobs all the light spilling off him.

It does the same, and the strange divide down the middle of the room resides. Two figures, standing off.

Light, and dark.

It seems strange, that the classic showdown depicted in almost every myth is really happening, like when that stupid movie trope happens in real life.

And they rush toward each other, colliding in a flash. Their hands are locked, pressing against each other, as they both grin an inch from the other's face.

Raito's smile falters, and he turns toward us, now grouped together.

"GO! Get out of here!"

"We're not leaving–"

"GO!"

His confident smile returns, and I can see something in his luminous eyes. Some sense of accomplishment as he inspects the expression on our faces. His voice is soft now, despite the shaking in his muscles as he holds the devil back.

"Please, go. Leave it to me."

Hearing his tone, we go fall silent. Ikari signals for us to follow him, and he leads us out of the room. As we reach the exit, we look back. Him and the devil have broken apart, and are dashing around the room, just like when he and the devil of storms clashed in the sky.

Kuro looks at him, and his voice is barely a whisper.

"Why, why would he take on a fight alone? Why would he put himself on the line to guarantee our safety?"

Ikari is the first to leave the room, but when he speaks from just beyond the doorway, we can all hear his words.

"Because it's what a hero would do."

***

Raito watches them leave, and breathes a sigh of relief. He turns back to the walking shadow before him, sizing him up once again. The shadow curls his clawed hands into fists, beckoning him forward.

The man bathed in light smiles once again, and does the same.

He knows there's only one way to win this, only one way to bring down the devil standing across from him.

His light simply has to be faster than its shadow.

In a flash, the two of them rush forward, meeting in the middle. The shadows oncoming fist meets directly with the man's open palm, and the man counters. The shadow twists out the way, and the man releases the shadows fist, before springing backward. He raises his hand, and a wave of luminous knives spring forward out of thin air, forcing the shadow to wrap its wings around itself defensively.

The man grins, and rushes in again.

Jab.

Cross.

Uppercut.

Cross.

Hook.

His barrage of punches causes the shadow to briefly stagger, but after a moment it snarls and recovers. The man barely avoids the kick aimed at his head, and launches a kick of his own–

Before he can get his leg up, the shadow's open palm smashes into his chest, and he finds himself flung against the wall.

Just like Shoto.

But he staggers to his feet, and wipes the blood that just coughed up away from his mouth. He mumbles to himself, barely a whisper.

"Faster."

Almost a blur, his fist rushes toward the shadow's throat, his teeth bared in a grimace. The shadow smirks, and side steps. The man slows, but still stumbles past. He turns on a dime, spinning his heel through the air, aiming the shadow's throat. Slipping his attack, the shadow stalks forward, only to be met with the man's rushing fist once again.

Cross.

Cross.

Hook.

Overhand.

Hook.

Losing its footing for a moment, the shadow almost falls, but recovers with a flap of its dark, leathery wings. It hisses, and one of its hands begins to morph. The fingers conjoin, the thumb melts away, the palm narrows.

A blade, perhaps a foot long, its darkness glinting in Raito's light.

"Tch. Bringing a knife to a fist fight."

The shadow, like always, has no response except a grin. Raito looks at his hands, and sees the harsh red skin on his knuckles. Small bunches of grey, lifeless skin surround them, as if he hand rubbed sandpaper on the back of his hand. He curls his fingers into a fist, and winces at the stinging pain.

Regardless, he turns his attention to the mass of humanoid shadow striding closer and closer, turning the hand-blade back and forth eagerly.

The man with luminescent skin comes to meet him, fists curled so tightly his red knuckles turn white.

As it arcs in the direction of his neck, the man raises a glowing forearm in defence. It strikes the glowing skin with a scraping sound, and the man lets it slide off his elbow. In the same motion, he pivots around till his back faces the shadow, before lashing a backfist behind his back.

Reeling from the blow, the shadow lurches back.

Seeing this, the man rushes forward–

A flash of red flies through the air, and the man staggers backward, losing his footing completely. As he hits the ground with a thud, he clamps a gleaming hand to his neck, feeling the cut.

A few centimetres deeper, and it would have been over. Cascades of red pour onto the hard floor, spilling from his neck.

Just like Kiaran.

The man stumbles to his feet, and despite the searing sensation, speaks under his breath.

"Faster. Have to go–"

He hacks up something crimson coloured.

"Faster."

And he disappears.

There's a deafening boom, and a cone of wind fans out from where he was–

Before he blurs into view again, grinning.

Jab-cross-uppercut-hook-cross-jab-elbow–

The light from him becomes almost blinding, as the shadow whips its sword wildly–

Left–right–down–up–stab–

The man barely avoids the attacks, feeling blood seep into his clothes from the ones that still graze him.

Crying out, sounding just like Yuno–

He hits the ground again, and sees the blade flashing toward him–

Whispering under his breath, he speaks again;

"Faster. Faster than the shadow–"

As if teleporting he bursts into existence behind the shadow, raising his fists–

Ja–cro–up–ho–ja–kic–

Too fast to track, to see, he seemingly pops in and out of existence around the shadow–

But still, the shadow keeps up, its sword matching the radiant fists that rush toward it–

Le-ri-up-dow-stab-le-ri–

Blow after blow, cut after cut. They move at speeds almost incomprehensible, and certainly too fast for the naked eye–

"But it's not fast enough."

The man speaks as he backs away from the supersonic encounter, his knuckles ripped to shreds, his shirt turned red. The shadow too reels from the encounter, jagged rips in the darkness that forms it beginning to appear.

Despite not really knowing why, the man begins to speak. He doesn't plan his words, but they just feel right to say.

"Y'know, there's only one way for this to go my way."

The shadow twists its face in what seems to be confusion, but it doesn't attack.

"Can you guess? Well, I'll tell you - Speed, so much speed you simply can't keep up. So much speed that light outruns its own shadow. Now, I know you can't speak–"

The man bathed in light smirks.

"–but I think you could guess at what point an object's light outruns its shadow?"

The shadow snarls momentarily, and its dark face creases as if narrowing its eyes. Still the man's smile remains confidently wide, and the challenge of his question hangs in the air. A stark tension settles over the two of them, neither moving. They watch each other closely, warriors of light and dark.

And the man speaks again; he speaks, and the words just flow out. He doesn't know why he says them, but they just feel right.

"The speed of light. The speed at which the principles of reality break down, the speed at which that previously could not happen, happens. The speed at which,"

His smile widens.

"An object outruns its shadow."

And then, the strangest thing begins to happen to his body. Like an object glitching on a computer screen, small parts of him separate and rejoin, as if his structure is beginning to break down entirely.

"When an object breaks down so completely, there is nothing left but light. And after that happens, if even a gram of mass remains, the impact it will have will be devastating."

He bounces on the balls of his feet, an electric light in his luminous eyes. A childish grin on his face, bloodied knuckles curled into fists. Hair flopping as he moves around, muscles loose yet ready to spring.

"And now rejoice, and relish my existence, for it sheds a hopeful light on the world."

The 'glitching' of his body gets more and more frequent, and something new happens. On the tips of his fingers, layers of skin and bone crumble away into a gold dust, sparkling as it falls to the ground. His voice lowers, and he looks at the shadow with a predatory gaze.

"Soul projection–"

The golden dissolving has started on his face now, his left cheekbone slowly breaking away. The air thickens with power, and the light flares up from within him. His skin goes beyond the usual glow, a blindingly bright hue covering him head to toe. But you can still see his face, his wild hair, his narrowed eyes.

And above all, you can see his smile.

"–Lightspeed."

***

–IKARI–

Do you really think that boy can handle the devil of darkness?

Yeah, I do. And please be quiet.

I shut out Kurayami's incessant voice, and concentrate on the long hall ahead of me. All of us are on edge, springing like scared bats at every tiny creak or pitter. I can feel this hall sloping downward, taking us deeper and deeper into Tartarus.

But, in the back of my mind, the thought of Raito is overbearing. To think he would so brazenly send us away, taking on such a being alone. Even after the way he struggled to put a dent in that shadow earlier.

But something changed in that split second. Like he... let go of something that's been weighing him down

In fact, something similar has happened to the other three alongside me. They've changed, not in a massive way, but more subtly. Slight differences in their mannerisms, slight changes in their way of speech. The biggest one...

Tengen.

What was that earlier, that cage of flames?

Since when could he fight like that?

And the way he looks at us has changed. It's minor, a barely noticeable change. I doubt he's even noticed it himself. But it's there, that tiny difference; he lacks the admiration that his eyes used to be so full of. The warmth is there, the friendliness, the hope, the confidence.

But no admiration.

As if he's just stopped looking up to us, as if now he sees us as below him. No. Not us.

Me.

He looks at the others just the same as he did.

So what changed?

Have you considered that it's something similar to what happened to you?

I told you to– What do you mean?

I mean that he's reached some kind of agreement with his devil.

The boy in question walks slightly in front of me, and I look at the back of his ear. I suppose that would explain everything.

What happened, why he's changed that slight bit.

Why they've all changed.

***

Everything turns white. Nothing to see, except blinding white light. In every corner, every direction.

Then it returns to normal, and the man is gone.

The shadow whips its head back and forth, searching for the man's presence with a hint of desperation–

A fist breaks outward from the centre of its pitch black chest, and it coughs a liquid that looks a lot like tar. It looks down at the fist, watching as if slowly dissolves into glowing nothings.

Still grinning, the man disappears again.

And a fist sends the shadow staggering, colliding into its jaw with a sickening crack. As he stands before the shadow, the man reaches up a hand and feels his face. It crumbles beneath his fingers, glowing wisps cascading down. He sighs, and curls his hand back into a fist. Sensing something it can't beat, the shadow shrieks in pain, and rushes toward the ceiling, wings beating wildly as it prepares to smash its way to the open air above–

And time stops for all except the man.

The shadow, frozen in place. Dust, suspended mid air. Rubble, stuck in place just before it could separate from the ceiling.

He wanders amongst all of this, perhaps an inch off the ground, feeling his body slowly dissipate into the air. His right arm is now gone, and the left one has disappeared up to the wrist.

He finds it funny how slow everything seems when you move this fast.

Now nothing but a torso with one leg, he sighs. The white steam of his breath is snatched away instantly, a reminder of what's really happening here. Moving at this speed, all it would take is one tiny piece of mass to impact anything, and...

The rest of his body slips away, and he breathes his last words.

"Even now, without a stage, without a crowd… *I'm still a real hero.*"

The last thing to go is his smile.

He's gone.

No trace of him, bar one thing.

His necklace, safe from dissolving into light, tumbles toward the floor. The small silver pendant of a nail passed through a circle.

It seems so slow for something moving so unfathomably fast.

The force of a thousand bombs in tiny silver chain and pendant.

And, able to escape turning into massless energy, the only thing left of that great hero hits the ground at lightspeed.

***

–IKARI–

A deafening explosion followed by a great rumbling fills the air, the walls around us shaking.

"What the hell was that?"

Yasei looks up, concern etched into her face.

"Whatever it was, it was powerful. Like some huge bomb just went off."

"Could it be–?"

Kuro finishes my sentence.

"Raito."

He too looks to the ceiling, and closes his eyes.

"We can only pray that he won, whatever it cost him."

Smiling, he meets each of our eyes, lingering on Yasei's for a moment longer than the rest.

"That's what he wanted right?"

Tengen smiles longingly at the roof of the subterranean tunnel.

"To be a real hero."

***

As the rubble rolls to a stop, and the dust settles, silence returns.

A few burst pipes splutter water weakly, trickling down to the bottom of the crater.

A gaping wound in the underground, unbelievably wide, like a globe shaped bite was taken out of the just beneath the surface.

The ground beneath the compound is nothing but empty space, and all that remains are the deepest levels of Tartarus and a faux level of grass and dirt, suspended above a gaping spherical chasm.

Nobody hears the soft clink of metal on stone as the silvery necklace settles on a piece of rubble.

And nobody sees the flurry of luminescent flecks that fill the air, shimmering like endless god rays.

The final parting gift of a true hero.

The man bathed in light.

The man called Raito.

20: REMATCH

A tense silence overcomes us as we near the end of this tunnel, our footfall echoing in all directions.
To my side, Ikari clutches the handle of his blade tensely. Just behind me, I can hear Kuro's bated breath as he stalks nervously. Yasei runs her fingers over the vines imprinted on her hand, the way she does when preparing for something. The rumbling has stopped now, a gentle yet harsh reminder of yet another lost companion. I'm just glad he did things on his own terms and gave us the parting gift he always wanted to.
Thank you, Raito. Thanks to you, we *will* win this.
"Wait."

Ikari's voice is abrupt, but we all come to a halt.

"Listen."

Calming our breathing, we listen closely, ears pressed to the air. It seems silent, even the hum of lights can't be heard. I suppose that's due to this place getting seemingly less and less advanced as we go deeper and deeper, the rickety lights replaced by flickering lamps that line the edges of the rounded tunnel–

A soft growling emanates from somewhere ahead, just beyond the door that waits in front of us. It rises and lowers in pitch, almost like speech. Yasei walks up to the door, and places a hand on it. The muscles in her arm tense as she strains, pressing into the door. It doesn't budge, but something begins to happen at the seams.

Tiny leaves and vines, minute weeds or tiny flowers. They fill the seams, giving the door an almost decorative floral outline. The wood groans slightly as plants press in on it, small cutesy flowers morphing into seething vines and creepers. Hairline cracks begin to appear, and she steps back.

Shaking from effort, she curls the fingers of her splayed palm inward, and the groaning grows to a series of cracks and pops. The steel lining bends, and the wood splits completely.

Ikari watches with a face of mild concern, and backs away slightly as he speaks.

"I think that's about to–"

Wood flies all over as the door collapses on itself, metal screaming as it buckles under the force of Yasei's choking plants.

It all happens so quickly, and after a moment, the clattering of splinters fades.

"–Explode."

Ikari finishes his sentence dryly, stepping forward into the space where the door was. He draws his blade, waiting for whatever was making that growling sound.

Silence.

I creep forward, standing beside him. He briefly looks over to me, before returning his gaze to the shadows beyond the shattered door. When he speaks, it's barely a whisper.

"You reckon it was bait?"

"Maybe... But if I can guess who's behind this, that's not their style."

He looks at me again, his brow wrinkled.

"You're telling me you know the next devil?"

Before I can respond, he cocks his head as if speaking to somebody else. His eyes narrow for a moment, and he gulps. Looking back into the empty space ahead, he speaks again.

"Oh. I see."

He sighs, and subtly tightens the grip on his sword.
Suddenly, that same growling sound can be heard again,
this time more aggressive.

And undoubtedly closer than before.

Behind me, I hear gentle footsteps as Yasei and Kuro step
up to be in line with us. One of them takes a deep breath,
and the other exhales heavily.

A pair of beady blue eyes materialise out of the wreckage,
followed by a silvery mane. A pair of paws pad the ground
softly, each step carefully placed.

Two scarred and clipped ears slicked back on top of its
head, and a tail juts straight out behind it. Dripping with
saliva, the lips around its snarling maw peel back with each
low snarl. In an almost snake like way, a long tongue slides
between curved yellow teeth with a haunting joy.

A beast? Down here?

And alone too.

Kuro steps forward, hands open in a gesture of surrender.
He lowers himself to one knee, eye to eye with the snarling
beast. He speaks in a low tone, yet there's a softness to it,
like a parent calming their child.

"A wolf without a pack has no place in caves like these."
The beast stops in its tracks, one paw halfway to the
ground.

"Relax…"

As the growling falters for a moment, its grey lips side forward briefly. Closing its maw, the ears spring up. Kuro creeps closer, extending his hand before him. And very slowly, very gently, he places his fingers between those beady eyes. The wolf cocks its head slightly, almost like an inquisitive dog. Kuro twitches his fingers, scratching the silvery fur. It wags its tail, and its back legs slowly curl down into a hunch. It sits on its hind legs, looking at kuro, panting–

There's a hissing sound, and the wolf goes still. The panting stops, and it topples onto its side. Frantically, Kuro places two fingers on its throat. His hand recoils, and he looks into the darkness with murder in his eyes.

"Oh, what a talent that is."

I know that voice.

Clear, pronounced, and yet there's a tinge of age to it. Kuro's eyes bury into the approaching silhouette. Without thinking, my hands curl into fists.

Clack.

Clack.

Clack.

A wooden cane taps against the hard ground, the fingers wrapped around the handle adorned with rings and wrinkles.

Dull hair. Pinstripe suit.

Wisps of grey poking out from the sides of a stark white surgeon's mask.

"To think that a mere boy could turn a rabid animal docile with just a few words."

The bagginess under his eyes bunches up as he smiles.

"Kids these days, ah?"

Ikari steps forward, eyes narrowed, jaw clenched.

"You."

"Yes! Me."

"Old man."

How could Ikari remember him? When we fought, he wasn't Ikari. He was Kuraymi.

And when he explained the two of them to me, he described it as two completely different people. Different memories, different knowledge.

So how could he know the representative by face–

Ikari swipes at the old man, his blade whistling past that white mask. It arcs back again, and the man slips backward.

"Wait! I do not wish to fight!"

Ikari pauses, but his blade remains primed to strike. The rest of us slowly surround him, tense. Kuro's knuckles are white, but he can still hold himself back. Yasei glances at him, then turns to the man.

"So what do you want?"

He peels the mask away from his face, revealing a smile
that doesn't reach his eyes. He jabs a finger toward me.
"Hand him over, and you can walk right past me."
What–
Me?!
"Not happening." Ikari's instant response surprises me, and
I see the man reach for something strapped to his hip.
"Well that's a shame. It really is–"
Flame roars from my open palm, and the man grunts in
pain as it washes over him–
"You bastard!"
–The man yells out, hands blocking his face. Stumbling, he
knocks into the wall with a thump. Running his tongue
over blackened lips, he snarls in a way eerily similar to the
wolf.
"Now fear me, for the world shall feel the terror of my
existence!"
No!– I know those words.
But where's the fog?
The grey snow?
The roots?
Is he bluffing–
No, we have to stop him, even if he's lying. But I'm too
far, I can't cover the distance in time. Ikari too. And
despite his anger, Kuro has no insects to command, which
means…

The old man smiles.

Could it really end here? Another one of those monstrous abilities, released in a space like this… we would have no chance.

I can't let him finish that ritual, but how?!

In the end, I can only watch as he speaks again.

"Soul project–"

He stops, and doubles over, before snapping back upright as if his back was spasming–

"argh– arkh–"

A spurt of crimson rushes from his mouth, splattering on the floor in front of him. Then another. Then another. It pools around his feet, soaking into his brown loafers.

Thorns burst from his chest, ripping out of his shirt as a sickening crunch rings out. He coughs one final time, head hanging low. Branches begin to enclose on his limp body, wrapping around him like a straightjacket. A rock strikes his nose, drawing blood.

The branches complete their incarceration, reducing the man to a bunch of thorny bushes.

A stunned silence washes over us, and all we hear is Yasei's heavy breathing. Amidst the sound, there's a soft–

Shhh…

-as Ikari sheathes his blade. Still, nobody speaks as the events that just passed really hit us.

After so much struggle in that first encounter…

To think it would be over in a few short moments.

It seems... anticlimactic.

I suppose we've gotten far stronger.

All of us.

I sigh and turn toward the hallway ahead.

"He's not here to say it but..."

I look over my shoulder at the three of them.

"Four down–"

Three rugged smiles. Three fighters. Three friends.

"One more."

***

–IKARI–

Hated that guy.

Oh, can you please shut up about the fact you fought that old geezer a while ago! All you've been speaking about is him!

Hmph.

Admittedly, it's been on my mind too. Was that it? All that the representative of the first devil had? It just seemed so... weak.

You should have seen him last time.

Was he really that strong?

Yeah. He really was.

The four of us stride through the hallways, still delving deeper and deeper into the earth. That fight was maybe half an hour ago now, and still none of us have said a word since Tengen did. Our footsteps pad softly, just like that wolf. Discreetly glancing at Kuro, it's clear that he's still feeling that. It's sad, so sad.

It really is bittersweet how quickly people can bond with animals, animals they just met. Hell, animals that were rabidly convinced they wanted to kill you a minute ago. I suppose I've been doing a lot of thinking lately.

Amidst the worst of battles, or simply staring at the ceiling at night. About a load of different things. But one thing I haven't been doing is thinking back. In fact, I don't think I've thought about the past since that talk with T. Most of my thoughts have been about a conclusion I came to a while ago.

'We are insignificant. But we don't care.'

Do I still agree with myself? Are we really that insignificant? And do we really not care?

I don't even know anymore. I can remember thinking, right at the end of that mental ramble on the liminal mountain:

'Perhaps I'm just going mad.'

Yeah. That I can agree with.

I really does feel like I'm just going mad. Like I'm just… slowly losing it. One thought at a time.

You think you're going mad, huh?

Well, you're definitely not helping.

I guess you make a fair point.

So how long are you going to be in my head exactly?

To be honest, I don't know.

Well that's great isn't it.

But, if I had to guess, the next time you get knocked out and wake up, I'll be gone.

Huh.

The next time I get knocked out.

We slow as the four of us come to another door, this time a vault of solid metal. We stop, looking up at the towering silver face before us. All around, the jagged stone of the tunnel drips murky water into small puddles.

Drip.

Drip.

Drip.

I place a hand on the metal, a shock of cold running through my skin. Rapping a single knuckle against it, a series of low thuds.

"It's deep. Ten inches, maybe a foot."

Yasei groans.

"Brilliant. Now what?"

Tengen grinds his jaw visibly, sweeping his gaze up and down the mass of metal. This deep underground, there's no turning back. We need to get past this door, one way or another. But what can we do? A solid foot of metal. Not even T could melt his way through. Yasei can't strangle this one with plants. And Kuro has slowly been amassing insects, but...

And what about you? What can you do?

What can I do?

The blade won't make it all the way through, it might not even pierce it at all. And a brute strike would never work, it's just too solid. My hands bunch into fists, twitching to lash out. But, it wouldn't do anything anyway.

Damn it.

What can I do?

You can think.

Think. He's right. I can think. But... think about what? Not the past. Not the future. I splay my fingers again.

What can I do, right now?

In the present. I mean, it seems stupid, but...

The door towers before me, some hulking mass of solid metal. Impenetrable. Unbreakable. Impassable.

A scuttling mass flings itself towards the door, slamming into it with a sound similar to throwing a handful of marbles at a wall. Dispersing, the insects scurry into any possible cracks or crevices. Seconds later, heaving branches and thorns press against the vertical sheen, like ants attempting to burrow through concrete.

But to no avail. For a moment, silence once again blankets us. Kuro breaks it with a sigh, his heavy breath filling the cave.

It seems stupid, but...

I raise a fist in front of the door, tensing it—

You'll break your hand.

—and turn my knuckles toward the door.

Knock.

Knock.

The sound of bone on metal echoes around the cave, an almost eerie thudding that spirals past our ears and into the shadows behind us.

Knock.

Knock.

Knock—

A soft hiss, like gas escaping a chamber, or a snake encircling its prey. A heavy clank sounds from somewhere within the door. Then another. Then another.

And with a final hiss, the metal face splits down the middle, sliding open with an almost relaxed slowness. A soft click, and the doors are fully open. Beyond their gaping maw, a sea of shadow. And then a flame burns to life, showing the start of a hallway. More and more flames light up, running down the hall. A crimson carpet lines the way, a river of blood leading to its source.

And at the end of it, barely visible:

A marble throne waits.
And a figure, shrouded in black fabric, lounges lazily.
That's when it hits me.
This sense – this sense that–
Death awaits us all.

21: A FIGURE IN BLACK FABRIC

"What– what is this?"

This… this pressure in the air. Like a fist curled around me, pressing me inward on all sides – a diver swimming hundreds of feet underwater. Every move takes so much effort, even lifting a finger.

"I think–"

Tengen raises a laboured arm toward the end of the hallway.

"–I think it's that figure causing this."

With great effort, Kuro takes a step forward.

"Then there's only one thing that we can do."

He lifts his leg again, shaking from the strain, and takes another step. And he grits his teeth, walking down the hallway, step by step. Yasei takes her first step through the doorway, and follows him. Tengen looks at me, and I nod. Step by agonising step, the four of us make our way further and further down the hall, our faces bathed in the flickering light of the fires that line the walls. Underfoot, the carpet gradually gets redder and redder, slowly turning from an orangey hue to a vermillion, and soon to a shocking crimson. All the while, that black spot at the end of the hall gets clearer and clearer, morphing into a distinguishable body. Their feet are crossed almost daintily, but the rest of their reposing figure rests against the chair with an unbothered confidence.

After what feels like forever, muscles burning, we come to a stop some ten metres before the figure.

The throne is clearer now, a towering chair of carved white marble, swirling marks running across its surface, and intricate patterns adorning every side. A cushion of emerald green supports the veiled head, and armrests of the same vibrant hue line the low sides of the seat. But now, the majesty of the throne is an afterthought.

For the person that rests on it is far more enthralling, in a petrifying way. Throes of inky fabric drape their every limb, and a midnight black cloak covers their torso. Hidden by a dark veil, their face is nothing but a sheer plane of nebulous textiles. This close, that pressure feels less like something physical, but more like some kind of subconscious screaming. Like standing in front of an oncoming train, where every instinct you have tells you to get up and run as far as you can.

No devil, no matter how strong they were, has ever had this effect on me. No devil, no matter what the situation was, has ever felt so all encompassing.

No devil, no matter how scared I was, has ever been so petrifying. And mixed in with the fear, there's some subtle sense of inevitably. As if all roads lead to here, all the possible paths we could have taken would end here. Before this figure. Before this throne. All the fights we've had so far, all the trials and tribulations.

They served only one purpose.

To bring the four of us here, and to set us before this throne.

And now, in the flickering torch light, standing on a river of blood, it feels like some kind of destiny has been fulfilled.

But, as I look at the masked face of this figure, I can't help but feel like that destiny is nothing but a death sentence.

You need to run. Now.

Run- I can't just run!

Listen to me, Ikari. You need to RUN.

RIGHT.

NOW.

No, I can't just run. Even if I wanted to, this immense pressure… Besides… I cast my gaze across the veiled face of the figure. Something tells me they won't let that happen.

You'll die, Ikari. And I'll die with you.

I– yeah. I probably will. But there's nothing else that can be done at this point. No time to run. No time to negotiate. Slowly, deliberately, the figure raises a gloved hand in greeting.

Time to fight.

***

–TENGEN–

Raising a hand?

Is that some kind of–

A flick of crimson flashes through my peripheral vision, and when I place my fingers to my cheekbone, they come away red.

What– how? What cut me?

The draped fingers of the figure twitch, and I see Kuro clutch his forearm as a few drops of vermillion hit the floor below him. Moments later, Yasei's fingers brush her temple, and she shivers at the damp warmth seeping down into her eyebrow.

"I SUPPOSE A 'HELLO' IS IN ORDER."

The voice that comes from the figure is soft yet deafening, but almost gentle. And yet, hidden in the undertones, there's something uncanny. Something threatening, like just hearing it triggers some primal fear.

"I DON'T BELIEVE I'VE HAD THE PLEASURE OF MEETING ANY OF YOU YET."

That voice. It feels like I know that voice. As if this figure is somebody I used to know, somebody I haven't spoken to in years and years.

"BUT I'M SURE YOU'VE HEARD OF ME. I'M SURE YOU'VE HEARD ALL ABOUT ME IN FACT."

I can hear the smile in their words.

"THE FIRST DEVIL. THE ANCIENT ONE. THE WEAVER OF FATE."

So, this is–

"I'M SURE YOU'VE HEARD AT LEAST ONE OF THOSE   NAMES. IN FACT, I KNOW YOU HAVE. BECAUSE AFTER ALL, EVERYTHING YOU'VE DONE SO FAR HAS BEEN TO REACH ME."

They cock their head playfully, shifting the inky fabric like water changing course.

"RIGHT?"

None of us speak, and a heavy silence falls across the scene. In the flickering light, it seems our fate is becoming clearer and clearer by the minute. Kill or be killed, I suppose.

"NOT FEELING VERY TALKATIVE? WHAT A SHAME."

And very slowly, every movement coated in tension, they rise to their feet. Waves of midnight fabric roll off them, floating through the air and draping over the now vacated seat. But the veil remains, and still their face is nothing but a sheen of dark cloth.

And they extend a hand before them.

Click.

The sound of their finger hitting their palm, a simple snap of the finger. For a moment, nothing happens.

What was that? Were they signalling–

And I'm falling, the ground beneath me turned to air–

Tumbling through shadow–

The ground rushes up to meet me–

And I slam into it, the breath knocked out of me. Moments later, three more dry thumps as what I can only assume are my companions hit the ground beside me. A chorus of groans, but one by one, we pick ourselves up to our feet.

"What is this place?"

Yasei raises a good point.

Just where exactly are we?

And now that I think about it, the journey up to this point has been a bit weird too. Surely as we travelled deeper into Tartarus, we should have seen prison equipment, cells, canteens. And yet, after we entered the prison from the JSDF surface entrance, we haven't seen a single sign that this place is a prison. There were doors sure, but behind them was just more hallway. And then it was caves and caves, no semblance of technology.

Until that towering metal door. Then, a hallway that leads to nothing except a throne. And finally, a pitfall into… whatever this is.

We find ourselves in a circular room, high vaulted ceilings, walls once again lined with torches all the way around. Above us, the chute that dropped us here closes with a grinding scrape as stone rubs against stone. Underfoot, smooth black stone, so glassy it looks back at you. Every breath, every tiny sound echoes through the room, turning a simple step into the beat of a heavy drum. And, in the centre of this great ring, there they are. No longer coated in drapes of fabric, their almost slim figure can be seen as a long cloak billows out behind them, blown by some undetectable wind. The inside lining is glossy black, just like the stone that surrounds us, and it reflects the metallic purple of their armour into jagged refractions that splay across the floor. They bear no weapon, but their gloves are gone, revealing well-manicured slender fingers. The only thing that hasn't changed is the veil that covers their face from the neck up, but in this new attire one thing is clear. A cascade of black hair spills down their shoulders, flowing with a stunning lustre.

To my left, the silvery length of Ikari's blade seems to stretch for the entire room, and each minute movement creates a kaleidoscope of silver. To my right, Kuro and Yasei stand together, shoulders brushing as they shuffle with tension.

And as for me, small wells of fire hover at each fingertip, and without really thinking about it, I bend my fingers, ready to flick.

This is it.

To think that after everything we've been through, this is where our story comes to a close.

One way or another, it will end in this room.

We set out with eight, and now only four remain.

Just as I'm about to attack, Kuro's voice fills the room.

"Take the mask off."

The figure cocks their head in that same playful way.

"OH? AND WHY IS THAT?"

He grits his teeth.

"Just humour me."

The figure laughs - a cold, empty sound. In fact, it sounds eerily similar–

"ALRIGHT THEN."

The figure concedes to Kuro's request, and curls their fingers around the base of the veil. With a short, sharp tug, it falls away from their–

From her face.

She smiles, and my own shocked eyes are reflected in her exposed teeth. I mean, it shouldn't be surprising - of course the first devil could be a woman. But... I find my eyes lingering on her face. Beautiful yes, stunningly so. But there's something else.

The tilt in her eyebrows. The high set cheekbones. The rounded yet prominent chin. And her eyes. Yes, hers are purple and not orange, but... the resemblance is there. I know it is.

This woman.

She looks like–

"HOLD ON A MINUTE."

Those purple eyes rest on the fires burning at my fingertips, and she frowns for a moment.

"I KNEW YOU TWO WERE CONTRACTED, BUT THAT METHOD OF USING FIRE..."

Our gazes meet as hers flickers up to my eyes.

"What is it, si–"

Was I just about to call the devil 'sister'? But I've never even met her, bear in mind be related–

Suddenly, a wave of understanding fills her eyes, and she laughs again, but this time in genuine amusement. She peers at me again, but it feels like she's looking at something just beyond my eyes.

"YOU'VE MADE YOUR MOVE FASTER THAN 1 EXPECTED, BROTHER."

Brother?

Wait.

Could she mean–

"Brother? What the hell does she mean Tengen?"

Yasei's voice is filled with surprise, and the looks that Kuro and Ikari are giving me matches her shock. I jab a finger at my chest.

"Not *my* sister."

I indicate to the fire that spills from my fingertips.

"*His* sister."

"You mean that–"

Ikari looks at the woman, seeing himself in her grin.

"That's Azoth's sister."

I nod curtly.

The figure laughs one final time, before spreading her arms.

"WONDERFUL, WONDERFUL. BUT NOW THAT WE'RE ALL ACQUAINTED–"

She smiles, but not out of joy. Now, nothing but malice fills those purple eyes.

"–SHALL WE BEGIN?"

And so I flick all my fingers, a barrage of fireballs rushing toward her–

She clasps her hands together, and some invisible force snuffs them out mid-air. A wave of entangled branches and brambles surges from the ground, piercing the glassy rock–

But with another wave of the hand, they fall to the ground in little pieces. Ikari advances forward, sprinting full speed–

And blood spurts from his thigh, causing him to stagger and fall to the floor. The devil raises a boot above his head, stamping down–

The ground where he was implodes in a shower of black fragments, sparkling with reflections as they tumble through the air. His blade arcs up from his new position, aiming for her calf–

But he goes skittering across the floor, flung by something unseeable. Yasei charges forward, fists enclosed with vines–

And the woman rushes to meet her, burying her fist in Yasei's gut–

There's a low rumbling echo as she smashes into the wall, a cloud of dust billowing up around the impact. The woman advances toward her, a killer's glint in her eyes. Suddenly, a cloud of insects rushes to meet her, swarming through her hair, biting at her face–

She bunches her hand into a fist, and the cloud disperses as something sweeps through them, hundreds of sliced bugs hitting the floor. Ikari rushes back in, the tip of his blade aimed for the back of her neck–

Without even looking, she splays her fingers, and his sword clatters to the ground as a series of cuts open on the back of his hand. Akin to an angry horse, she kicks one leg out behind her, and Ikari lets out a strangled wheeze as he hits the floor, panting to recover the air that was knocked out of him.

The figure laughs as she brushes off each and every attack, barely breaking a sweat.

"IS THIS ALL YOU HAVE? I'M SHOCKED YOU'VE MADE IT THIS FAR–"

She flings an arm out to the side and makes a series of complex finger movements, as if she was wrapping string around a ball–

A large chunk of rock disconnects from the wall and flies toward me, thrown by an invisible hand–

I cross my forearms in an X, and at the last possible moment flames rush up to meet the boulder mid-air, shattering it on impact. I breathe sigh of relief, and the flames disperse–

A hand shoots out from the smoke, and I see my wide eyes reflected in a broad grin for a split second before fingers close around my neck–

I feel myself lift from the ground, suspended only by the choking grip on my throat. Gasping for breath, the edges of my vision begin to darken as the smoke finally clears fully. The woman smiles up at me as I scratch and pummel her outstretched arm, desperately trying to dislodge her grip. Just before my vision fully closes, I see Ikari rushing toward us having recovered his sword–

And the air returns to my lungs as I fly through the air, smashing into Ikari with a sickening thud. The two of us hit the deck, groaning from the collision. Through dazed ears, I hear her laugh as she brushes away another of Yasei's attacks.

"GOOD TO SEE THAT TOSSING MY LITTLE BROTHER INTO THINGS IS JUST AS FUN AS IT USED TO BE!"

Her laughter fills the room as she battles Kuro and Yasei, both of them giving everything they have.

I pick myself up to my feet and try to steady my ragged breathing as I help Ikari up. Breathlessly, we talk.

"Sorry."

"No worries. Any- any idea how she's doing all this?"

We glance at the devil, watching as each twitch of her fingers opens another cut or blocks another attack. I look back at Ikari.

"I got one."

He looks at me, fully focused.

"She gave it away when she flung that boulder at me. She had to take a moment, and she was moving her fingers like she was wrapping something. And one of the names she listed: *Weaver* of fate."

"I see. What you mean is–"

He smiles dryly as he watches her manipulate some unseen force to toss the other two around.

"–Threads."

I nod, and turn to the devil.

He raises his fist between us, and I knock mine into it.

"They're fast, so watch her hands."

"Yeah. Let's go."

And we re-enter the fray, my flames scorching the air as Ikari uses them as cover to rush in–

Her fingers curl inward, like plucking a guitar string–

Which means-

"From in front!"

Ikari slashes in front of him, and low and behold; an almost hair like string of silver thread flutters through the air, cut cleanly in half-

And a flash of red arcs from the woman's bicep as Ikari's blade finally reaches its mark. She staggers back, and snarls as she speaks.

"WELL WOULD YOU LOOK AT THAT."

***

–IKARI–

I press forward, unfazed by her words–

Her index finger flicks to the left–

And I slash to the right, smiling as another thread is severed. This close, rushing right up to her, time seems to slow.

Watch her fingers.

Yeah. I remember.

With that tiny realisation, what once seemed like some untouchable power is now just another ability. And every ability has a counter. If her fingers go one way, the attack comes from the other.

It's that simple–

I cough as her boot slams into my chest, knocking me back–

Her elbow thumps into my jaw, and reeling from the blow I raise my sword in an attempt to ward her off–

But still she rushes in, her heel arcing for my temple as she spins into a kick–

And a wall of vines catches it, thorns digging into her ankle. Yasei grinds her jaw as she wrestles with the outstretched leg of the devil, more and more plants piling on. Snarling again, the woman leaps into the air and smashes her other leg into the mass of plants, dislodging Yasei's hold for just enough time to free herself–

But yet another rush of insects piles onto her–

She swipes her hand wildly, cutting them to shreds, and turning to face Kuro–

Wait. How–

In his hand, palm slick with blood, he grasps a thread, having wrapped it around his own hand. The devil's eyes widen in surprise, and Kuro yanks left–

She staggers left, wrestling to release that thread–

Kuro yanks right–

And she stumbles right, dragged by her hand–

Straining from the effort and wincing as the thread cuts his hand to shreds, he digs his feet in and yanks the thread up and over his head, turning around as he does–

There's no way he could–

But the devil sails through the air, yanked by her own thread–

And smashes into the ground with a deafening–

CRASH!

–sending stone and dust all around.

Gasping, Kuro lets the thread slide from his hand, having turned both the thread and his hand utterly crimson.

For a few seconds, there's no sound except our laboured breathing, and the buzzing of insect wings. Between panting breaths, Yasei speaks.

"Is, is it– Is it over?"

None of us dare respond, we only keep our gaze locked on the cloud of dust that slowly settles. And–

No.

No way.

Rising amongst the dust, there she is. Smiling, she wipes a smear of blood from her mouth, and spits out a small glinting object that may have been a tooth. The dust clears fully, and I look at my wide eyes in her smile for what feels like the thousandth time today.

Dents and scratches cover her once shiny purple armour, turning it dull and lifeless. Her cloak is ripped all over, and her once flawless hair is caked with dust, dirt and blood. But still, the way she stands is unchanged. And only now, looking at her, do I realise that the moment we entered this place that invisible pressure vanished completely. Was that her doing? Or is it just a side product of where we are? Either way–

"I THINK IT'S TIME I TOOK YOU ALL SERIOUSLY."

Her voice is almost sultry, and yet that statement chills my blood.

She spreads her arms out wide, and there they are.

The threads, finally revealed.

They extend from each and every fingertip and fill the air around her. She pulls one of them back, and lets it go.

Almost too fast to see, it slices through the air, coming to a stop inches before my face. Like a tree of a thousand hair-like razor blades, and she's the epicentre. Quite literally, the one tugging on the threads. Her smile widens amidst the thousands of silvery lines.

"THIS WORLD ALREADY FEARS ME, SO ALLOW ME TO DEMONSTRATE WHY."

The threads begin to vibrate, shaking from tension.

"IF YOU CAN SURVIVE THE NEXT FIVE MINUTES, YOU WIN."

What? If we can–

No, she can't be about to–

"SOUL PROJECTION–"

23: FIVE MINUTES

No.
No.
No.
She can't use that. If she does, it's over. The soul
projection of the first devil would be–
The air thickens with power, every molecule charged up.
Shaking from tension, the threads that fill the space around
her begin to lash like wild snakes, arcing aimlessly through
the air. Her cloak billows out behind her from the wind that
it creates, and I raise my forearm to protect my eyes from
the dust flung toward us–

Suddenly, she closes her hands into fists, and the threads freeze; stuck out in every direction, almost like some ungodly porcupine. The wind, the power, the wildness. It all stops.

Silence, as we can do nothing but wait and see what happens next. She sighs, and completes the ritual–

"–VOID SPINDLE."

In an instant, the four of us are flung back by the explosion of force, dust and rock sent flying in all directions. As the energy in the room surges, the shadows seem to come to life. Darkness seeps from the rock and climbs up her body, coating her arms. And then, like ink staining paper, it begins to climb the threads.

And slowly, almost hypnotically, the once silvery threads find themselves overcome by those liquid shadows. The tree of silver turns to a tree of ink, lines of midnight reaching out into the open air.

She exhales heavily, and the threads begin to crackle like power cables. With a playful grin, she tenses the now onyx threads.

"YOUR TIME STARTS..."

The threads shake from withheld force, like charging bulls barely restrained.

"NOW."

They seem to disappear, reduced to a mix of black blurs
that rush towards us. No time to read their paths–
I cast all the fire I have out in front of me, a last-ditch
effort to slow them even slightly.
But still they slam into me, cutting my chest all across like
claws of some animal.
Kuro yells out as they strike him too, and I hear strained
groaning as Ikari attempts to hold them off with his sword.
The first devil's laughter is as cold as ever, filling the room
despite the constant booming as the midnight threads
smash into the walls, ripping huge chunks of rock out.
Each second is taken up by fighting for my life and I can
only hope that the others are holding out as well. Blood
seeps through my clothes, and each step, each motion
sends a spasm of pain through my body.
The threads are seemingly endless, lashing from all
directions one after the other–
Flames spew from my hands constantly, and for the first
time ever it feels like I'm doing more than just scooping
water from that lake.
Now, the lake flows directly into me, a never ending
supply of flames. But despite that–

Every moment is a struggle, and I don't know how long my body can take this–

From the left.

Right.

Right.

Behind.

Each attack by the threads feels like a supersonic whip cracking across my skin, but–

I won't fall. I won't let myself die here.

After so much. After so long. Losing so many friends. Losing family. This pain, this pain I can deal with. I wonder, what if dad had never got involved with the gangs. I mean, I don't even know what he was borrowing money for, so…

How nice would that have been?

To be in a regular household. Me and Ikari, mom and dad. Me and Ikari could have walked to school together, could have gone to play in the park. When it was the other's birthday–

Hold on. When is Ikari's birthday?

When's my birthday?

Which one of us is older?

Even now, getting slammed around by this overwhelming power, hanging onto life by an inch, I find that funny.

We'll never know who the older brother is. Maybe it's for the better that we don't. My smile fades as I pull myself

from my imagination and face the scene before me,
looking out at the battlefield.
To my left, Ikari grits his teeth, both hands on the handle of
his sword, pressing a single thread away from him–
Another thread slams into him from the side, and he
smashes into the wall–

–3:57 REMAINING –

–IKARI–

The breath is slammed from my lungs as I hit the wall,
crumpling on impact. I can feel the stone cracking, and as I
tumble to the floor small chunks of it roll over my back.
Groaning, I pick myself up, only to see–
On pure instinct, I raise my sword–
The thread presses against it, and my shoulders scream
from the force. But there's no other option, no other path
forward.
All I can do is grit my teeth–
A thread swipes for my legs, and I jump to avoid it–
The thread in front of me slams me back into the wall, but
this time I'm ready–
That cold laugh fills the room again, and I finally manage
to direct the thread off my blade into the wall–

My back burns, spasming with each and every movement.
But still I have to press onward.

Some five metres away, Yasei's plants are constantly
rising and rising only to be shredded by the relentless
barrage of midnight black whips. I can't hear it over the
endless sounds of destruction, but I can see her ragged
breathing, her overwhelming exhaustion.

How long has it been now?

Another thread, arcing toward my neck–

I duck, and it carves a gouge in the stone behind me–

The mirror-like floor is so covered in craters and cracks
that every reflection is turned to a kaleidoscope of its
colours, and as the battle plays out it looks eerily similar to
some kind of dance floor.

What a funny thought–

Two threads forming an inky X rush directly for my torso–

I move my sword to block but–

Too slow. Everything seems to slow to a crawl as they tear
into my clothes, and then my skin–

I cry out, two scythes of red splattering onto the floor
before me–

A warbled choke escapes my throat, and a spasm runs
through my body–

I hear my name cried out, and I stagger–

–TENGEN–

My cry seems to fall on deaf ears as Ikari shows no
recognition, staggering like a drunkard–
The floor turns slick and red before him, his head hands
low–
Yet another thread whips toward him, bearing down on his
torn up chest–
A soft clink rings out as his blade rushes into the path of
the thread, and stops it in its tracks–
But now I find myself relentlessly assaulted by the trails of
darkness, as they curl in from every direction. A
subconscious desperation to survive, a desperation to live
is all that keeps me going–
Blinded by hope, all you see is a chance.
Where did I hear those words again? They feel like a
distant memory, some sense of deja vu being triggered as
they roll through my mind over and over, sparkling cloth
spinning in a battered tumble dryer–
But that chance is seeming slimmer and slimmer by the
moment, a tiny sliver of light hidden amongst a sea of
dark–
And somebody yells, a guttural, wrenching cry–

The air clouds with buzzing shadows, the ground seethes with scuttling legs and clicking mandibles–
Changing course to batter down the most prevalent threat, the threads gift me a moment of peace. Whipping my head around, I search for the man that I know is the source of this chaos–
And there he is–
Wait–
A long cloak of translucent wings ruffle behind him, interlocking mandibles around his neck like a necklaces clasp–
The simple clothes that wrap his body are gone, layers of scale and stinger forming armour in their place–
And he raises his head, black hair tousling as he moves, and ash grey streaks that were never there before run through it–
His eyes focus on the devil–
One warm brown, just like Kuro-
And one beady and midnight black–
Like an insect.
And his insects rush ever forward, hounding the woman. But her laugh never falters, the all encompassing destruction never slows. It only picks a new target, cutting through the ranks of creatures with terrifying ease–
For now, I can catch my breath. This awakened Kuro can take the weight, even if only for a moment–

Black threads pierce the cloud of insects, and wrap around him like a straightjacket–
The scales on his chest shimmer as he writhes within their grip–
The wings on his back flutter madly–
But still the threads lift him away from the ground–
And slam him back and forth, left and right, each impact shaking the cavern–
Left.
Right.
Left.
Right–

–2:10 REMAINING –

–IKARI–

A series of booms echo throughout the room and fragments of rock fly all over as Kuro's slammed against the floor repeatedly–
And it seems that despite that... awakening he just went through, he's still no match for the strength of the threads–
Left.

Right.

Left–

And the now mauled plate of shining stone cracks once again, but this time for a different reason–

They curl up ferociously, writhing through the air toward Kuro–

And they wrap around him tightly, attempting to wrestle him back from the maw of threads–

Great seething vines, adorned with flowers–

But they can't overpower the threads, not by themselves. The threads need to be dislodged by…

Standing at the forefront of the chaos, the first devil bears an eerie grin on her flawless face, and the way those teeth reflect the madness that unfurls around her sends a shiver down my spine. Regardless, if the threads need to be dislodged–

My feet seem to skim across the ground as I close in on the devil, knuckles white on my sword hand–

And just before I enter striking range, her head whips toward me as her hair flows wildly–

Her fingers twitch backwards–

A line of shadow seems to materialise before me, cutting across my vision like a censor bar–

But the devil is tiring, and she was ever so slightly too slow–

Because I can still stretch out my leg, feeling the pain rocket through my shredded chest with each movement–
Slamming my shin into her ankle with all the force I have–
I'm thrown backward, swatted away like a pestering fly.
But I think I did just enough to make her lose focus, even if only for a fraction of a second. And I close my eyes, preparing for the oncoming impact with hard stone–
Yet what I hit is soft, almost like–
Vines.
Regardless of their softness however, the sudden impact sends a jarring flash of pain through my body that radiates outward from my back and chest all the way to my fingertips–
A groan escapes my mouth as I slump forward, feet once again returning to the hard ground for a moment before I land flat on my back–
"Ok?"
I flit my eyes about in search of the voice–
Huh?
Not her too.
She extends a hand, and I take it, feeling the solid and yet floral gauntlet that covers all the way from her fingertips to halfway up her forearm. As I get hauled to my feet, my eyes skitter over her figure and widen at the changes.
Unlike Kuro, the only difference in her clothing is those gauntlets, but…

Her eyes, once brown, quickly inspect my condition as luminous green pupils jut up and down. As she turns, the forest green ends of her hair sail through the air like a fan opening. She pats me on the back, turning to the fight–
And in a split second she crosses her forearms in an X, the thread slamming into the gauntlets–
Sparks fly as the two forces press against each other, but just like Kuro, even this stronger Yasei can't hold out for long–
She slides further and further back–
But the pressure on her falters for a second as Kuro and T launch a barrage of fire and insects at the devil–
Each attack is just swatted away, but they don't stop, they don't let up–
And I too leap into the fray, slashing wildly–
Her threads occupied with the other three, she matches me in hand to hand combat for the first time–
And it feels like I'm drowning, every attack I try closed off in an instant–
But still I slash and slash, even in the face of such overwhelming speed and power and technique. She piles on the pressure, and each second a new attack flashes past my face as I step back and back and back–
And stupidly I leave my arm a bit too far forward–
Her heel connects with my wrist, and there's a sickening crack–

My sword is tossed from my hand, clattering to the floor beside me–

And still her attacks push me further and further back as the blood that cascades from my wrist and torso turns the floor slick–

"IKARI!"

Sparing a second to look in the direction of the yell, I see something arc through the air toward me–

I feel the cold solidity of the wall against my back as I run out of space to back away–

And blindly, I grab at the blur–

My fingers curl around a distinct handle, my thumb brushes against an oddly bumpy guard–

And I instinctively whip the sword around in an arc before me–

–1:06 REMAINING –

–TENGEN–

Seeing Ikari slash blindly at the devil, determination painted on his face–

Seeing Yasei and Kuro push their contracts to the limit, reaching the next stage of power–

Seeing the overwhelming strength of the weaver of fate, the power that has commanded the greatest fear of this world since the very beginning–

Ikari grabs at his old sword, and settles into a stance I've never seen before; left hand grasping the metal blade in reverse grip, right hand gripping the plant-insect sword in the way he used to.

Seeing the final moments of our story unfold–

'We can do more, there is a path we take in which we walk out into a new world at the end of this! So will you walk to the light, or wallow in the darkness!?'

Old friend–

'We'll be the heroes of the story, dammit! When the dust settles and the sun rises with refreshed hope, we'll be the ones who usher on a new dawn!'

–Thank you.

And the banks of the lake burst, the power once withheld floods forward. It surges like a wild flood, each nerve overrun with nothing but that flaming water–

Smoke rises from my skin in wisps as the hair singes. My eyes meet my own in the reflection of the devil's teeth, and amidst the whites of my eyes two suns burn. Like forest fire cleansing the ground of dirt and shrub, the dark colour of my hair slowly recedes as a line of smouldering ember runs through it. And when the last of it burns away–

A swirling sea of red and orange ruffling with each movement like a burning flag in the wind.

Ikari grits his teeth and battles furiously, fighting in two different styles simultaneously, and he and the devil are an even match for the moment.

Yasei pounds fists into the oncoming storm of threads, but even she cannot progress.

Kuro's insects surge over and over again, but each time they get shredded like fruit in a blender.

The whole battlefield is fighting at a standstill.

Something needs to tip the scales.

Something needs to give us the final boost.

Something needs to be the difference maker.

And now, hair like wildfire, eyes like suns; that something is me.

A great fire to sweep the field, to burn away the shrubbery and leave the great pillars standing tall.

Blinded by hope, all you see is a chance.

Well I've been seeing that chance for a while now.

I think it's high time I took it.

And when the words flow, I don't think about them.

"And now prepare, for the ashes have settled, and the phoenix is ready to rise."

At once, the devil's gaze snaps to me, as an expression of horrified realisation blooms on that all too familiar, beautiful face. My hands settle into a butterfly, thumbs intertwined, bloodied knuckles facing outward.

"Soul projection–"

All the things that have led up to this. All the lives lost. All the words spoken. All the blood, sweat and tears. All the fear. All the joy. All the despair. All the thoughts. All the love. All the hate. All the fights.

All of it is what defines our story.

And now, I'll make sure it gets the ending it deserves.

To always scorch the earth for those you love.

I haven't forgotten.

I never will.

"–Phoenix of hope."

–0:05 REMAINING –

–IKARI–

An inferno.

An inferno sweeps the room, smouldering vermillion tendrils creeping through every corner.

And there is my brother.

Right in the centre of it all.

Four flaming wings hold him above the ground, and fire-like hair flows in the wind of his own blaze.

Those butterfly hands flutter, each flap of them stoking the flames higher and higher. But when they wash over me, they're warm. Pleasant to the touch, like a gentle hug.
And as for the devil–
She doesn't scream.
She doesn't cry.
She simply stands amongst the fire, despite her skin charring, despite her hair burned to a crisp. She simply stares at Tengen, a faint smile playing on her lips.
It's now or never–

–0:01 REMAINING –

The swords feel light as air in my hands as I rush closer and closer, fire washing off my skin like water falling from a leaping fish–
She turns to me, and the threads of darkness rear up behind her–

–TIMES UP–

With a great flash, the shadows splinter away from the threads, and their original silvery nature is restored–
But still the devil sends them flying toward me–

And yet, having gone through the hell of those black threads–

I cut the threads down, and reach the devil–

She raises a fist–

And coughs up a shock of red as two blades pierce her heart–

Her eyes meet mine, and that faint smile never falters–

My voice is barely a whisper–

"All these devils, and you fall to a human in the end."

And she smiles properly now, and places a hand around the back of my head gently.

She pulls me in, her breath like ice on my neck–

She reaches behind her–

Falls away for a moment–

And leans forward again, pressing something into my palm–

And the warmth of her hand vanishes as it slips away–

With a tug, my swords come free of her body–

And with a soft thump, the weaver of fate falls to the ground.

The greatest fear of all has fallen.

And as my wounds finally catch up to me, it all goes black.

23: SUNRISE

Darkness fades to light as my eyes peel open, the warm sun spilling down onto my face. Straining, I sit up, and let my vision focus on my surroundings. A woman is leaning over me, looking down with a concerned expression.
Yasei?
But I focus on her face, peering up, and realise that she isn't Yasei. Her hair is brown, cut short in a bob that brushes the base of her neck. When her eyes meet mine, she springs up and gestures toward something I can't see. Another figure enters my vision, another woman. Her hair

is pulled back in a taught bun, and she brings her eye right up to mine, filling my gaze with her watchful iris. She straightens up, and looks down at me.

"Can you understand me?"

I go to reply, and nothing but a parched croak escapes my lips, Looking away, the woman gestures for something. Moments later, a hand passes her a small bottle. Gently, the original woman slowly raises my back until I'm sitting up.

She unscrews the bottle, and hands it to me.

Weakly, I grasp it, and my eyes settle with surprise on the mass of white fabric that coats my hand from fingertip to wrist. With great strain, I lift the bottle to my face, and tip the contents down my throat.

A feeling of relief fills me as the water cascades down my gullet, pooling in an empty stomach. Experimentally, I open my mouth, and it feels slightly better. Despite that, my voice is barely a whispering croak.

"The others–"

"–Are perfectly safe. Most of them fared as badly as you, and will be in a similar condition. One boy lost almost a litre of blood, and has only just woken up. Unfortunately, whatever happened down there has put the four of you in an exceptionally nasty state

"Where are we?"

"You're on a stretcher at the top of a hill, in a JSDF field hospital overlooking Tartarus."

"What– what does it look like down there?"

She scans my legs for a moment, and seems to make a split second decision.

"Come have a look for yourself. The others are already there."

***

"Wow."

And I can't help but agree with Kuro. Looking down from the top of this hill, the once great compound of Tararus looks like nothing more than a pile of rubble. Smoke curls from embers that still smoulder amongst the fallen brick, and masses of workers swarm the site, the dawn light reflecting off their hi-vis coats.

"What happened?"

The lady beside me scoffs dryly.

"As hard as it is to believe, an airstrike. We don't know who's responsible, but there are people working on it. And also, a rather unexplainable spherical chasm. In fact, it was when we were evacuating the chasm that we discovered a series of tunnels not on the official site map. And those tunnels led us to you."

She looks at the four of us through narrowed eyes.

"Along with a trail of corpses. Most of which are still down there, as the underground sections are far too volatile to traverse for their collection."

I swallow hard, and turn back to the smoking mess of rubble. To them, I can't imagine how bad this must look for us. A group of young people, armed to the teeth, and a trail of corpses. Of course, there's no way to tell them the truth. We can only hope that–

"Now sit tight. An envoy will be arriving shortly from a private company listed as a hunting firm. They will be transferring you to the military hospital."

With that, she strides away, some hint of annoyance in each step. But, if a company listed as a hunting firm is coming…

Good to see that old bag cares enough to put us in a proper hospital. And hell do we need it. My knuckles are effectively gone, my back roars with pain at each shoulder blade. The others have various wrappings of white too, most noticeable the huge mass of bandages around Ikari's chest. No surprise there, I suppose.

The horizon glows with a gentle golden hue, as the sun begins to crest above it.

I open my mouth to say something, and decide against it.

So we stand there, the four of us.

After so much, it's over.

After so much, we can stand here as survivors. We can finally grieve those who fell, and we can finally start looking forward again.

There's the sound of rustling cotton, and I look over to see Kuro's hand gently clasped in Yasei's. I meet her eye, and she smiles. I smile back, and watch as she leans in and speaks softly to Kuro. The two of them wave briefly, and walk slowly away, Kuro leaning his head on her shoulder. I smile again, and see Ikari doing the same.

For a while, all that surrounds us is the open air, and all we feel is the warmth of dawn, and the wind against our bruised and battered skin.

"I guess that's it, huh."

"I guess so. It seems…"

"Strange, doesn't it?"

"Yeah. It really does."

The soft whistling of the wind swirls amongst my ears, as the sky turns more and more gold, with streaks of soft pink and purple breaking through as well.

"Hey Tengen?"

"Hmm?"

"Do you not feel like…"

He pauses.

"Like at some point, all of this… *stuff* will come crashing down, and it'll catch up to us? All the things we've done are… well they're not normal things for seventeen year olds to do, y'know?"

"Yeah. I do think about that, about all the death and destruction. About all these devils and contracts and abilities and soul whatevers. And most of all, I think about the people swept up into it all."

He sighs, and speaks toward the dawn.

"And the people who lost their lives in it."

"They're the ones I'll never forget. I swear it."

The grass under foot ripples in waves of shifting green, and the grey smoke of the rubble is blown softly into the ever-brightening sky. Like a hopeful hand reaching out, trails of purple reach across the golden cracks of lit up clouds.

And finally, there it is.

After so long…

"Hey Ikari?"

"Yeah?"

"What did the weaver of fate hand to you?"

He turns serious.

"It was a piece of paper. Just one sheet, folded in half."

We ponder in silence for a moment, but the smile returns to his face as he continues.

"It says on the front of it-"

He reaches into his pocket.

"-To whom it may concern."

"A letter?"

He unfolds the paper.

"It would seem so."

Here we are. A new dawn at last. A chance to get things back to how they were. A chance to thrive, and a chance for the nation to feel hope again. And just like in the cave, I plan to take that chance.

And I'll bring my brother and friends along for the ride.

"Well, what does the letter say?"

EPILOUGUE

Hello, my killer.
I had lived a long life. Longer than most. In fact, I had lived one of the longest lives out of any living being. And so, I'd seen a lot. Been through a lot. Witnessed civilisations rise and fall, witnessed empires conquer half the world only for their reign to vanish into thin air. Witnessed the growth of humanity, witnessed people change and evolve.
And as I watched them, I realised something.
Humans live for emotions. They live for happiness, for joy. But also, they live for sadness, and for hardship.
Because they see life as ups and downs, not a straight line. They rise and fall, alternating everyday from the highest of highs to the lowest of lows.
And somehow, they keep on going.
In that regard, I was always jealous of humans.
And don't get me wrong, I've done some horrible things to them. I've done horrible things to all the world. And I don't regret any of it.
But, if I was to go back to the start, if I was to do it all again…

I think I would try to live how humans live. Try to feel that joy, that sadness, that happiness, that hardship.
All my life, I had been on the giving end of emotion, of dark and twisted emotion.
I think…
I think it would have been nice to be on the receiving end.
To feel all those emotions for myself.

And finally, a warning for my killer.
They're coming.
The angels are coming.
And trust me, they're not so angelic as the name implies.

In pursuit of heaven, hell is
created

Angels

OF

FEAR

COMING

2026

© ELIAS VIRKAR-YATES

Final words from Yours truly.

I think that once again, I owe you thanks.
Whatever that story was to you, whether you simply
skimmed it, or even if you've just skipped ahead to this
page, I'm glad you're even holding this book.
And again, thanks to everyone who helped me, because
there are many more than I mentioned at the start. In fact,
if I listed all of them, we would be here for *quite* a while.
Well, I sure hope it was worth your time.

See you in the sequel.